ALPHA

REGAN URE

Cover Design: © L.J. Anderson, Mayhem Cover Creations

Formatting by Mayhem Cover Creations

ISBN:978-0-9932864-2-1

This book is dedicated to my mom. Thank you for believing in me.

CONTENTS

Chapter One	1
Chapter Two	11
Chapter Three	21
Chapter Four	31
Chapter Five	41
Chapter Six	51
Chapter Seven	62
Chapter Eight	72
Chapter Nine	82
Chapter Ten	92
Chapter Eleven	102
Chapter Twelve	112
Chapter Thirteen	122
Chapter Fourteen	132
Chapter Fifteen	142
Chapter Sixteen	152
Chapter Seventeen	162
Chapter Eighteen	172
Chapter Nineteen	182
Chapter Twenty	192
Chapter Twenty-One	203
Chapter Twenty-Two	213
Chapter Twenty-Three	223
Chapter Twenty-Four	234
Chapter Twenty-Five	244
Chapter Twenty-Six	254
Chapter Twenty-Seven	265
Chapter Twenty-Eight	275
Chapter Twenty-Nine	286
Chapter Thirty	297
About the Author	307

CHAPTER ONE

SCARLETT

I swung my fist toward my opponent's face, but he ducked out of the way at the last moment. Sweat beaded my forehead. I raised my tightened fist, ready to deflect a blow as I stepped backward.

I didn't watch his fists. I was taught to watch my opponent's eyes to be able to anticipate their next move.

"Too slow, Scarlett," my opponent teased with a challenge. I would make him eat that comment soon.

For a few moments I watched him carefully, studying his eyes, which flickered to his right, betraying his next move. This time I had more than enough time to move out of the way and attack with a well-placed kick to his side. My kick wasn't hard enough to incapacitate him, but I heard a grunt of pain.

"Did that hurt?" I teased as I bounced lightly on my feet a safe distance away from him.

Instead of some cocky reply, he glared at me and I grinned.

His eyes narrowed as he planned his next line of attack and I watched him carefully as I anticipated his next move. Like before, his eyes flickered to the left and I ducked out of the way as his fist swung for my face. I stepped closer and landed a punch to his abdomen. The grimace on his face told me it had hurt.

"Now who is the slow one?" I teased.

If you compared my five-foot-seven lean frame to my opponent's six-foot muscular build, you would think I'd be at a disadvantage, but I wasn't. At the age of sixteen, I'd started to develop heightened senses and, along with that, my physical strength had also increased.

The changes had been subtle at first and as time passed they'd become stronger and stronger.

I got in a few more hits before my opponent threw up his hands in defeat.

"I'm done," said Gary as he bent down and reached for a towel next to the gym mat. He wiped the sweat from his forehead with it.

"You're showing your age," I teased as I reached for a bottle of water beside the gym mat we were sparring on and took a couple of gulps from it.

He glared at me because of the reference to his age. He was no spring chicken, but at the age of thirty-seven, he didn't consider himself old. To my seventeen years, he wasn't exactly young.

He'd been my father's best friend and I'd known him my whole life. After my parents died when I was ten, Gary had become my legal guardian. To me, he'd been the unofficial uncle who had become my only family. He loved me like a daughter and I loved him like a father.

At the age of sixteen, I'd made the decision to get emancipated. Gary had understood my need for independence and my wish to control my own affairs. When

I'd sat him down and explained to him what I wanted to do, he hadn't been surprised. In fact, he'd supported the idea.

Although I was now considered an adult and able to make my own decisions, Gary had remained an important part of my life. He was family—the only family I had.

"Come on, there are some boxes with your name on it," said Gary as he turned to leave the gym. I followed him, wanting to do anything but unpack boxes. It was such a tedious task.

"I don't want to," I whined like a five-year-old. He shot me a warning look and I glared back at him playfully.

"The moving company unpacked everything, except your personal boxes," he informed me as he left the gym and walked upstairs to the reception and the entrance of the house.

My house was quite big. I'd resorted to naming the lounges according to their use: game lounge, casual lounge, formal lounge and the upstairs lounge.

The house also had a gym with an indoor heated pool. It had its own tennis court and a huge landscaped garden. I had enough staff to run the house, though I rarely used the driver because I enjoyed driving.

"Has my new car been delivered yet?" I asked as I followed him up the stairs to the first floor.

"Not yet." He turned to smile at me. I'd been driving him nuts, asking about the new car.

I returned his smile with a cheeky one.

"Go unpack some of your boxes and I'll see you downstairs for lunch in an hour," he instructed as he turned to the left into the hallway to his bedroom.

"See you in an hour," I replied as I took a right and followed the hallway down past some of the guest bedrooms until I got to my bedroom, which was the main bedroom of the house. I opened the double doors.

I loved my new room. I'd hired someone to help me with the decorating and she'd really done a good job. I loved the colors purple and blue so my whole room, which was the size of two bedrooms, was decorated in those colors.

As I stepped into my room, I felt calmness settle over me.

The only things that stood out in my bedroom were the four boxes at the foot of my bed. It would take me forever to get through them all.

We'd just moved into the house a couple of weeks before. The movers had sorted through all the other boxes. Initially, I'd been left with ten personal boxes and I'd only managed to unpack six of them in the last two weeks.

I decided to shower before I punished myself with the task of unpacking the remaining boxes. Normally, I would have gotten the movers to do it but the fact that they contained my personal items made it hands-off to anyone but me.

As I walked into my adjoining bathroom, I stripped off my gym clothes and threw them into the laundry basket. I turned on the shower and adjusted the water temperature as I got in.

I closed my eyes and savored the feel of the water running down my body. I was stalling, but the boxes wouldn't unpack themselves.

Once I'd finished showering, I got out, determined to finish the unpacking in the next hour.

I changed into a pair of jeans and a shirt before I walked over to the boxes. There was another reason I'd been putting it off. Inside these boxes were memories of my parents.

Although they'd been gone for seven years, it still hurt to think about them, and how much of my life they'd missed. I swallowed hard, trying to keep memories of my grief at bay.

I still remembered the last time I'd seen them alive. They'd planned an evening out, leaving me home with the babysitter.

My mom had kissed me goodnight as she'd tucked me into bed. I closed my eyes for a moment as I remembered her warm and loving smell. God, I missed her.

My father had stood in the doorway.

"We're going to be late," he'd informed my mom as he'd walked into my room and stopped beside my bed.

"Night, princess," he'd whispered gently as he'd kissed my forehead. I could still feel his lips on my face.

The thickness in my throat grew. My dad had given me the nickname princess.

As I'd clutched my childhood teddy, Norman, I'd watched them leave. That had been the last time I'd seen them alive. They'd gone out that night and they'd never returned.

The truth was that they hadn't just died, they'd been murdered. And now, seven years later, their murder was still unsolved. Initially, the coroner had ruled it an animal attack but later it had been changed to unknown.

At a young age, I'd learned that life wasn't guaranteed and that anyone could be taken away at any moment. This had pushed me to live my life to the fullest. It had also made me fiercely independent, and my need for control had grown.

It was one of the reasons I trained so hard, to keep fit and to be able to protect myself. I didn't want to meet with the same fate that my parents had.

It also made me keep people at a distance. By being standoffish and cold, I kept people from wanting to get closer to me and kept myself from getting hurt.

I let myself wallow in the memories of my parents and their deaths for a few more minutes. Then I took a deep breath and released it as I opened the first box.

It contained photo albums of my parents. I didn't open any of them because it hurt too much to look at the photos and be reminded of what I was missing in my life.

All the big portraits of my parents, I had put into the attic. Someday, I hoped that I'd be able to display them in the house and look at them without feeling the heartbreaking loss of their deaths.

I was relieved when I finished unpacking the albums and I moved on to the next one. I was determined to finish by lunchtime. The next couple of boxes were filled with my personal books, which took forever to get through. By the last box—which was filled with clothes, like underwear and pajamas—I was tired and hungry.

All the boxes were now empty, although there were still items on my bed when I heard a knock on my door.

"Time for food," Gary announced through my closed door.

"I'm nearly done. I'll see you downstairs as soon as I'm finished," I replied, folding my silk pajama top.

"You'd better hurry up or there may not be any food left," he teased.

I just laughed in response.

I turned my concentration back to finishing up my unpacking. Once I was done, I felt relieved as I made my way downstairs to the kitchen. There was a massive dining room but I liked to eat at the table in the kitchen; it had a more casual atmosphere.

Gary had already started to eat when I dropped into the chair next to him.

"You unpacked all four boxes?" he asked in disbelief.

"Yes, all four boxes," I confirmed triumphantly as I surveyed the food in front of me. On the kitchen table, spread out in front of us, was a variety of sandwiches and salad. I selected one and placed it on my plate.

"Wow, that was quick," he murmured as he took a bite of his sandwich.

"I hate moving," I muttered as I dished up some salad onto my plate.

"At least everything is done," he reminded me. He was right. Everything had been unpacked. The only thing I was still waiting for was my new car.

"And I don't know why you're complaining about moving. This was your idea, remember?" he reminded me.

It had been my idea. From the time I'd turned sixteen, I'd begun to develop a need for nature and the wilderness. This had coincided with my senses becoming more powerful.

So, here we were.

"When is my new car arriving?" I asked as I took a bottle of water from the table and opened it to pour into a glass.

"I phoned to check and they said it was on its way. They guaranteed it would be here before the end of today."

I was so excited, I was like a little child on Christmas Eve and I couldn't wait to open my presents.

"Are you looking forward to starting your senior year tomorrow?" Gary questioned.

I shrugged.

"Not really."

I wasn't excited about my senior year or starting a new school. It was simply a task that had to be completed. I hadn't quite thought about what exactly I wanted to do once I graduated.

The thing was, I had more money than I could probably spend in a lifetime, so I had the time and money to take my time deciding.

When I'd gotten emancipated, I'd started learning about finances from Gary. It was crucial to keep track of how my inheritance was being invested and I'd learned a lot. Initially, Gary had sat in on the meetings with my financial advisors, but nowadays I held those meetings without him.

I'd spent most of my life going to private schools and I'd

decided with my move to attend a public school for the first time. I might not have wanted to go, but I had no doubt it was going to be interesting.

I'd been told many times that I was attractive, and I had money, so most girls didn't like me much. Guys tended to be intimidated by me and there weren't a lot of guys who would take on someone who was as strong-willed as I was.

It didn't matter to me. I didn't need a man to define who I was.

I spent the rest of the day waiting anxiously for my new car to arrive as I flipped through the channels on my flat-screen in my room. There was nothing to watch.

I finally heard the faint sound of an engine and I bounced off my bed in excitement. My new car had arrived. I ran to the window in the upstairs lounge, but I couldn't see anything from the window. I knew the truck was near. Like I said, I had really good senses.

I only had to wait for about five minutes before I saw the truck drive down the driveway headed to the house. It was still early enough to take it for a drive.

Gary was already waiting outside the front door when I joined him.

"I don't think I've ever seen a girl get this excited about a car," he remarked with a smile.

"Not every girl gets to drive a Maserati," I shot back with a grin and he laughed.

"You going to take it for a drive now?" he asked.

"You even have to ask?" I replied as the truck pulled up in front of us.

The driver got out of the truck and gave me some documents to sign while another guy reversed my car out of the back.

Beautiful.

I'd opted for a sleek, silver-gray color. Once I signed the

necessary documentation, the driver handed me the keys to my new baby.

I only had one final question before I got in my new car.

"Insured?" I asked, to which Gary replied, "Of course."

Not that it really mattered, but I didn't want to waste money if I did total it. I was a little bit of a speed freak and battled to keep to the speed limit.

There was no way I was going to be sticking to the speed limit in my new car. I slid into the driver's seat as the truck left. The car smelled like expensive leather and I took a deep breath.

I started the car up and revved it. Gary just shook his head at me.

He knew me too well. Thankfully, through the years and since I got emancipated, he had begun to let me make my own decisions even though he didn't always agree with them.

I pulled out of the driveway with a screech. I didn't know the town very well but I had GPS so I couldn't really get that lost. I took a right and pressed my foot down, loving the thrill of the car purring beneath my hands.

I had probably an hour before sunset and I was going to make good use of every minute of it as I began to drive around the new town. The residential areas around the town were sparsely populated. There were a few properties similarly sized to mine but, other than that, it was forests and fresh air.

Putting down the window, I took a deep breath of the fresh air. I felt free.

I loved every minute of getting to know my new car as I drove around for nearly half an hour. I was on my way back when I spotted a red Porsche tailing me. It accelerated until it pulled up alongside me. The darkened windows on my car made it impossible for the driver to see me, but I could see him.

He obviously wanted to race and I smiled as I sped up,

ready to kick his ass. I was used to driving fast cars and Gary had made me take an additional driving course to make sure I was equipped to handle them.

I pulled ahead of the Porsche as I pressed down on the accelerator. The Porsche lost some ground, but after a sharp right corner it accelerated and pulled up beside me again. Shaking my head at his attempts to keep up with me, I pushed down on the accelerator again as the road straightened up in front of us.

My Maserati was faster. I pulled away from him, leaving him unable to overtake me so he pulled in behind me. I smiled triumphantly.

Playtime was over. I could see my house coming up and I was done racing. I slowed down a few feet from my driveway with the Porsche still hot on my tail, but before he could make another attempt to overtake me, I pulled hard on the steering wheel and turned into my driveway without slowing down any further.

The tires screeched on the surface but my baby stuck to the road without losing traction and I slowed down as I entered my property. In my side mirror, I saw the Porsche hit the brakes just outside just outside the wrought-iron gate that stood at the driveway's entrance

Still high on the thrill of the race, I pulled up in front of the house.

CHAPTER TWO

SCARLETT

One thing I hated most about school was waking up early. Why did school have to start so early? I loved to sleep in and I rarely got out of bed before eleven most mornings when I didn't have to wake up for school.

I yawned when my snooze time ran out and my alarm began to buzz again. I sat up and rubbed my face. I'd set my alarm for earlier than normal so I would have the extra time to get my schedule and find my locker.

I kept promising myself once school was finished, I'd make sure I never had to wake up early again.

Unlike most girls my age, I wasn't interested in fashion and what the latest trend was. I dressed in what I liked irrespective of whether it was considered fashionable or not.

I pulled on a pair of black hipster jeans and a button-up dark blue shirt, then I finished off my outfit with a pair of black, flat, strappy sandals. The only makeup I wore was some lip-gloss. These days I never bothered with jackets or a jersey because I never got cold anymore.

When my senses had grown stronger, my internal body heat had increased as well.

Gary had suggested I get some tests run to discover why I'd suddenly developed changes when I'd turned sixteen, but I'd refused. Physically, I felt fine. I didn't see any reason to get tests done, and I'd learned to live with the new changes in my body.

The smell of fresh coffee caught me as I descended the stairs and I followed it into the kitchen. Most mornings I couldn't function until I had my first cup of coffee.

"You're up," I heard Gary say as I entered the room.

"Yeah, I'm up," I muttered as I went straight for the coffee. I poured some of it into a cup and took a sip.

"Mmm," I murmured as I took another sip and felt the caffeine begin to take effect in my body. Gary just shook his head at me and laughed. He knew better than to try and interact with me before I finished my first cup.

"Are you taking your new car or do you want the driver to take you to school?" Gary asked, sitting at the kitchen table as I finished my coffee.

"I'm taking my new baby," I answered.

"I've installed a tracker on the car," he notified me. I nodded my head. It was something I was used to and it was his way of keeping me safe. If I let him put a tracker on the vehicle I was using, then he wouldn't have to send a bodyguard with me. There was no way I was going to school with a massive bodyguard following me around. If Gary could, he'd keep me locked up at home. I wasn't going to live my life in fear of what could happen, though.

My parents' deaths had been tragic, but there was no proof that their murderers were out to get me, too.

I was running late so I skipped breakfast and I grabbed a protein bar, which I shoved into my school bag.

I bent down and gave Gary a quick kiss on his cheek.

"I'll see you later," I said as I dashed out of the kitchen.

My new baby was parked in the driveway, ready for me, when I opened the front door. Gary knew me too well, so he'd made sure she was parked outside for me.

I got into the car and programmed the address of the school into the car's GPS. I hummed along to the song on the radio as I started the drive to my new school for the next year.

The parking lot of the school was starting to fill up when I pulled in. I found a parking space in the front row of the parking lot. I grabbed my schoolbag and got out of the car.

As I walked away, I pressed a button on the remote of the car and I heard the door click closed. There weren't many students at school yet but I did get a couple of curious looks as I made my way to the entrance.

The school wasn't exactly as big as the schools I'd been used to. It was a fair size, but I wasn't in the city anymore and the thick forest that surrounded the school reminded me of that.

The single-story brick building with large windows had a sign above the entrance that read "Parkland High School". A large double entrance to the school was preceded with a small set of stairs that led straight to parking.

Once I entered the school, I passed a couple of students. A smell hit me and I faltered for a minute, trying to figure out what the smell was. It smelled like fresh rain.

Two students standing close by turned to look at me with curiosity as I pushed myself past the smell to the reception room. Behind the counter in reception sat an old, plump lady with a pair of glasses on the edge of her nose.

"Hi," I greeted her.

"Hello," she greeted me back with a warm smile. "How can I help you?"

"I'm a new student and I've come to collect my schedule and locker number," I answered.

"What's your name, dear?" she asked as she began to sift through some of the papers on her desk.

"Scarlett Hayes."

"Here you go," she said as she handed me my schedule. On the top of the sheet was my locker number and she also handed me a map of the school.

"Thank you," I said with a friendly smile as I walked out of reception and began the hunt for my locker.

I rotated the map around a couple of times, trying to figure out which direction I was headed in. Someone had told me once that women were supposed to be good at reading maps, but I wasn't convinced that was true.

After twenty minutes, I was still walking up and down the hallways trying to find my stupid locker. That distinctive smell that had hit me when I first entered the school seemed to be all over this place. I couldn't explain why. Fresh rain intermingled with the distinctive smell of a forest.

The strange smells kept hitting my nostrils randomly as I walked around, trying to find my locker.

"Do you need some help?" I heard a voice ask, taking me by surprise.

"You scared me," I said as I tried to catch my breath. My heart hammered in my chest.

"Sorry," the stranger said, standing in front of me and watching me with amusement. He was a good-looking guy.

He was a little taller than me. His light brown hair was long enough to fall across his green eyes as he studied me with a smile.

Yeah, scratch that. The confidence this guy oozed kicked him up a level to gorgeous. His confidence also screamed player, which was the type I avoided at all costs. Players were normally male whores who thought they were God's gift to women.

The distinct smell of a forest hit me again as he stepped

closer to me and took the map from my hands.

"What are you looking for?" he asked as he studied the map and his eyes flickered back to me.

"My locker," I mumbled. I wasn't used to asking for help; in fact, I hated it. I normally persevered until I figured it out on my own.

"I'll show you where it is," he offered as he folded the map and handed it back to me.

"Sure," I forced myself to say. I'd wasted enough time looking for my stupid locker and, as much as I hated help, I didn't want to spend the next twenty minutes still searching for it.

"I'm Blake," the stranger offered as he headed down the hallway and I followed behind him. A couple of the students turned to stare at the two of us as we walked past.

"Scarlett," I muttered.

"So where did you move from?" he said, trying to start up a conversation, but I wasn't interested in small talk.

"None of your business," I shot back. I wasn't one to open up to strangers.

"Aren't you just a nice warm teddy bear," he teased with a devilish smile and I just glared at him.

"Here's your locker," he said as he pointed to it. It was a dull gray color and had seen better days.

"Thanks," I muttered as I stepped around him to my locker and opened it.

"You're welcome, Scarlett. See you around," he said as he began to walk away from me and hitched his schoolbag over his shoulder.

"Not if I can help it," I muttered under my breath as I shoved a couple of my schoolbooks into my locker.

"I heard you," Blake chuckled, almost halfway down the hallway already. Geez, he had good hearing. It was nearly as good as mine.

I didn't have a lot of experience with guys. My straight black hair reached my shoulders and my eyes were a silver-gray color that darkened when I was angry. With all the working out I did, I was slender, and I wasn't really tall or short.

I'd had plenty of guys try asking me out, but my life had been too busy with training and taking over my responsibilities of my inheritance to do the usual teenage dating thing.

I wanted to have the type of love my parents had shared. I remembered the way my parents used to look at each other. One day I wanted to find someone to look at me that way.

In the meantime, I was going to finish school and then decide what I was going to do with the rest of my life.

I closed my locker and opened my schedule to see what and where my first class was.

As I tried to hunt down my first class for the day, I noticed the unusual looks I was getting from the other students as I walked down the hallway.

Being the new girl, I expected some curious looks, but the students who glanced in my direction looked at me with a watchfulness I'd never encountered before.

It was almost like they were wary of me. I shook my head. Perhaps I was imagining it. It didn't make sense—why would they be wary of me?

I ignored their watchful gazes and held my head high. I walked confidently into my first class of the day, taking a seat nearest to the window.

Students began filtering into the class as I flipped through my textbook. When my eyes drifted to the doorway of the classroom, I saw two male students watching me closely just a couple of feet from the door.

I didn't know what it was about this school, but most of the guys were gorgeous and well-built. Maybe there was something in the water.

The one with short blond hair crossed his arms over his chest as he watched me with open hostility. I was not one to be intimidated, so I glared back at him.

My response must have been unexpected because instantly the hostility vanished and he smiled at me. The guy next to him with the dark auburn hair let his eyes glance between the two of us before his eyes settled back on me. There wasn't any animosity in his eyes; he acted more curious than anything else.

My attention was pulled away from them when the teacher walked into the classroom and began the lesson. Thankfully the teacher wasn't interested in making me stand up and make a little speech about myself to the class. I was relieved.

I ignored the eyes that I could feel watching me and paid attention to the teacher. I was here to learn and pass my senior year. I wasn't here to worry about why most of the school population was watching me like I was going to try and attack them at any moment.

In my next class, Blake walked in to the room and when he spotted me he smiled and shook his head.

I narrowed my eyes at him as he walked over to the empty desk beside me and dropped down into the seat.

Was there no escaping this guy? He seemed to be everywhere and it was starting to annoy me.

"Miss me?" he asked with a smirk.

"I can't miss you if you won't go away," I retorted and he laughed.

"Cade is going to love you," he murmured to himself with a grin and I rolled my eyes at him. I had no idea who he was talking about and I didn't care.

"What pack did you belong to?" he asked under his breath.

Pack?

"I don't know what you're talking about," I replied, slowly but surely losing my patience with him.

He studied me for a moment, looking a little shocked as he leaned forward in his seat.

"You really have no idea, do you?" he asked softly.

"Did you forget to take your medication today?" I asked, studying him with faked concern and he laughed.

"I can't wait for Cade to meet you," he murmured to himself, clearly enjoying his private joke. He made absolutely no sense to me.

I made a point of turning slightly away from him, signaling to him I was done with the conversation.

For the rest of the lesson, Blake watched me quietly but didn't talk to me again. Even after the lesson ended and I stuffed my books into my bag and walked out of the class, he remained seated, watching me with a grin.

I had to force myself to leave before I turned around and wiped that grin from his face with my fist. He was so annoying and the majority of what he'd said didn't make a lot of sense.

At my locker, I leaned my head against the cool surface and took a deep breath to get my temper under control.

Between the strange looks, weird smells and Blake's odd conversation, I was so confused. There wasn't much that was making sense at the moment.

I took another deep breath before I straightened up as I felt my anger begin to subside. I opened my locker and took a book out before I closed it with a bang.

After another pep talk with myself, I made my way to my next class. I could do this.

By lunchtime I still had no answers to all the strange things I was noticing. I got myself some lunch and made my way to an open table in the middle of the cafeteria.

The strange smells that I'd smelled from the time I'd walked through the school entrance this morning hit me full force as I sat down at the table.

The distinct forest, woodsy smell came from the group that Blake sat with and the fresh-rain smell came from another group sitting on the other side of me. How was that possible that all the people in the specific group all smelled the same?

That was odd.

As my eyes connected with Blake, he smiled and waved at me. I ignored him and began to eat my sandwich.

I wondered how long it would take to get a restraining order against Blake? All it would take would be a phone call to one of my lawyers. I was really tempted.

"Can I join you?" a soft-spoken voice asked. I looked up to see a pretty girl with long blond hair that nearly reached her waist and wide, expressive blue eyes flashing me a friendly smile. She was dressed in a denim miniskirt and a white button-up shirt.

"Sure," I said and she sat down opposite me, sliding her tray onto the table.

"My name's Keri," she told me before beginning to eat.

"I'm Scarlett," I replied, and then took a sip of my diet soda.

Surprisingly, I liked Keri. There was something about her that just clicked with me.

"It sucks being the new girl, doesn't it?" she said as she opened her soda.

"Yeah, it does."

"I was in your shoes not so long ago," she told me. "I started a couple of months before last year ended."

We had something in common to bond over and I liked her even more.

"This school is a little strange. Most of the students seem

to be divided up into two groups. Blake Stevens is head of the one group and Cade Presley seems to be in charge of the other group," she said as she inclined her head to the two different groups on either side of us. "They don't really mix and they're not really friendly to students outside their groups."

She'd just summed up the strange things I'd noticed so far.

"I met Blake," I revealed, to which she raised her eyebrows at me.

"He spoke to you?" she asked, sounding surprised.

"Yes, he showed me where my locker was this morning," I answered with a shrug. I didn't know what the big deal was.

"Wow, he never speaks to anyone outside of his group."

"You're not missing anything. He's just annoying and he really didn't make much sense." I was still toying with the idea of getting a restraining order.

By the end of lunch, I decided I liked Keri. She was very direct and straight to the point—no beating around the bush. It was like whatever popped up in her mind came straight out her mouth. Most people would be offended by it, but I thought it was charming.

CHAPTER THREE

SCARLETT

The rest of my first day at school went by quickly. Most of the students still watched me warily and every time I saw Blake he would grin and shake his head at me. He was really annoying me.

By the time the end-of-school bell rang, I was ready to leave. I'd had enough and if I saw Blake once more I wouldn't be responsible for my actions.

I made a quick stop at my locker before walking back out into the parking lot.

When I saw my new car parked in the parking lot, I felt a calmness settle in me at the thought of driving my baby home. I really needed it after the day I'd had.

I adjusted the strap of my school bag over my shoulder as my eyes met a set of stunning blue eyes. For a moment I stopped and took in the sight in front of me.

If Blake was a gorgeous, confident male whore, then this guy was sinfully stunning and the king of all male whores. He oozed sex appeal and an air of confidence that commanded attention. Immediately, I knew he was the leader of the other group, Cade Presley. I felt an air of authority around him and the only other person I felt that around was Blake.

I recognized him as the driver of the red Porsche I'd raced and I felt a smug smile tug at my lips as I held his gaze.

His hair was black like mine, although his was short on the sides and had a longer section on top that fell across his forehead. When his deep piercing turquoise eyes settled on me, I felt my body shiver at the intensity of it. Butterflies began to flutter in my stomach as I held his gaze.

I didn't have to know him to be able to tell that he was dangerous and ruthless. It was something I could sense.

Even dressed in a plain white shirt and faded jeans, he was gorgeous and looked ready for a photo shoot. It should be against the law for someone to be that good-looking; he was lethal.

I reminded myself that hot guys normally knew it and carried around an ego to match. He might look good on the outside, but I'd bet money he was not so good on the inside.

He was leaning against the side of his red Porsche.

I wouldn't let him intimidate me so I held my head high as I confidently walked toward my car. There were a couple of girls surrounding him, vying for his attention, but his eyes were fixed on me.

I watched as his eyes widened in surprise when I opened the door to the Maserati. The girls who were trying to engage him in conversation realized that his attention wasn't on them anymore and when they noticed that he was staring at me, they crossed their arms over their chests and glared at me.

As I slid into my car, I noticed the guy from earlier, the blond one with the short hair who had initially glared at me in my first lesson of the day. He walked up to Cade and stood by him. Both of them watched me intently as I started up my car and revved slightly as I backed the car out of the parking space.

I glanced back once more before I pulled out of the parking lot. The strangeness I'd encountered and gorgeous boys were forgotten as I raced home. The feel of the car gliding around the corners made me feel relaxed because I was back in control. By the time I arrived home, I was relaxed.

I parked the car in the garage and slid out. I still loved my other cars. I had various other cars but the Maserati was my favorite. When I needed to relax and drive fast, I drove the fast cars; when I wanted to go unnoticed, I normally used my Range Rover or Jeep.

Gary was in the kitchen when I walked in and dropped my school bag on the floor.

"So, how was your first day at school?" he asked with genuine interest.

"It was okay, but some of the students are a bit weird," I told him as I grabbed an apple and pulled up a chair next to him at the kitchen table.

"How were they weird?" he asked as he sipped his coffee.

"They kept watching me the whole time and it was almost like they expected me to attack them," I explained with a shrug. It still made no sense.

"Maybe they were just looking at a pretty girl," he explained with a smile and I rolled my eyes at him.

"There is definitely something up at that school. There are two different groups that seem to be run by two different guys," I tried to explain.

"You think they're some type of gangs?" Gary asked with concern.

"Maybe."

Gangs. I hadn't thought of that. That could explain why there were two groups that stuck together and didn't mingle with the other students.

"I don't like the sound of that," Gary said with a crease

in his forehead.

"Relax, I know how to protect myself," I reasoned with him. He knew what I was capable of because he trained me himself. Despite what I said, I could see Gary getting that determined look.

"I'll be fine," I assured him.

I knew Gary well enough to know that if he thought there was something dangerous in my environment, he wouldn't hesitate to yank me out of the school and make me move to another place he considered safer.

"I can't let anything happen to you," he stated as his eyes softened. He took the responsibility of keeping me safe very seriously.

"Nothing is going to happen to me. Other than two tight groups, I didn't see any weapons or any fights. I think you might just be over-reacting. I don't want to move; I like it here."

"Fine," he muttered. "But if anything happens that I'm not happy with, we're moving."

I gave him a brief nod. Even if he was right and the two groups at school were gangs, if I had nothing to do with them and kept my distance I wouldn't have anything to worry about. I still couldn't figure out why they had given me strange looks, but I was sure after a while they'd forget about me.

As soon as I was done with my homework that afternoon, Gary started with my training. I knew it was the fear that something could happen to me that had spurred it on.

He was normally very strict and determined with my training, but this time he pushed me harder than he ever had before. By the end of it my legs were wobbly and my arms hurt. I lay on my back on the sparring mat with the sweat pouring off of me. I'd definitely be feeling it the next morning.

Gary stood above me and gave me a hand up.

"Are you trying to punish me?" I teased as I wiped the sweat from my forehead.

"I'm just making sure you know your stuff," he stated with a smile, but I knew him well enough to see the worry hidden beneath the grin.

"Don't worry," I told him as I walked out of the gym, leaving him standing there drying off his face with a towel.

If it kept him from hiring a bodyguard to protect me, I'd do double the training I normally did to keep him happy. I didn't want some bulky guy following me around at school.

I was so sore that the first thing I did when I went upstairs to my room was head straight to my bathroom to run a bath.

With a sigh, I stripped my clothes off and sank into the warmth of the water that eased my tired muscles. I lay in the bath until my fingers started to wrinkle and the water began to cool.

Once I got out of the bath, I put some clothes on and then headed downstairs for an early dinner. It was one of the perks of having a chef: I got him to make all my favorite meals.

It was late when I went back upstairs to my room and Gary disappeared into his study. The sun had set already and it was dark outside. I stood by my bedroom window, looking up at the bright stars in the sky, admiring at how beautiful it was.

I inhaled the distinctive smell of fresh rain. I searched for the source and my eyes widened in shock when I saw a huge wolf sitting on the inside of my property by the boundary wall.

It was a massive black wolf—I'd never seen a wolf that big. I even rubbed my eyes and looked again to make sure I wasn't seeing things. It was completely black and its amber eyes glowed in the darkness as it watched me.

Feeling vulnerable, I shut my window and took a step back.

I had more questions running through my mind. Why on earth did a wolf smell like the group of students at my school? And, why was it so large? I knew it wasn't possible that a wolf could be that big, but I had seen it with my own eyes. Maybe someone had fed it steroids.

Also, why had it been on my property, watching me? I felt a shiver run down my spine.

It was creepy.

There was no way I was going to tell Gary any of this because he'd make me move and I liked it here.

That night, I fell into a restless sleep and I dreamed about the massive black wolf with the glowing amber eyes that had been watching me.

The wolf chased me through the dark forest. No matter how fast I ran, it was faster. In the next moment, I felt myself fall and I lay face down in the damp grass. Fear spread through me as my heart hammered in my chest. I closed my eyes for a moment and I smelled fresh rain.

Something inside of me that I'd nurtured for years refused to allow me to lie on the ground and tremble in fear. No matter what life threw at me, I wasn't one to cower from a challenge.

I pushed myself up onto my knees and then I stood up. The smell of fresh rain surrounded me as I struggled to hear any sounds. Slowly I turned to see the wolf watching me with its amber eyes.

The forest was dark, but the streaks of moonlight illuminated the massive wolf in front of me.

My heart pounded in my ears. The fear in me fought against my actions; it made me want to turn and run, but I kept rooted to the spot.

I knew none of my training would help me against this massive animal in front of me. It was the first time I felt vulnerable because I couldn't defend myself.

The wolf sniffed the air before it took a step forward. Against all my instincts, I remained unmoving with my eyes fixed on the wolf that was slowly approaching me.

It sniffed the air again as it stepped closer. It was only a couple of feet in front of me but I stood my ground, my heart still hammering with fear in my chest.

Slowly it pressed its wet snout into my hand. I held my breath, unsure of what the wolf wanted from me. I opened my hand and the wolf angled its head so my hand rested on its head.

I felt a tingling sensation start up in my hand as I touched the wolf. It was the strangest thing I'd ever felt.

You've got to be kidding me! I thought when I realized it wanted me to stroke its head. I gently moved my hand over its fur and it nuzzled my hip.

This made no sense. The wolf didn't want to hurt me, and suddenly I felt safe even though I'd feared for my life just a few moments ago.

I bent down on one knee and it brought its eyes level with mine. It licked my face and I felt a smile tug at my lips.

"Why are you here?" I asked in a whisper. I knew it was ridiculous that I was talking to a wolf. Don't ask me how, but I knew without a doubt that it could understand me. If anyone saw me, I had no doubt they would lock me up in the looney bin.

I watched its eyes as they began to change. Slowly, they changed from the amber color to a turquoise-blue color. I'd only seen those eyes once but I would recognize them anywhere.

Cade.

I shot up in my bed, tangled in my bed sheets. My heart hammered in my chest and it felt like it was going to take off.

I rubbed my temple, trying to sort through the remains of my strange dream while I tried to calm my breathing.

There had to be a logical reason why the wolf and Cade were plaguing my subconscious. I'd seen a wolf before I'd gone to bed so that explained why the wolf had followed me into my dreams.

What stumped me was why the wolf's eyes changed to Cade's piercing ones. It made no sense. Somehow my first and brief encounter with him had left a bigger impact on me than I'd first thought.

My dream had felt so real that I could still feel the fur under my hands. I remembered the strange sensation of tingles when I touched the wolf. It had been a strange dream.

I shook my head, trying to rid myself of images of the dream. I knew it was created from my subconscious thoughts, and I pushed them away. Dreams weren't really supposed to make sense, so I wasn't going to look for something that wasn't there.

I reasoned that it had been all the strange behavior from my first day at school that made me experience such vivid, weird dreams.

Tired and still struggling to wake up, I dragged myself into my bathroom. After a quick shower, I was feeling better but I needed my caffeine fix. While I dried my body off, my fingers brushed over my birthmark on my hip. It looked more like a tattoo, but I'd been born with it.

It was two teardrops side by side. One teardrop was bigger than the other.

I finished getting ready and went downstairs to get some coffee.

"You look awful," Gary informed me as I walked into the kitchen. He sat at the kitchen table with a half-eaten plate of food and holding a newspaper. I just glared at him then walked over to the coffee machine and poured myself some. The rich aroma began to clear my tired and foggy mind.

"Didn't you sleep well?" he asked as his eyes softened.

"No, I didn't."

The dark bags under my eyes wouldn't allow me the white lie so there was no point in lying. Normally, I wore very little makeup, but I'd put a little more on than usual in the hopes of hiding my lack of sleep. I hadn't been able to cover it up, though.

His eyes held mine. I knew what he wanted to know and I shook my head.

After my parents had died, I'd suffered from night terrors and after a while the night terrors had faded into nightmares. After a few months and some therapy, I began to experience the nightmares less often until a few years later they stopped completely.

It had been years since I'd had a nightmare and I could see the concern in Gary's eyes. His first thought at the mention that I hadn't slept well was that I'd had a nightmare about my parents. There was no way I was going to tell him about my dream. He'd think I was crazy.

"It was probably first-day-at-a-new-school nerves," I tried to explain. I took a sip of my coffee.

"Okay," he said. He didn't look convinced, but he let it go.

This time I wasn't early so I had to park my baby farther away from the school. I hitched my bag over my shoulder and walked to the entrance.

Just as I got to the front, someone stepped into my path. My eyes went to the obstacle.

He stood in front of me with his arms crossed over his chest. Vibrant eyes held mine.

There was an unmistakable power in him that demanded attention, but I wasn't your typical girl. I tilted my heard upward and held his gaze confidently, refusing to be intimidated. The truth was I felt it, but there was no way I'd show him that as my stubborn streak kicked in.

In his eyes I saw surprise at my reaction to him.

Yeah, pretty boy, I think you've met your match.

CHAPTER FOUR

SCARLETT

I held his gaze for a few moments before he took a step closer to me. I felt an electric shiver through me as I felt my body react to him. I'd never felt that type of reaction with anybody else before.

The smell of fresh rain hit me full force. I took another deep breath but there was no mistaking that smell; it reminded me of my dream last night.

Ignoring my body's reaction to his piercing eyes, I returned his stare without revealing the havoc he was causing me. The outside world around us disappeared into the background as we continued to glare at each other.

He might think I was one of those many girls who would be in awe of him and his devastating good looks, but he had another thing coming. It didn't matter that he made butterflies in my stomach come alive. I was stronger than this.

I wouldn't be one of those girls who fell at his feet and allowed him to treat me like a fleeting attraction before he moved on to another willing girl. There was that saying 'never judge a book by its cover' but in this case I'd bet he was exactly what I'd summed him up to be. He was arrogant and in his case the book cover had warning signs telling me to keep well away from him.

"We need to talk," he said as he folded his arms across his chest. Dressed in dark jeans and a black shirt with a leather jacket, he looked badass—but I wasn't scared of him. I could see from the way the material molded to his lean chest that he worked out, possibly as hard as I did.

"I don't even know you, so why would we need to talk?" I asked as I took a step forward, placing me only a few inches away from him.

I was so close that I could see his dark eyelashes framing his turquoise eyes. His dark, raven hair hung across his forehead and I had an urge to run my hands through it.

Mentally, I shook myself. It felt so wrong to find him so attractive when I didn't even like him.

Something dark flashed in his eyes, then his forehead creased as his jaw tightened. Just from his body language, I could tell he was angry. He wasn't used to being questioned. He was the type who spoke and everyone obeyed, but I was no follower.

"Don't play dumb with me," he hissed, his eyes darkening with anger. The unmistakable power rolled off of him in waves and I felt that power hit me in the chest. I took an unsure step backward.

There was something different about him.

He didn't know me and I had no idea what he was talking about. It reminded me of my strange conversation with Blake. I couldn't figure out why both of them kept talking to me about something I was supposed to know but didn't.

If I didn't know better, I'd think I was going to a school for crazies.

Straightening my back, I stepped closer and pushed a finger into his chest. Although he was taller than me and without a doubt physically stronger than me, I refused to back down from him.

"Listen here, buddy, I don't know you or what I'm supposed to know but I can guarantee you that I have no idea what you're talking about," I said to him angrily as I continued to poke my finger into his chest. "Understand this: if you don't back off, I'll make you sorry you tried to mess with me. Keep to the vacant bimbos and leave me alone."

His eyebrows shot up in surprise and then his eyes pierced mine. Then, unexpectedly, he cocked his head to the side and studied me for a moment before the one side of his mouth tilted upward in a half smirk.

His devastating smile made my knees weaken.

I was so over this. As much as he affected me on a physical level, there was no way I was going to let him get the better of me or push me around.

I stepped around him and entered the school, ignoring his eyes on my retreating figure. The butterflies were going crazy inside my stomach and I couldn't deny the physical reaction he caused.

He was dangerous and I needed to be very careful of him.

The strangeness I'd experienced yesterday had just upped a level to downright weird. I couldn't help my thoughts going back to my dream from last night. Cade smelled like fresh rain, like he had in my dream.

By the time I made it to my locker, I'd pushed all the crazy thoughts from my mind. I wasn't going to allow anyone to ruin my second day at a new school.

"Hey."

I turned to see Keri standing beside me. Like her personality, her clothes were bold and colorful. The blood-red mini skirt teamed with black boots and green shirt on most people would look mismatched, but she pulled it off. It actually looked stylish.

"Hi," I greeted as I closed my locker, stuffing the books I held in my hand into my school bag.

"What's your first class for the day?" she asked.

"Math," I answered with a sigh. Math was not one of my strongest subjects but I had to work hard at it, especially when I was doing my own finances now.

"I've got English but it's next to your class," she informed me.

"Cool."

I was usually a loner, but I liked Keri. There was something about her that put me completely at ease in her company. I knew I hadn't known her for long, but I felt she was someone I could trust.

"I saw you had a run-in with Cade this morning," she said as we started walking down the hallway to our first classes.

My eyes darted to her curious gaze.

"He's like Blake; he never really talks to anyone outside of his group. What did he say to you?" she asked.

"Honestly, he didn't make much sense," I revealed. "He said he wanted to talk to me and told me I knew what it was about. I'm not sure he's playing with a full deck of cards."

Keri laughed and I couldn't help the smile that spread across my face.

"Only you would think the hottest guy in school was crazy."

She hadn't known me long, but she knew me well already.

"He's not the only crazy in this school," I added, remembering Blake's conversation with me had been just as weird.

"Do tell," she instructed.

"Blake also made no sense," I told her.

She laughed again as she shook her head.

"Let me correct that: only you would think the two hottest guys in this school were crazy," she restated, trying to keep a straight face.

"Maybe it's something in the water," I said with a shrug.

I wasn't going to waste any more time thinking about those two idiots.

"Have you seen any wolves before?" I asked when I remembered the wolf I'd seen watching me last night. Even memories of the dream were still fresh in my mind.

She stopped for a moment, my question clearly taking her by surprise.

"Yeah, I've seen a couple. I once saw a huge—and I mean huge—black wolf," she said as she held her arms out to give me an idea of the size she was talking about.

"I didn't think that wolves could get that big," she added as her arms fell to her sides and she started to walk again.

"I think I saw the same wolf," I murmured. It was nice to know that the wolf I'd seen last night hadn't been a part of my imagination.

"Did its eyes glow like an amber color?" she asked in a whisper, like anyone who overheard us would think we were nuts, and then we'd be joining those two crazy idiots in the white-padded room.

My eyes met hers and I nodded. A foreboding feeling settled in my stomach at the confirmation that we'd both seen something that wasn't possible. Instinctively, I knew that there were too many strange coincidences for all of this to be nothing. There was definitely something strange going on.

In my first class of the morning, my annoyance grew when Blake breezed into the room and dropped into the seat at the desk next to me.

I glared at him and he smiled back. He was deliberately trying to annoy me and I could feel my temper spring to life. Not wanting him to get the reaction he was working for, I turned to look out of the window and ignored him as best I could.

"Not talking to me this morning?" he asked in a teasing tone. Ignoring him wasn't helping, so I swung my gaze back to him as I gripped my pen in my hand tightly to try and keep my temper under control.

He leaned back lazily in the seat, smiling at me when he noticed I was trying to keep my temper under control. I so wanted to wipe that smile off his face.

"Leave me alone," I hissed at him in a whisper, not wanting to cause a scene. The class was starting to fill up.

"I wish I could, but I can't," he said cryptically as he leaned forward. His smile began to wane. I could see the joking was over and he was very serious.

"We can't leave you alone," he added.

I was about to ask him who was the 'we' he was referring to and why they couldn't leave me alone when the teacher walked in the classroom. Blake's gaze held mine until I turned to face the teacher.

I wasn't going to let him say things like that to me without explaining further, so when the class ended I made sure I grabbed his arm just as we exited the classroom.

"You need to explain what you meant earlier," I told him as he turned to face me. His usual light-hearted and teasing look was gone as he looked at me.

"I can't tell you," he explained and then added, "Just know that Cade and I are the good guys."

With no further explanation, he turned and walked away from me and I was tempted to throw a book at him.

If I was confused before, I was even more confused now. They kept spinning one riddle on top of another. I had no idea what they were talking about and they wouldn't explain.

Frustrated, I stalked to my next class. Like the day before, I kept getting strange looks from most of the students.

By lunchtime, I was tired of going around in circles in my mind. On my way to the cafeteria, I made up my mind. I wanted answers and I was going to get them.

I walked into the cafeteria and spotted the person who was going to give me the answers I wanted.

Cade was sitting at the large table on the one side of the cafeteria where the strange smell of fresh rain was the strongest. I still needed to figure out why most of the students smelled so distinctive.

I walked determinedly to the table. This morning he'd wanted to talk to me and now I was ready to talk. His eyes fastened onto me as I reached the table. The conversation died down when the other students sitting with him noticed me.

I recognized that the blond guy who had stood beside Cade yesterday was sitting across from him. He looked to Cade and arched an eyebrow.

"I want to talk to you," I informed Cade. He glanced to the blond guy and it was like they were having a conversation without words.

"I thought you didn't want to talk," Cade said as his eyes locked with mine. A shiver of awareness ran through me; I hated the way I reacted to him.

"And now I do," I said, feeling my temper beginning to grow. I crossed my arms over my chest to keep myself from slapping him.

I'd never met such an infuriating man and I seemed to lose my temper around him more easily than usual.

"Don't get your panties into a twist," he said as he stood up.

"Leave my panties out of this," I threw back at him as I followed him out of the cafeteria. If I weren't so desperate for some answers, I'd have stormed off.

Just outside the cafeteria, he turned to face me. The hallway was quiet so we wouldn't have anyone listening in on our conversation.

"So, what changed your mind? I was pretty sure after your little outburst this morning you weren't interested in what I had to say." He cocked his head slightly to the side as he studied me.

"Yeah, well, I'm tired of having these cryptic conversations with you and Blake," I said as my hands went to my hips. Cade smiled at the gesture.

"So what did you want to talk to me about this morning?" I asked when he remained silent, watching me with veiled eyes. I breathed in the distinct smell of fresh rain. I needed to ask him what type of cologne it was because half the school was using it.

He watched me quietly for a few moments before he started to talk.

"I want you to come to my house this evening," he said.

My eyes narrowed at him.

"Why?" I asked as I looked at him suspiciously.

"I need to tell you some stuff and I can't do that here," he explained softly, looking around to see if anyone was close enough to hear our conversation.

"I don't know you and I don't trust you," I told him as I shook my head. I didn't know him well enough to go to his house alone tonight. For all I knew he would be a serial killer lining up his next victim—me.

"It's simple. If you want answers, you'll meet me at my house," he stated confidently and I wanted to kick his shin. He was so arrogant, so sure of himself, I wanted to flip him off and tell him to get lost.

I was about to tell him to go and play in traffic when he leaned forward and under his breath and close to my ear he said, "I can explain why you started to change when you turned sixteen."

I couldn't help my mouth from opening in shock as I stared at him. How did he know about that? I hadn't told anyone except Gary.

"How...?" I asked, still bewildered.

"Be at my place at seven," he ordered and then turned to leave. He rattled off an address to me before he disappeared back inside the cafeteria.

Still in shock, I leaned back against the lockers and tried to figure out what had just happened. He knew about the changes. How did he know that?

Well, as much as I didn't want to, I knew the only way to find out would be to go meet him at his house.

I couldn't concentrate for the rest of the day so by the time school ended, I was relieved. Cade and Blake had been scarce since I'd had my conversation with Cade. I hurried home.

Even during my training, Gary picked up on my preoccupied mind.

"Everything okay?" he asked as he wiped the sweat off his face with a towel.

"Yeah," I replied. I wasn't ready to tell him about my short conversation with Cade. If he knew about it he would try to stop me from going and I couldn't let that happen. I wanted to know, to find out why I'd experienced the changes, and for once the answer was within my grasp.

As soon as training was over, I jogged upstairs. I tried hard to concentrate on my homework but it took me forever because I kept watching the time, wishing it would go faster.

After I finally finished, I showered and changed. I wore dark blue jeans and a white baby-doll shirt. There was no way I was dressing up for my visit to Cade's house, so instead of a pair of high heels, I settled for flat, black ballet pumps.

I decided against wearing makeup because I didn't want Cade to get the wrong idea, so I only put a little lip-gloss on.

Gary was already seated at the kitchen table when I entered. At the sight of me, he raised an eyebrow.

"Where are you going tonight?" he asked as I sat down across from him.

"I'm going out to meet a friend," I answered vaguely. Gary wasn't stupid; he knew I was trying to avoid telling him, and I knew him well enough to see he wasn't happy about it.

When Gary had become my guardian, he'd been very protective of me and he still was, even though he wasn't my guardian anymore.

"I'll be fine," I assured him as I got a plate of food.

He didn't say anything further on the subject as I sat down and ate my dinner.

"I'll see you later," I said to him as I left the kitchen once I'd finished eating. My last check of the time told me I still had half an hour, so I headed to the garage. I got into my car and programmed Cade's address into the GPS.

My answers weren't far away. It would only take twenty minutes, according to the GPS, to get to Cade's place.

CHAPTER
FIVE

SCARLETT

I felt a little apprehensive as I followed the GPS instructions to Cade's house. It didn't take long before I pulled up in front of big black gates that were connected with a ten-foot wall around the property. It kind of looked like a fortress.

Actually, it suited his personality from the little I'd seen; he was hard, powerful and used to getting his own way.

I looked to find some sort of intercom system, but there was none. Then I noticed a video camera on the wall. I watched it angle lower to fix on me and then the gates began to open.

Geez, and I thought I had a thing about security. I had nothing on this guy. I drove slowly down the driveway, taking in the sight in front of me. Although it was dark, the lights along the driveway lit up the way and then my eyes fixed on the mansion in front of me.

His house was massive, but it wasn't unexpected. Porsches weren't cheap. There were a few lights along the driveway and the front area of the house was well lit with a few outside lights.

I parked in front. With my eyes still fixed on the house, I slid out of my car and closed the door. The front door opened and Cade filled the doorway.

"You came," he said like he'd expected me not to show.

"You sound surprised," I said dryly as I walked to the front door and stood before him. He was taller than me but I didn't let that intimidate me as I raised my eyes to hold his gaze. An awareness of him shivered through me again and I felt a flutter in my stomach. I hated the fact that I was physically attracted to him. Why couldn't he be a hunchback with warts?

"I didn't think you were going to show," he said with a shrug as he stood aside for me to enter. I eyed him up and down before I stepped past him and into his house.

Where my house was decorated with furniture with sleek lines and a more modern look to it, Cade's house was the opposite. It had older, more antique-looking furniture and with the Persian carpets it was way too busy for my liking. I believed less was more.

"This way," he commanded as he walked through a doorway to the right. I glared at his back as I followed behind him reluctantly. I hated being given orders and it seemed to happen often when he was around.

"I'm not going to stay long," I told him as I followed him into a formal lounge. "I just want the answers you promised to give me."

"Are you always this impatient?" he asked with a frown as he turned to face me with his feet apart and his arms crossed over his broad chest.

"Yes," I answered without hesitation, walking past him to take a seat on the sofa. I didn't believe in beating around the bush. I crossed my legs and tilted my head to look up at

Cade, who'd turned to face me.

"Spill," I commanded him and I could see it irritated him. He was used to giving commands, not following them.

"I'm waiting for someone to arrive," he informed me coldly.

"Who?" I asked, curiosity getting the better of me.

At that moment a doorbell rang and Cade left to answer it. I'd find out soon enough who he'd been waiting for. I was surprised, though, when Blake followed Cade in a few moments later.

"Yay, it's Tweedledum," I said sarcastically as I rolled my eyes. Cade narrowed his gaze at me but Blake took no offense, laughing instead.

"Constant entertainment," he said, still with a grin on his face as he sat down on the sofa across from me.

"Are you always this bitchy?" Cade asked as he stood in front of the fireplace facing us with his eyes on me.

"Nope, I took an extra bitchy pill this morning," I replied sarcastically.

"Do we have to do this?" Cade turned to Blake and asked. There they were, at it again, talking cryptically about me and I had no idea what was going on.

"You told me you'd give me answers," I reminded him, starting to feel my temper rise. "I'm here, so start talking."

Cade ignored me and kept his attention on Blake. Blake shook his head and turned to Cade with a grin and said, "Yeah, we have to."

"I'm pretty sure she doesn't need our help," Cade argued and continued to ignore me. I could feel my temper rise even further.

"She needs our help," stated Blake seriously, all joking aside as he held Cade's glare.

"I'm done," I said as I stood up and stalked back to the front entrance. I wasn't going to sit there all night while the two of them debated whether or not to tell me what I wanted to know.

I would have to figure this out on my own. I didn't need their help.

"Wait," I heard Blake call from behind me, but I didn't stop and by the time he made it to the front door I was already sliding into my car. I slammed the door shut and started up the car.

I drove down the driveway and, at the gates, I waited impatiently for them to open but they remained closed. I revved the engine but the gates never budged.

My anger began to build and I felt like I was going to combust. It had taken a lot for me to put aside my dislike for Cade long enough to make the trip to his house so he could give me the answers I'd been searching for. I'd made the effort only to watch Tweedledee and Tweedledum argue cryptically in front of me.

And now they were preventing me from leaving. I took a deep breath and released it, trying to rein in my temper.

Then, just when I was about to turn around and drive back to the house and go ballistic at those two idiots, the gates finally opened. I pulled out of the driveway and onto the main road.

Too preoccupied with my thoughts as I drove away, I didn't notice the figure standing in the center of the road until it was too late. I slammed on the brakes, desperately trying to avoid the person but I felt something smack the front of the car and crash into my windshield before it rolled over the roof.

Too shocked to try and control the car, it spun out of control and I hit something with so much force that my head flew forward, hitting the steering wheel before I was flung backward.

Dazed and shaken, I tried to move and I winced when I

felt my head throb. Gently, my fingers touched my forehead and I felt blood. A pain in my chest told me I was either badly bruised across my chest or I had hurt a rib. It hurt to breathe.

I'd hit someone.

Terror gripped me when I realized I'd actually hit a person. Shock began to set in and I began to shake as I struggled to release my seatbelt. When the seatbelt finally opened, I tried to open my car door but it was stuck.

I felt tears of pain and fear sting at my eyelids as I tried to push against the door with all the strength I had and the door finally opened. I bit down on my lip to keep from crying out in pain as I climbed out of the car.

My car had hit a tree. It was then that I noticed a dark and foreboding forest on either side of the road.

It was dark and a couple of the streetlights were out so it wasn't well lit enough to see much. I began to panic when I scanned the road, but I couldn't see anyone.

There was no way the person I'd hit could have gotten up and walked away. Where were they?

I began to scan the trees on the side of the road, trying to find the person I'd hit. Panic began to rise up in me when no matter how hard I looked, I couldn't find the body.

I dropped to my knees beside my car when the pain in my chest grew. Tears of frustration and pain began to slide down my face.

Everything began to spin and I put my hands to the ground to keep myself steady. I closed my eyes and then opened them again, trying to keep it together, but the world tilted again.

I felt hands reach for me.

"I got her."

It was Blake. His gentle hands turned me around and laid me gently on the ground as I winced in pain. I closed my eyes and tried to open them. Blake's concerned face spun in front of me. My body continued to shake as the shock set in.

"I hit someone," I confessed to Blake, trying to stop my body from shaking. "They rolled off the car, but I can't find them."

"Don't worry about that," he told me softly.

"How can I not worry? I hit someone," I said angrily, but he ignored me.

"He was here," I heard Cade say angrily and then I heard something growl. I clutched at Blake's arms at the sound of the animal growling.

"It's okay, you're safe," he assured me gently. The pain in my chest worsened and I groaned. I felt his gentle hands as he began to check my injuries.

"How did you guys know I had an accident?" I asked Blake when the realization set in that we were too far away from Cade's house for them to have heard it, so how had they known?

"Where does it hurt?" he asked softly, ignoring my question as I felt his fingers brush over my temple.

"My chest," I gasped as he lifted my shirt to check, but my hands held it. "Go and get a cheap thrill somewhere else, Blake."

He let out a sigh.

"I'm trying to check your injury," he assured me. I looked at him without his image spinning and I could see the concern in his eyes.

"Fine," I relented and I released the hold on my shirt.

He lifted it and I felt his fingers brush over the right side of my chest where it hurt the most. I nearly hit him when he pushed down gently along my rib and I felt the pain flare again.

"It's bruising already, but I don't think you've broken anything," he informed me.

"Thanks," I muttered, because even though I hadn't broken anything, it still hurt.

"We need to get her back to my house," Cade said with concern as he knelt beside me. Even lying on the road in pain, I couldn't help the flutter when I looked into his eyes. *Damn the jerk!*

"We need to call the cops," I insisted. How could they want to take me away from the scene of a crime?

"We can't, we need to get you back to Cade's house," Blake insisted.

"I just hit someone. They could be lying injured or they could be…" I said. I couldn't say the word.

"The person you hit isn't dead," said Cade with steeliness in his voice as his eyes looked toward the dark forest.

"How do you know that?" I asked. The more time I spent around these two, the more I was convinced they were crazy.

"I just do." His eyes settled back on me. I could see it was pointless trying to argue with him.

"What about my car?" I continued to argue.

"I'll send someone to come and get it," Cade assured me.

"But—" I tried to argue.

"You need to trust us," Cade said, cutting me off with a hard look. I was in pain and still shaking, not exactly in a state to fight him on this.

Blake's hands slid under me and he lifted me up into his arms. I winced and held my right side as it ached.

Cade hurried to the passenger side of a black Grand Cherokee that was parked a few feet away and opened the door. Blake slid me onto the back seat and I bit down on my lip to stop me from screaming out in pain.

Once I was in, the door was closed and Cade got into the driver side and Blake slid into the passenger side. The trip back to Cade's house felt like forever because every jostle of the car ripped through me and I bit down to keep from crying out.

When we pulled up in front of Cade's house, he and Blake got out of the car. I tried to shift out of the backseat, but it hurt too much.

"Is she okay?" I heard an unknown voice ask and I looked up to see the blond guy who always seemed to be with Cade.

The door opened and Blake climbed into the back seat and helped shift me out while the blond guy held my legs. Once I was out of the car, the blond guy lifted me effortlessly into his arms and carried me into the house with Blake following closely behind us.

Cade was already in the house when we entered and halfway up the stairs. The blond guy carried me up the stairs as Blake followed.

I wasn't exactly heavy, but I was surprised when the blond guy didn't seem to strain at all when he carried me up the stairs and to a bedroom.

The bedroom was huge and decorated similarly to the rest of the house. The bed, table and chairs were all antique furniture.

Cade pulled back the comforter as the blond guy gently put me down. I winced and then I slumped backward onto the pillow, feeling emotionally and physically exhausted.

"Jake, go and get Ross to help you get Scarlett's car," Cade ordered the blond guy to which he gave a brief nod and disappeared from the room. So, the blond guy's name was Jake.

Cade disappeared into the adjoining bathroom and returned with a box that looked like a medical kit. He opened it up and got some cotton out. He put some liquid onto it and then began to clean my head wound. I winced when the liquid burned the cut.

Once he was finished, he took the stuff back into the bathroom and reappeared back in the room moments later.

"I think the two of you have some explaining to do," I suggested as I looked up to Cade and Blake. They shared a look for a moment. I could see Cade was the one who was reluctant to tell me, but he let out a sigh.

"You have to keep an open mind and promise me you're not going to freak out," he told me as his eyes pierced mine. I gave him a brief nod.

What could be so bad?

"We're more than human," he began.

Yeah, they were idiots. I couldn't help but giggle. Cade glared at me and I stopped. I felt like a little kid who had just been put into my place and I pouted. Blake just shook his head at the two of us.

"We are supernatural creatures," he explained while he held my gaze. I blinked and then I looked at Blake. He wasn't laughing; he looked as serious as Cade did and I thought they were both crazy.

"We are werewolves," he stated. They both watched me as I processed what he'd told me. I began to look around the room.

"What are you looking for?" Blake asked, a little confused at my behavior.

"The cameras," I replied.

"What are you talking about?" Cade asked as he threw his hands up in the air. He was exasperated with me.

"This has got to be some sort of joke," I replied, still looking for the cameras, but I couldn't see any. Maybe they were built into the roof with only a small hole to capture what they needed to. These guys were good.

"It's not a joke," Cade said angrily. I could see he was about to lose his temper.

"I think you guys have been reading too many teen-girl

books," I remarked, trying to sit up, but my chest hurt too much. Blake leaned forward and helped me sit up without jarring the injury.

"Thank you," I said to him.

Cade turned to glare at Blake and then he stalked off to the one side of the room and leaned against the wall. His eyes darkened with anger as he crossed his arms.

"We're not joking," Blake tried to explain to me as he sat down on the edge of the bed.

"Do you guys honestly think I'd believe that rubbish? Do I look that gullible?"

I didn't know what their deal was. Why did they keep talking about crazy, unbelievable stuff?

"We're telling you the truth," Blake insisted again.

"We're wasting our time with words, we're going to have to show her," Cade said to Blake as he pushed off the wall and walked closer to the bed.

"Yay!" I remarked sarcastically while clapping my hands like a little kid.

"Show me the big, scary werewolf." I cheered enthusiastically.

Cade disappeared with a growl and in his place stood a massive black wolf with amber eyes. It growled as it stepped closer to the foot of the bed.

My eyes remained glued to the impossible image in front of me. There was no disputing it—there was a massive wolf standing on all fours growling at me.

CHAPTER SIX

SCARLETT

My eyes traveled over the massive beast that watched me with its unusual amber eyes. Its teeth were bared but it had stopped growling. Blake sat calmly at the edge of the bed, watching my reaction.

I laughed and clutched my side when the pain shot through me. Despite the pain, I continued to laugh until I had tears running down my face.

Blake looked at me like I was crazy and shifted closer.

"Are you okay?" he asked as he gripped me by the arms.

"Yeah… I'm fine…" I tried to tell him in between my laughter. "I just can't believe… my hallucination would… be this good."

"You're not hallucinating," he insisted.

Finally, I managed to stop the laughter and I turned to face him, wiping the tears of laughter from my face.

"I bumped my head pretty good," I argued with him.

"You didn't hit it hard enough to start seeing things," he assured me, shaking his head.

"But if I'm not hallucinating, then…" I paused for a moment as my eyes shifted back to the wolf watching us. "It's real."

Holy crap! The wolf is real.

Blake watched me closely as my eyes remained on the massive beast at the foot of the bed. After I got over the initial shock, I peered closer and realized it was the same wolf that had been watching me the previous night.

I sucked in a breath as the realization hit me that Cade had been stalking me in wolf form and my anger began to grow. Common sense would dictate I'd be more concerned with the fact that Cade had turned into a wolf in front of my eyes, but the only thing that my mind would concentrate on was that Cade had invaded my privacy.

"You," I said angrily as I pointed an accusing finger at the now-growling wolf in front of me. Feeling my blood boil with anger, I slipped out of the bed, holding my injured side as I stepped closer to the wolf.

"I wouldn't do that if I were you," warned Blake but I ignored him as I stepped closer to the wolf, whose amber eyes watched me closely.

"You were watching me," I stated angrily. The hilarious thing was that I was talking to a werewolf like it wasn't something out of the ordinary. Clearly, I needed my head examined.

"You came onto my property and you were watching me," I accused as I stood a few feet away from Cade—well, wolf-form Cade. The growling stopped as his amber eyes held mine.

"We were watching you." The explanation came from Blake.

"Why?" I turned to face Blake, who was standing beside the bed. He ran a hand through his hair.

"You need to sit down and we'll explain," he suggested as

he flickered a glance to the wolf and then back to me.

"Don't treat me like I'm fragile, I can handle it," I assured him, feeling that independent streak rise up in me. I'd worked hard to make sure I didn't have to depend on anyone, even Gary.

Whatever these two threw at me, I would be able to handle. In my short life I'd experienced some dark times and I'd managed to get through them. Those moments had made me stronger and they'd made me the person I was.

"I don't think you're fragile, trust me," he said cryptically. "But the explanation might take a while and no matter how tough you're trying to be, you're injured."

He had a point, and sometimes I was too stubborn for my own good.

"Fine," I relented and sat down on a nearby chair that faced toward Blake and Cade, the massive black wolf.

"You can change back," Blake said to the wolf.

In the second it took me to blink, the wolf disappeared and Cade stood tall, dark and domineering. Amber eyes were replaced with his signature turquoise eyes. Thank goodness he was fully clothed when he shifted back into human form.

I was annoyed when I felt the flutter again inside my stomach at the sight of Cade. I hated how I felt around him. Maybe it was one of the reasons I went out of my way to annoy him. He made me feel things no one else had ever made me feel, and I had no idea how to deal with it.

"Spill," I instructed Blake.

"You're in danger," Cade spoke. My eyes shifted back to him and he held my gaze. I couldn't help a tiny bit of fear that soaked into me at his words. From the time my parents had died I'd been looking over my shoulder expecting the same thing to happen to me. It was one of the reasons I trained like I did.

"Why would I be in danger?" I asked, trying to mask the

fear I felt, but my voice wavered for a split second.

"Let's start from the beginning," Blake said with his arms folded over his chest.

I looked at him expectantly as I tapped my foot against the carpet. These two took forever to get to the point and I was running out of patience.

"When I asked you what pack you were from, you told me you had no idea what I was talking about," he reminded me.

"Yes, I remember."

These guys had said a lot that didn't make sense. Then the penny dropped; he asked me what pack I'd belonged to—pack, as in a pack of wolves.

"I'm not one of you," I stated fiercely.

They remained quiet.

"I'm not a werewolf," I added as I stood up, wincing when pain shot up the side of me.

"Take it easy," Blake said as he came forward and tried to gently push me back down into the chair. When I glared at him, he dropped his hands and stepped back.

"Stop arguing," Cade said fiercely as he stepped in front of me. "You're one of us whether you like it or not, and arguing about it isn't going to change that."

"But how is that possible?" I asked out loud, taking a step back. I felt the chair at the back of my knees and I sank into it.

A werewolf.

"Both, or at least one, of your parents are werewolves," Cade informed me.

"My parents were murdered when I was ten," I revealed to them. At least one of my parents must have been a werewolf and that thought was hard to wrap my mind around.

"So that explains why you have no idea what you are,"

muttered Blake.

"How were your parents murdered?" asked Cade gently. It was the first time he'd spoken to me without sounding angry or exasperated. My eyes flickered to him.

"Initially, the coroner had ruled it an animal attack but later he'd changed it to unknown," I mumbled, still trying to process what they were telling me.

Even deep in my own thoughts I didn't miss the look Blake and Cade shared. They knew something.

"What?" I asked, frowning at them.

"It sounds like they were killed by another werewolf." My head reeled at that thought. A werewolf had killed my parents? Why? I couldn't stop an image of a fierce, massive werewolf tearing into my parents with its sharp razor-like teeth. I closed my eyes briefly, trying to push the image from my mind.

"I don't understand," I said, looking at the two of them to explain it for me.

"Most werewolves stay in a pack, some larger than others. The werewolves that don't belong to packs are called rogues."

"Am I a rogue?" I asked softly. Clearly, I didn't belong to a pack.

"Yes, but technically you weren't forced from your pack or left it of your own free will," Cade informed me. "Your situation is different. Until five minutes ago, you didn't even know you were a werewolf."

"Rogue werewolves are usually werewolves that struggle to fit into a pack. They have issues with following rules and commands. Humans that break the law are put into prison; werewolves that break the law are forced from the pack and made to live on their own," Blake explained.

"So you think my parents were killed by a rogue werewolf?" I asked after a few minutes' silence.

"Yes," answered Cade.

"But why?" I asked softly. Having to bring up the memories of my parents and their violent deaths left a lump in my throat and a sting of tears in my eyes. It was hard to keep it together.

In front of me, Blake bent down on one knee to bring his eyes level with mine.

"We're not sure," he said as he looked at me with sympathy.

"All of this still doesn't explain why I'm in danger," I reminded them.

"To explain properly, I need to give you a bit of information about werewolves," said Blake as he stood up. He grabbed a nearby chair and angled it toward me before sitting down in it. Cade remained where he was, sitting on the edge of the bed with his legs stretched out in front of him.

"Most werewolves are born and raised within a pack. Up to the age of sixteen, werewolves are pretty much human. From the time a male werewolf turns sixteen, their senses strengthen and they are able to shift into wolves. But when female werewolves turn sixteen, only their senses strengthen —they are not able to shift into a wolf."

He allowed me a moment to digest the information.

"So that explains why I started developing stronger senses after I turned sixteen," I murmured.

Blake and Cade nodded their heads at me.

"Only from the time the werewolf turns sixteen can it be smelled and identified by other werewolves. It's a way to keep young werewolves safe from rogue werewolves until they get to an age where they are able to protect themselves," Blake explained further.

Smelled and identified. I realized the distinct smells I'd smelled since I'd gotten here were the different werewolves. If I'd been a part of a pack, I would have known what the distinct smells meant.

"Why do some werewolves smell like forest and some smell like fresh rain?" I asked the question that had been bugging me for a while.

"The werewolves that smell like fresh rain belong to the storm pack and the others belong to the silver moon pack," Blake explained.

"So if werewolves have scents according to their packs, what do I smell like?" I asked.

"Like wild daisies," said Cade, looking a little uncomfortable. Blake threw him a look and smiled.

Flowers were good; it could be worse, I could smell like old shoes.

"So if I had to join a pack, would my scent change to that of the pack?" I asked. Cade raised an eyebrow and I rolled my eyes at him.

"It's a hypothetical question. I don't want to join either of your packs," I stated heatedly.

"Yes," answered Blake.

"I don't know much about werewolves. The only stuff I do know is what I've read about in teen books or learned from movies like *Twilight*. But aren't werewolves too territorial to have two packs so close together?" I questioned. Questions were forming in my head faster than they would be able to answer them.

"In most towns that would be correct, there would only be one pack, but here things are different. I'm the alpha of the silver moon pack and Cade is the alpha of the storm pack. The only reason why we are able to run our packs together in one town without trouble is because we've been best friends from the time we started to walk."

"When you say alpha does that mean that you're in charge?" I asked.

"Yes," answered Cade. "Our job is to keep the pack

running smoothly and to keep everyone safe. The alpha of the pack is the person who gives the orders and the rest follow our orders without question."

I didn't like the sound of that one bit. I didn't want to be a part of a pack if it meant I had to follow orders from an alpha. I wasn't ready to kiss my independence goodbye.

"You said male werewolves shift at the age of sixteen but female werewolves don't—why?" I asked. It seemed a bit sexist, if you asked me.

"Female werewolves only start to shift once they find their mate," he began to explain and I frowned.

"Why?" I asked the question, but I was pretty sure I wasn't going to like the answer to it.

"There are a lot of things that get triggered in the female werewolf when two werewolves mate. Once the werewolves mate, the female werewolf begins the cycle of going into heat until she falls pregnant. It's like nature's way of ensuring the female werewolf has a male werewolf to take care of her needs and keep her safe."

Oh, hell no!

My frown deepened. I didn't like the sound of that at all.

"When the werewolf belongs to a pack, the werewolves are able to talk to each other in their minds, like a mind-link."

That sounded cool. It was pretty much the only thing that sounded cool.

"With two werewolves that have mated, the link between the two runs deeper and the two mates are able to feel each other's emotions and stuff like that. It ensures the male werewolf knows when the female werewolf is in danger."

"How do werewolves find their mates?" I asked, wondering if it went along the same lines as *Twilight*. What had they called it? Imprinting? And it happened when they looked at each other, didn't it?

"Unlike what most books or movies portray, finding one's mate isn't accomplished by just seeing them. The mates have to touch each other. The touch has to be skin to skin."

"What happens when they touch?" I asked, curiosity getting the better of me. It wasn't like I was going to be hoping and praying that I'd find a mate; I was happy on my own, and I wasn't interested in finding a mate.

"They know straight away."

"If we have to go into that much detail, we'll be here all night," Cade said as he stood.

"I've just found out I'm a werewolf and I'm entitled to ask all the questions I damn well please, so if you don't want to listen to it, then leave," I said, putting him in his place. Momentarily surprised at what I had said, his eyes widened and then they narrowed in anger.

"Fine," he said angrily as he sat back down on the bed.

I looked to Blake.

"Finish," I instructed, ignoring the other seething alpha in the room.

"All werewolves are born with a birthmark on their hips and mates have matching birthmarks."

I couldn't keep my fingers from straying to the place on my hip where I had a birthmark of two teardrops. It was a lot of information to digest. I could feel my head begin to throb and I rubbed my temple.

Cade pushed off of the bed and strode from the room. I looked to Blake, who just shrugged.

"So how do werewolves mate?" I continued with my questions.

"The male werewolf marks the female werewolf and then the mating is completed with sex," Blake explained without batting an eyelid. This was probably so normal to them.

I couldn't help the blush that set into my cheeks at his answer.

"How does the male werewolf mark the female werewolf?" I asked.

"He bites her."

That was barbaric. There was no way in hell some male werewolf was going to bite me.

At that moment Cade strode in with painkillers in his one hand and a glass of water in the other.

"Here, drink this," he instructed as he dropped the tablets into my hand and gave me the glass of water. I didn't argue; instead, I put the pills into my mouth and swallowed some water. The throbbing in my head had gotten worse and it was just a matter of time before it turned into a full-blown headache. It also probably had something to do with hitting my head in the accident.

"Thank you," I said, still holding onto the glass of water. Cade remained quiet as he sat down on the bed, facing us.

"You still haven't answered my previous question," I told Blake.

"Werewolves that don't belong to a pack are always more susceptible to attacks by rogues because there isn't a pack to protect them. It makes them easier targets."

"Why would a rogue want to attack me?"

It made no sense.

"It's what they do. Some have a reason, others do it for fun. It is easier to attack a lone werewolf that doesn't have protection from a pack, especially a female werewolf."

The picture they were beginning to paint for me started to scare me a little.

"It's worse for a female werewolf—they'd probably keep you to use your body." Cade dropped that bit of information into the conversation.

"Are you saying what I think you're saying?" I asked him, feeling the shiver of fear up my spine.

"Yes," he confirmed, watching me for my reaction.

Oh, crap!

"So the person I hit tonight..." I took a moment to get myself together, "was a rogue that wanted to..."

I couldn't finish the sentence.

"Yes."

The confirmation scared me because I knew no matter how much training I had, there was no way I would be able to fight off a werewolf. I simply wasn't strong enough.

"When you first got here we knew you were a werewolf. We knew you didn't belong to a pack so we've been keeping an eye on you to keep you safe," Blake explained further.

So they'd been trying to protect me, not stalk me. I felt a little bad for going off at them.

CHAPTER SEVEN

SCARLETT

"Do you think the rogue will come after me again?" I asked as I bit down on my bottom lip to keep it from trembling.

Everything that they had told me was a lot to take in and I was still trying to process it along with the shocking events of my earlier run-in with my first rogue.

"Yes." The answer came from a stern-looking Cade.

I tried to regain whatever composure I still had left under the watchful eyes of the two alphas.

"So, what happens now?" I asked.

"Ideally, it would be easier for us to guard you if you joined one of our packs," suggested Cade.

"Not going to happen," I replied, shaking my head without even considering it.

"You'd be stronger and more able to defend yourself if you could shift," said Blake.

"But I'd only be able to shift if I found my...mate." I could barely say the word.

"Look, let me explain something to you guys," I started as I stood up and faced both of them.

"All this werewolf stuff is normal for you but up until about half an hour ago, I didn't even know werewolves existed. This stuff might be normal for you, but it's all new to me."

I paused for a moment.

"I'm not interested in being a part of a pack or finding a mate. I've worked hard to build my life and I'm not giving up on it."

Blake watched me thoughtfully while Cade was shaking his head at me.

"You can't fight the inevitable," Cade stated as he stood with his arms crossed.

"You don't know me very well," I warned, holding his gaze. "I'll up my security and if need be I'll get a bodyguard."

"You don't get it, do you?" Cade growled at me as he stepped forward so he was standing directly in front of me. "Humans won't be able to keep you safe."

Nervously, I bit down on my bottom lip and Cade dropped his gaze to my lips. Even in the middle of an argument with him, when all I wanted to do was slap his arrogant face, I could feel the flutter of butterflies in my stomach. Annoyed, I took a step backward.

"I guess we can at least provide protection and in the meantime we could train you," suggested Blake quietly.

"It's not enough and you know it," said Cade as he turned to glare at his friend.

I looked hopefully at Blake.

"It can be enough for the time being," he muttered to Cade. I didn't like the sound of that because no matter what, I wasn't going to change my life.

Some noise from in front of the house that sounded like a car pulled Cade's attention to the window.

"Jake is back with your car," commented Cade as he peered out to the driveway.

"You see if you can talk some sense into her. I'm going to check in with Jake," Cade muttered to Blake before he stalked out of the bedroom.

I let out a big sigh.

"Is he always like this?" I asked, feeling exasperated.

"Yeah, he is," replied Blake with a half-smile.

I hadn't known them for very long, but I could tell Blake was the laid-back one out of the two. Cade always seemed so intense and serious all the time. He was draining.

"Cade is right," he said, running a hand through his hair. I didn't want Cade to be right, I didn't want to have to join a pack, and there was no way I was interested in finding a mate or anything like that.

Surely a werewolf could live without a mate?

"Watching over you without you joining a pack is only going to be a temporary fix for the moment, or at least until we catch the rogue that is after you."

That sounded like a plan.

"We will get this rogue, but remember there will always be others," he warned me. He was telling me that he could only give me a temporary reprieve, but that there would come a time I'd have to join a pack.

I didn't like the sound of that one bit.

"Did you manage to talk some sense into her?" Cade asked Blake when he returned.

Cade rolled his eyes when Blake shook his head.

"Jake and Ross cleaned up the road and they brought your car here," Cade informed me.

"So what do we do now?" I asked. I hated relying on them for stuff, but clearly they were better at covering this type of thing up than I was.

"Without a police report, you won't be able to collect

from the insurance so I'll replace your car," said Cade.

"No, it's fine, I can replace my own car," I assured him as he raised a questioning eyebrow. "I have my own money."

"Whatever," he muttered with a shrug.

"Who do you live with if both your parents are dead?" asked Blake.

"My dad's best friend and my guardian up until I got emancipated," I explained.

"Emancipated, I can't say I'm surprised," muttered Cade under his breath. I glared at him.

It was a lot to take in and I was still in shock from the accident. I needed to call Gary and let him know what had happened. He was going to freak. I couldn't remember where I'd put my phone, though. It was probably in my car.

Just thinking of my shiny new baby in the state she was now in nearly made me cry. I'd waited so long for her and now she was damaged.

"I need to make a call," I said to Blake. He pulled a phone out of his front pocket and handed it to me.

I wasn't sure how I was going to explain any of this to Gary. I had two options. One, I could tell him the truth and he could have me committed; or two, I could lie. Lying to Gary wasn't going to be easy. I'd always been truthful with him.

But the reality was I couldn't really lie to him. There was no way I could explain the damage to my car and the lack of a police report to go along with it.

"Do any humans know about what you guys are?" I asked.

"There are a trusted few," said Cade.

"I need to tell Gary," I revealed, expecting Cade and Blake to both disagree with me.

"If you must, but make sure he is trustworthy because if he isn't, we'll have to deal with him," warned Cade. I didn't want to know what 'deal with' entailed but I trusted Gary more than I'd ever trusted anybody.

"We'll give you a minute," Blake said as he headed out of the bedroom and Cade followed reluctantly behind.

"Thanks," I murmured, trying to rack my brain for a number I'd known for most of my life. Just when I was about to give up and give the phone back, I finally remembered Gary's number and dialed it.

"Hello," he greeted after the third ring.

"Gary," I said.

"Why aren't you calling me from your cell?" he asked. I could hear the unease in his voice. Immediately he knew there was something wrong.

"I'm calling from a friend's cell," I answered, although I didn't really classify Blake or Cade as friends.

"What's wrong?" he asked before I could continue.

"I had an accident," I blurted out and then I waited for him to go off at me.

"Are you okay?" he asked anxiously.

"A little banged up but I don't think I did any serious damage," I revealed, my fingers touching the bump on my forehead.

"Where are you?" he asked urgently.

I told him the address.

"I'm on my way," he told me and I could hear the jingle of keys in the background and then the call disconnected.

I held the phone in my hands for a few minutes afterward, trying to figure out how I was going to tell Gary what I'd just found out. I knew him well enough to know he wouldn't believe a word I said without thinking I was crazy so he would have to see it for himself.

Blake and Cade were going to have to help me show Gary the truth.

I never imagined that when I woke up this morning that

my day would be ending the way it was. This morning I'd been a normal girl going to school and now I was a werewolf whose life was in danger.

Gary made it to Cade's house in record time. He'd probably broken all the speed limits to get to me.

"Where is she?" he asked, looking desperately for me as Cade opened the door for him.

The moment he saw me, relief flooded through his features and he pulled me into a hug.

"Thank God," he whispered into my hair. After holding me tightly for a minute, he pulled away and gave me a once over with his eyes, looking for any visible injures.

"How is your head?" he asked with concern, seeing the cut on my forehead.

"I'm fine," I insisted. The headache tablets Cade had given me earlier had kicked in and my headache was gone.

"Are you hurt anywhere else?" he asked, checking my arms. Blake and Cade stood together, watching us with interest.

"I think I hurt my ribs," I owned up. He would find out sooner or later. From the time I'd lost my parents, Gary had become not only a father to me, he'd also become a surrogate mother and at the moment he was mothering me.

"We need to get you checked over," he insisted.

"I'm okay," I insisted and pulled out of his grasp.

"We checked her and she doesn't have any serious injuries," Blake said, trying to reassure Gary but he didn't look convinced.

"I've a doctor on the premises that can check her out," Cade revealed.

"Why do you have a doctor on the premises?" I asked.

"It's a long story," muttered Cade. He pulled his phone from his jeans and dialed a number.

"I need you in the house," he ordered and then ended

the call.

I couldn't help but wonder if he had a hospital at his beck and call as well.

Gary's attention was now focused on Blake and Cade, who up until then had been quietly watching our interaction.

He studied them for a moment before he turned to face me.

"Who are these guys?" he asked me.

"Guys from my school," I informed him. I did quick introductions between the three but they didn't shake hands; instead, they seemed to be sizing each other up. It was such a guy thing.

"What happened?" Gary asked, turning to face me. "I saw your car outside…"

That was what had probably freaked him out. The car was probably totaled.

I wasn't sure why but suddenly I began to feel tired. I don't know whether it was the adrenaline that wore off that made me suddenly feel dead on my feet, or something else.

"I think it would be best if she sat down," insisted Blake, taking note of my sudden paleness. Gary put an arm around my waist and followed Cade's lead into the formal lounge I'd been in earlier that evening before the accident.

With Gary's help I sank down into the sofa and leaned back. As much as I wanted to close my eyes and give in to the tiredness, the evening wasn't finished.

Moments later an older guy with gray hair beginning to show in his dark brown hair and dressed in a suit stepped into the lounge, holding some sort of leather bag in his hand.

"Curtis, please make sure she doesn't have any serious injuries," Cade instructed.

It was then that I noticed the stethoscope around his neck. He gave me a friendly smile as he walked to me. Gary stood up and Curtis sat down beside me. Under Gary's concerned eyes, the doctor checked my breathing and my heart. His fingers gently probed my injury by my ribs and my head.

He asked me a few questions, like if I had blacked out after hitting my head, and stuff like that to make sure I wasn't suffering from a concussion.

"She'll be fine," was his verdict. "She hasn't broken any ribs. They are just badly bruised and they should heal in a few days. I'd just watch her closely tonight to make sure she hasn't suffered a concussion."

"Thank you," Gary said with relief.

"Thanks, Curtis," Cade said before the guy turned and left. Gary seemed to be less anxious now that he knew I was physically going to be okay. Although after hearing what we were about to tell him, he would definitely be concerned for my mental state.

I took a deep breath as Gary gave me his undivided attention. It was time to tell him the almost unbelievable secret I'd just found out myself.

"You know that from the time I turned sixteen I started developing stronger senses," I began and he nodded, still not quite sure where I was headed with this. "Even my physical strength seemed to increase."

"What has that got to do with you having an accident?" he asked impatiently.

"Well, it seems Cade and Blake know why," I revealed.

I knew Gary wouldn't believe me if I just told him, so I needed Cade or Blake to show him.

"Show him," I instructed Cade and Blake.

"I've done my party trick for the night," said Cade as he stepped back and Blake took a step forward. Then in an instant, the body of Blake was transformed into a huge dark-brown wolf.

"Holy shit!" shouted Gary as he shot up and stood

protectively in front of me, putting himself between me and the dangerous animal.

Wincing, I stood up, clutching my injured side and pulled Gary back to look at me. His eyes were still glued to the wolf that was standing on all fours in front of us. Cade stood by, watching Gary's reaction with a smug half grin.

It took some talking to get Gary to sit back down and Blake shifted back into his normal human form. Thank goodness when they shifted, their clothes shifted with them, otherwise it would be all sorts of awkward with naked bodies. And I had no desire to see Blake or Cade naked.

I sat back down, pulling Gary back down beside me. Wide-eyed, Gary listened to Blake and Cade explain the whole werewolf thing. When they were done, he turned to me.

"You're a werewolf?" he asked, almost still in denial. But he couldn't deny what he'd seen with his own two eyes.

"Apparently," I said. I didn't feel any different and the fact that I couldn't really shift into a wolf also didn't help me feel more like one.

"So what does this have to do with your accident?" Gary asked.

I let Cade and Blake explain that a rogue was after me. They gave him the same rundown about rogues that they'd given me earlier.

I could see the fear grow in Gary's eyes at the thought of some supernatural creature wanting to hunt me down and kill me for no apparent reason. He was going to make me move.

"We need to move," were the first words that he spoke to me when Cade and Blake finished telling him about rogues.

"There's no point. If you run, he'll just chase you," Cade warned us.

"But we can't just do nothing and let him get her!" shouted Gary as he stood up to face Blake and Cade.

"We're not going to do nothing," said Cade angrily, glaring at Gary and taking a menacing step forward. Blake put his hand on Cade's shoulder. Cade took a deep breath and tried to get his temper under control.

The more time I spent around them, the more I noticed that Blake was the one to think before he acted but Cade was the complete opposite. He acted without thinking it through.

It did baffle my mind that two people who were so different were such good friends.

"So what is the plan?" Gary asked, looking to the two alphas.

"She's going to have to move in here," Cade said, laying the plan out.

"No way," I said, shaking my head. There was no way I wanted to spend more time around Cade than I already had. The way he made me feel when I was around him scared me and I knew spending more time around him would only make it worse.

"How long?" Gary asked, ignoring my protest.

"At least until we take care of the rogue," Cade clarified, shooting a dark look at Blake.

"I said no," I reinforced, standing up in between them so they couldn't ignore me.

"I don't know why you're fighting us every step of the way. We are trying to keep you safe, but you make it as if we are trying to punish you. I'm not going to beg you to stay, the choice is yours," Cade said angrily at me.

"We wouldn't ask you to do it if there was any other choice," Blake said, trying to reason with me.

My reasonable mind and my fear of the attraction to Cade wrestled with each other and after a little silence my mind won the battle. They were right; I needed their help.

"Okay," I mumbled to Cade.

CHAPTER EIGHT

SCARLETT

It was an hour later and I was standing in the guest bedroom I'd been in earlier.

I still wasn't happy about this arrangement but there was no use fighting it. They did have a point, though. I knew how to protect myself against an attack from a human, but I'd be useless going up against a vicious werewolf. It was hard to comprehend that the rogue had been powerful enough to go head-to-head with my car and survive.

So, for my own survival, I'd given in and accepted that I'd be staying at Cade's house until they managed to catch the rogue that was after me. Cade and Blake had assured Gary and me that there were enough werewolves on the property to protect me.

"There is a compound at the back of the property where a lot of the werewolves from my pack live," Cade had explained.

The fact that there was a huge compound in his backyard was a little weird, but wolves like to live in packs.

He'd briefly explained that Curtis, the doctor and one of the few humans who knew about the werewolves, lived in the compound. I suppose it came in handy, especially when werewolves got injured because in a normal hospital, questions might get raised that might jeopardize their secret.

I didn't know a hell of a lot about werewolves, but I was sure that if their blood got tested something would be discovered.

I still couldn't figure out why the rogue was so determined to harm me. I didn't have a lot of memories of my parents, but from what I could remember, they were kind and loving people. Why would a rogue have murdered them?

Gary was relieved I'd caved in and he'd gone back to my house to get some stuff, like clothes and toiletries, for both of us. I'd wanted to get my own stuff, but Cade had shaken his head at me.

"You're injured and you need to rest," he'd reminded me. "And remember, the rogue is still out there somewhere."

That had scared me enough to back down.

Once Gary and Blake had left, he'd showed me the kitchen so I could help myself if I was hungry and then he'd led me back upstairs to the guest bedroom I was in now.

"Gary can use the guest bedroom next door to yours," he'd told me.

"Thanks," I'd muttered.

"If you need anything, I'll be in my bedroom at the end of the hallway," he'd informed me before he'd turned and left.

I'd walked over to the bedroom window and looked out over the back of the property and I could see a massive building that was slightly hidden by a bunch of tall trees. I wondered how many werewolves stayed there.

It was a big building, but Cade's property was massive.

It was the first time it occurred to me that he hadn't said

anything about his parents. I wondered if they stayed in the house with him or maybe they lived in the compound with the other werewolves.

I made a mental note to remember to ask him.

I rubbed my temple as my head began to pound again and my side started to ache again. The painkillers were wearing off. Normally, painkillers worked for a certain amount of time but once I'd started to develop changes they only seemed to last for half the time they used to when I was human.

Wow! It was still sinking in that I wasn't human anymore.

Knowing I couldn't let the painkillers fully wear off, I had no option but to walk down the long passage to a set of double wooden doors. Cade's room.

I knocked on the door and seconds later Cade opened it. He was only wearing a pair of jeans that hung low on his hips. His chest was hard and defined and I couldn't help but stare.

No matter how hard I fought it, I was physically attracted to him. I wanted to reach out and run my hand over the smooth skin of his chest, but I tightened my hand into a fist and fought the urge.

"Do you need something?" he asked when I was too occupied with fighting my physical attraction to him to tell him that I needed painkillers.

"Y—Yes…" I stuttered. It was like I became a blubbering idiot around him, like my brain stopped working and my hormones went into overdrive. I was acting like a hormonal teenage girl and it revolted me.

"You're looking at me like you've never seen a naked chest before," he stated with a smirk. I felt mortified. My cheeks darkened with a red blush.

"Oh, please," I scoffed at him. His ego was unbelievable.

"For God's sake put some clothes on," I muttered to him, trying to cover up the fact that I was attracted to him.

He gave me a knowing smile as he stepped back and walked to his bed. I followed him into his room.

It was huge. The color theme of his room wasn't surprising. It was a dark blue—a very male color. The bed was massive. I was pretty sure it was the biggest one I'd ever seen. I couldn't help thinking of what probably happened in it.

Cade reached for a discarded shirt on his bed and pulled it over his head. I couldn't argue the fact that physically he was gorgeous. He was ripped and defined, and it was enough to make any girl's knees go weak, even mine.

It was as my eyes surveyed him that they fixed on a birthmark on his hip as he turned to pull the shirt down. There were two teardrops side by side, one bigger than the other. They were identical to mine. Shock locked the air in my lungs as I stared openly at the birthmark that confirmed something I didn't want to believe.

As his birthmark disappeared under the hem of his shirt, I racked my brain trying to remember what Blake had said about them. Slowly the realization sank in and I felt a wave of horror sweep over me.

Mates had matching birthmarks. Mates.

Oh. My. God.

It wasn't possible. It had to be some sort of joke.

I tried to remember what else Blake had told me about mates. It wasn't like in the movies or books, since werewolves had to physically touch to discover they were mates. I tried to remember back through the stressful events. Blake had picked me up when I lay injured in the road. The more I cycled through the events, the more I realized that Cade hadn't touched me at all.

"Are you okay?" he asked, watching me closely.

"Yeah… I'm okay," I managed to get out as I tucked a

piece of hair behind my ear, trying to pull myself together so he didn't suspect something.

"Well, you came here for something," he said as something changed in his eyes.

"Was there something you… *wanted?*" he said. Then it hit me: he thought I'd knocked on his bedroom door because he thought I'd come looking to get better acquainted with him.

"Oh, please," I scoffed at him and rolled my eyes. He was so conceited it was annoying. "I came to ask for some more painkillers."

"Sure you did," he said like he knew better and I wanted to smack him.

I couldn't believe he was supposed to be my mate. If that was true, I would end up killing him.

He disappeared into his adjoining bathroom and I heard him searching for something in the cupboards before he reappeared with a bottle of painkillers.

"Here," he said as he handed me the plastic bottle. I made sure I didn't touch his fingers as I took the bottle from him. I didn't want him to know that I was his mate until I had time to wrap my mind around it.

I knew I wouldn't be able to hide it forever, but I was going to try and give myself time to come to grips with all this werewolf stuff before I needed to add an egotistical mate to the equation.

Could the fact that he was my mate explain my unwanted attraction to him?

"Thanks," I murmured while still deep in thought about werewolves and mates as I turned to walk out of his room. I felt the heat of his gaze as he watched me leave.

By the time I made it back to my room with the painkillers in my hand, I felt the panic at the realization that Cade was my mate.

I was so screwed.

I sat down on the bed, still clutching the bottle of painkillers in my hand, as I tried to calm myself down.

I felt like a cornered animal that was unable to escape. Technically I was a werewolf and I was pretty sure I couldn't escape the whole mate thing. It was destiny, stuff that was written in the stars, so there was no way to get away from it.

There was no point in entertaining the idea of trying to leave because the rogue that was hell-bent on killing me was enough to keep me in place.

My head began to pound worse than before and I rubbed it, trying to ease the headache that was in full force now.

Some people might have a romantic idea about werewolves and mates—the idea that in an instant everything falls into place when you find your mate, the person you are going to spend the rest of your life with. In that moment, you find the person who is going to love and protect you forever and you in return feel the same about them.

There are no games or backing out. It is final and definitive. Soul mates.

It was hard to consider that I'd feel something other than loathing for him. He had a way of riling me up without even trying.

I hadn't spent tons of time thinking about boys or falling in love, but never in a million years had I expected this. I'd thought about meeting someone and feeling that instant attraction that after a while would develop into something stronger like love. Not touch someone and instantly I'm in love with someone I can't stand to be around. I didn't even like him.

One thing I couldn't dispute was the fact that I was physically attracted to him, as much as I hated that fact.

When he'd opened up his bedroom door without a shirt on, I'd wanted to run my hands over his perfectly defined abs.

I also couldn't help but wonder if his lips felt as soft as they looked. I'd never felt so attracted to the opposite sex. I, like any other girl, could appreciate a good-looking guy, but this attraction I felt for Cade was something else. I contemplated the whole idea for a moment. Perhaps it would work if he could keep his mouth shut, but I didn't see that happening.

Cade was a force to be reckoned with. He was all male, strong and dominant, and he wasn't the type to back down from anything. Despite the fact that I'd never seen him fight in wolf form, I knew he would be vicious.

I knew Cade well enough to know he would try to dominate me totally and it scared me. For so many years I'd been fighting to be independent and the thought of losing that independence in a moment when Cade discovered I was his mate filled me with dread.

I wondered whether his dominance was part and parcel of being an alpha but then I thought about Blake. Blake was also an alpha, but he was very different. From the short time I'd known him, he struck me as the easygoing type who would take people's feelings into consideration before making a decision, unlike Cade.

Even now I could see the independence I'd fought so hard to get was running like water down the drain.

The pounding in my head brought me out of my thoughts and back to reality. Despondent, I walked to the adjoining bathroom and took two of the tablets and drank them down.

The ache in my side was still so sore. I lifted my shirt and studied the area that hurt and saw a bruise was already starting to form.

Despite all my feelings about Cade being my mate, I couldn't change what was destined. I could delay it for a while, but that was all I could hope for.

Someone knocked on my door and I opened it to find

Gary standing there holding a bag.

"Thanks," I said as I took the bag from him and walked over to the bed. He followed me inside.

"How are you doing?" he asked with concern.

"As good as can be expected," I said. "It's not every day I find out I'm a supernatural creature."

I let out a sigh and turned to face him.

"Sorry, I don't mean to be so full of it. It's been a rough day and I'm sore and tired," I told him.

"I know," he said, pulling me into a gentle hug. I rested my head against his chest and closed my eyes for a moment. Gary was the only one who saw me at my most vulnerable. To everyone else I was tough and independent. He was the one who saw the vulnerable and scared little girl who had lost both of her parents.

After a few moments, I pulled away from him.

"I still can't quite believe that I'm a werewolf. Maybe it might feel more real when I'm able to shift," I said.

"I was your dad's best friend and I never suspected anything," he said, sounding mystified.

I was too young to remember much, so even when I worked through the few memories I had of my parents, I hadn't noticed anything that would indicate they were anything other than normal parents.

"It is what it is; it doesn't matter how we got to this," I muttered as I sat down on the bed, feeling a little drained from the events of the evening.

"All that matters is how we move forward," I finished.

"Blake and Cade seem to know what they are doing," he commented, watching me carefully.

"Well, they'd better or else it isn't going end well for me," I said with a sigh. It was the truth. My life and survival was in their hands. If they made a mistake, I would end up paying the cost.

It was frightening for my life to be dependent on the actions of others.

"I suppose this means I'd better start being nice to them," I said as I looked to Gary. A half grin tugged at his lips.

"Probably," he agreed, like he wasn't convinced I could do it. I couldn't help the smile that started to spread across my face.

"Cade said you could use the bedroom next to mine," I informed him as I tried to suppress a yawn.

"It's getting late. Go have a shower and try and get some rest," he instructed before he turned and left.

I had a quick shower before getting into my pajamas that Gary had packed in my bag. My mind was still too busy sorting through the events of the night so it took me a couple of hours before I drifted off to sleep and into a dream.

Dark and foreboding trees above me made me shiver with apprehension as I glanced around the dark forest.

The only light was moonlight that filtered through the trees. My heightened senses were on full alert. I had a feeling I wasn't alone in the dark forest.

I heard a noise behind me and I turned to find nothing but the wind blowing the branches of the trees. My fear began to grow as I took a tentative step back and then another one.

Then I stepped back and felt someone standing right behind me and I froze.

"Scarlett," Cade whispered seductively with his head bent down next to my ear. I felt a shiver of awareness run through my body. There was no point in fighting the inevitable, so instead of moving away from him I leaned back and closed my eyes. Reveling in the feel of him against me.

His arms wrapped around me from behind and I reached to touch his arm. Our first skin-to-skin contact sent a rush of adrenaline through me that felt like an electrical current.

I felt a rush of feelings and possessiveness for Cade.

"Mine," he growled possessively as he tightened his hold on me. Deep in the dark forest under the moonlight, he held me like he was never going to let me go. And deep down inside me, I didn't want him to.

"Yes, I'm yours," I whispered to him, giving in to the destiny that had decided he was my forever.

I shot up in my bed, breathing hard. My body was tangled in the sheets, showing I'd been restless in my sleep.

I rubbed my face with my hands, trying to remember what I'd dreamed about. When I remembered, I was mortified. I'd given in to him and I was disgusted with myself.

CHAPTER NINE

SCARLETT

I was still half asleep when I pulled my robe on and tied it around my waist. I slipped my feet into my slippers, thankful Gary had remembered to pack them. Coffee was the only thing I could think about as I left my room in search of my first caffeine fix.

The rich aroma hit me and I followed it to the kitchen.

"Morning," Cade greeted me cheerfully from the counter he was sitting at.

"Morning," I muttered, trying to stop myself from killing him with my death glare. I was grumpy as hell until I had caffeine running through my veins.

"Aren't you just a ray of sunshine first thing in the morning," he observed as I just turned and let my ice cold gaze sweep over him. He didn't get the message because he kept smiling.

I wanted to smack the smile off his face, but that would involve touching him, which I was avoiding at the moment. Would he find it strange if I covered my hand with a glove to slap him? It sounded so appealing, it made me smile secretly to myself.

A stronger whiff of the coffee pulled me out of my planning and I shuffled to the machine. I took one of the cups beside the machine and poured myself some.

I took a deep sniff of it and sighed before I took a tentative sip.

Yummy.

I turned to face Cade and leaned against the counter.

He didn't have a shirt on again. What was with this guy and going shirtless? Most girls wouldn't complain, they would just enjoy the view, but seeing him half naked just set off that familiar feeling inside my stomach. I liked to be in control and around him, I wasn't. My body's reaction went against any logical reasoning I could muster.

Then there was that other problem that he was my mate, he was meant to be my life-long partner. I couldn't help but wonder if my attraction to him had anything to do with him being my mate, even though we hadn't touched yet?

"Don't you own enough shirts?" I asked as I took another sip of my coffee.

"Does it make you uncomfortable? Most girls don't complain," he said with a smirk.

Can't slap him, I kept chanting in my head as I felt my temper start to rise.

"I'm not most girls," I muttered as I held his gaze.

I had to remember to try and be nice to him as hard as it was going to be. He was helping me by letting me stay at his house and I needed to appreciate it no matter how much I wanted to slap him or bring him down a peg or two.

He got up and walked to the coffee machine beside me. As much as I wanted to stay where I was, I moved away because I couldn't chance him touching me by accident. I wasn't ready to deal with a possessive mate just yet. Deep down I knew I couldn't avoid it for long, but I needed some time to get my head around it.

He smiled at the action. He probably thought I moved because he made me feel uncomfortable and he liked the fact that his presence affected me.

"You scared I'm going to bite you?" he said in a seductive tone as his eyes traveled over me appreciatively. I bet he used that line a lot.

"Who says I won't bite back?" I retorted.

"I don't mind," he teased with a smile as his eyes held mine.

"Does that line ever work?" I asked, annoyed.

"I don't have to use lines," he assured me with a satisfied grin.

He was probably right. I could see the girls falling at his feet without him having to utter a word. I was pretty sure one look from him would do it.

Can't slap him, I told myself again. It was going to be harder than I'd first thought as I clutched the coffee mug tightly in my hands to stop me from doing something I would regret.

"Morning," Gary greeted as he entered the kitchen. He was already dressed.

"Morning," Cade and I greeted at the same time.

I was relieved to have another person around and it seemed to ease the tension that had been building between Cade and me.

"How are you feeling?" Gary asked with concern as he checked the cut I was still sporting on my forehead. At least the swelling had gone down. He was in 'concerned parent' mode.

"I feel better. My ribs are still a little tender," I confessed. I wasn't one to complain, but I wanted him to know I was healing. It was only when I made sudden movements that I felt the pain.

"It's a werewolf thing," Cade commented, watching the two of us.

"What is?" I asked, turning to face him.

"We heal fast. You'll heal faster once you shift," he informed us.

That was a good thing. Maybe being a werewolf wasn't such a bad thing after all, but then I remembered the whole 'mate' thing and that put a damper on things.

"So what's the plan for today?" Gary directed the question at Cade.

"I've got some of my pack tracking the rogue but they haven't found him yet," he explained as he went back to the kitchen counter and sat down.

"How long do you think it will take?" Gary asked.

Cade shrugged his shoulders. *His shoulders are wide and strong,* I thought to myself. Angry with myself, I shook my head, to stop thinking of him in that way.

"It could be a while. This rogue is good at covering up his tracks and he is very good at keeping himself hidden," he answered. "He is probably an older werewolf."

Great! Not only did I have a rogue intent on doing me some serious harm, but he was older and more experienced. I had a feeling I was going to be staying at Cade's house for a long time.

Crap! It was going to be harder keeping my distance from him if I was living in his house. The odds were starting to stack up against me.

"Is there a chance that there might be more of them?" I asked. I wasn't sure what made me ask the question.

"Yes, there is." He watched me carefully for a reaction to his answer.

The thought that there might be more than one rogue terrified me, but I kept my outward calm facade firmly in place as I finished my coffee. I glanced down at my watch and realized I didn't have a lot of time before I had to leave for school.

"I'm going upstairs to get ready for school," I announced as I put my empty mug in the sink.

"You're not leaving the house; it's not safe," Cade informed me sternly. Gary looked more concerned as he shot me a look, which told me to play nice but he knew me better than that.

I didn't like being told what I could and couldn't do no matter what was at stake. I was stubborn to a fault.

"Why not?" I asked. "The school is filled with werewolves, so how can I not be safe there?"

This whole 'being in danger' thing really sucked.

"You're safer here, or do you want to chance another encounter with the rogue?" Cade asked, already knowing what my answer would be. Last night had scared me, although I wouldn't openly admit it to anyone. I hid my fear deep under my facade of confidence.

"I can't just skip school until you catch the rogue," I argued. "Like you said, it could take a while."

"At least give us today to try and strategize and put a plan into action," he said, surprising me. I'd expected him to tell me that I wouldn't leave the property until the rogue had been dealt with.

I was learning I needed to pick my battles. I gave him a brief nod, agreeing to stay put for the day.

"Tomorrow I'm going to school," I stated. There would be no negotiating.

"Fine," Cade agreed tightly. He didn't like being dictated to; well, that made two of us.

"Nice to see the two of you are getting along this morning," Blake remarked, standing in the doorway of the kitchen.

"I wouldn't say we were quite getting along," I muttered. I think the correct thing would be to say we'd negotiated some sort of truce for the moment.

Spending the day at Cade's house was boring. I'd gone back upstairs to shower and change. Then I'd lain down on the bed for a little while. I was so bored, even flipping through the channels of the TV didn't hold my attention for long.

My stomach rumbled and I let out a sigh.

As much as I wanted to hide out in the room to avoid any run-ins with Cade, I needed to eat. The kitchen was empty when I walked in. I let out the nervous breath I'd held, hoping I wouldn't run into Cade. Cade had instructed Gary and me to help ourselves to whatever we wanted in the kitchen.

I began to look through the cupboards. I had a craving for some sugar-coated cereal, which was strange because it wasn't something I normally ate. I found a couple boxes of cereal on the top shelf of the one cupboard and I tried to reach it on my tiptoes.

"No way!" I heard Blake exclaim.

Confused, I looked over to him, his eyes were fixed on my hip —my hip that had my birthmark. Mentally, I swore as I quickly pulled my shirt back down but it was too late. He'd seen it.

"What?" I asked, breathless, like I'd been caught with my hand in the cookie jar.

"This is going to be good," he murmured to himself with a grin on his face.

"What do you mean?" I pretended I didn't know what he was talking about as I clutched my shirt over my birthmark.

"You're Cade's mate," he revealed to me, shaking his head like he was truly amused by the information.

"Cade's my mate?" I asked, trying to feign surprise but he saw right through it. His eyes narrowed for a moment and he cocked his head to the side.

"You don't seem that surprised by that information," he observed.

I contemplated whether it mattered if I knew before and decided it didn't.

"Yeah, I know," I muttered as I shrugged my shoulders.

"How'd you find out?" he asked, watching me with curiosity.

"I saw his birthmark," I answered. I felt a nervous knot start to form in my stomach, and there went my appetite. He began to grin as he shook his head again, like he was laughing at some inside joke or something. It was annoying.

"Why are you laughing?" I asked, sounding as annoyed as I felt and I put my hands on my hips as I glared at him.

"Because I think the two of you are perfectly suited for each other," he answered, still with a huge grin on his face. "And it is going to be endless entertainment to watch the two of you figure all of this out."

I continued to glare at him but, honestly, he was only telling the truth. Cade and I were both strong-willed and we didn't back down easily, so the fact that we were mates was going to be a constant battle of wills.

"Are you going to tell him?" I asked, nervously biting my lip. Blake stopped smiling at me and looked a little taken aback.

"Why would you want to keep this from him?" he asked. It didn't take a genius to figure out he wouldn't be happy about keeping the secret from his friend.

"I just wanted a little time to get used to the idea before he finds out."

It was the truth. I couldn't keep it from him indefinitely. Was it so wrong to want a couple of days to get used to the idea? My eyes pleaded with his and after a few moments of contemplation, he sighed.

"Cade is my best friend and I don't like keeping things from him... but I understand you're new to all of this and want some time to get used to it so I'll give you two days."

I was about to argue with him but he gave me a look that made me shut my mouth.

"Two days is all I'm going to give you."

The finality in his voice told me not to bother arguing with him, and that I should be happy he hadn't gone looking to tell Cade straight away.

"Thank you," I said, relieved I still had some time, although two days didn't seem like a lot. At least it was something.

"Understand that if you don't tell him by the end of the two days, I will," he warned me seriously.

I nodded. *Two days.*

"I know it's a lot for you and I know Cade can be a bit domineering and stubborn at times, but I know him well enough to know that he is fiercely loyal and he'll be a good mate."

It was because he was domineering and stubborn that I was so hesitant to reveal I was his mate. He would try and dictate to me and that was something I wasn't willing to take from anyone, even someone picked out by destiny to be the person I was supposed to spend forever with.

"I feel I should also warn you," he continued as he sat down in the chair across from me, "just so you know what you're in for."

I felt the nervous knot in my stomach grow. Whatever was coming wasn't good.

"When Cade finds out you're his mate, he'll make sure he does everything in his power to keep you safe."

"That's not exactly a news flash," I replied sarcastically.

"You don't understand."

He took a deep breath and released it. It was like whatever he was going to say was something I wasn't going to like.

"At the moment, you don't belong to a pack and you can't shift into a werewolf. Both of these things make you weaker and therefore an easier target."

His eyes held mine, his face serious.

"So?"

"He'll expect you to join his pack."

That was the first bombshell. I didn't want to belong to a pack. I liked being on my own.

"He will want you to mate with him so you'll be able to shift into a werewolf."

And there was the atom bomb.

Ah, crap!

Slightly stunned, I walked over to the kitchen table and sank into one of the chairs. Thought upon thought of what was going to happen bombarded me and I felt the pressure weighing down on my shoulders. Blake watched me with concern.

"Are you okay?" he asked gently as he came to stand in front of me.

"I don't think I'm ever going to be okay," I mumbled. I felt like my life was busy spinning out of control and there was nothing I could do but watch it happen.

Blake was right. When Cade found out I was his mate, my safety would become his top priority. He would make me join his pack. I wasn't even sure how that happened, and then he would insist we mate.

Then I remembered what mating involved: biting and sex. There was no doubt about it, I was physically attracted to him, but that didn't mean I wanted to jump in the sack with him. And the biting thing, that would hurt. It was barbaric.

I shook my head. I wasn't ready for any of that and I doubted two days would change that.

"I know it's all a bit much all at once but it isn't that bad," he assured me gently. I looked up at him and threw a look that told him to go fly a kite.

"Just yesterday I was a single, independent, human girl starting her senior year. Today I'm a werewolf whose life is in danger, who has also just discovered she has a mate and, once he finds out, I'll have to join his pack. I lose my independence and on top of that I have to mate with him so I can shift so I will be able to protect myself."

Blake remained still and silent.

"Does that about sum it up?" I said, feeling my anger rise at the unfairness of it all. This was my life and it felt like since I found out I was a werewolf that it wasn't just mine anymore.

"It is what it is," was the only consolation I got from him. It meant no amount of anger was going to change the inevitable.

In two days, Cade would find out I was his mate. I knew, irrespective of how hard I fought him, my life was going to change. There was no doubt about that.

CHAPTER TEN

SCARLETT

After our conversation, Blake left me with my thoughts as I munched on some of the cereal. I hadn't bothered with a bowl and I was eating out of the box. It was something I normally did at home. My appetite was gone, but the munching seemed to ease my angst slightly.

My conversation with Blake played on my mind. Blake was right—when Cade found out I was his mate, he would do everything he could to keep me safe and I couldn't blame him for that. He'd make me join his pack and he'd insist we mate.

This was all so unfair. I'd just found out I was a werewolf yesterday. I hadn't even had time to adjust to that, so the thought of joining a pack and mating overwhelmed me.

I wasn't sure what joining Cade's pack would entail. I made a mental note to ask Blake some questions about it. But there was no way in hell I was ready to mate with Cade. Sex might not mean a lot to some people, but it meant something to me and I wasn't going to be forced into anything like that when I wasn't ready, even if my life was in danger.

With my decision made, I began to feel a little better. I'd be open to the idea of joining Cade's pack, but there was no way I was going to mate with him.

Images of the two of us getting hot and heavy flashed through my mind and it made me feel a little flustered. I was attracted to him, but that didn't mean I was going to sleep with him.

At that moment, the boy who had occupied my mind for most of the morning walked into the kitchen looking as hot as ever and as his eyes met mine, I felt the flutter of butterflies in my stomach again.

It was like my body came alive every time he was near. I wondered if he felt anything around me; if so, I hadn't picked up on anything. I tried to pinpoint if it was the way he walked or if it had something to do with the fact that he was an alpha—that he held that air of authority about him.

I wasn't a good liar and I wasn't good at keeping things from people. It felt like I had a neon sign above my head flashing that read, "She's hiding something!"

"You're so hungry you didn't bother with a bowl?" he asked as he pointed to the cereal box that I had on my lap.

"Sorry, it's a bad habit. I normally only do it at home," I said while standing up, intent on putting the cereal box back. Then I remembered that was how Blake had found out. No putting the cereal box back, so instead I set it down on the kitchen counter.

"I don't mind," he said as he walked to the fridge and got out a bottle of water.

"Do what makes you happy," he added with a shrug of his shoulders.

I watched him for a moment as he opened the bottle and took a couple of swallows. It was one of the few times he had spoken to me without being angry or annoyed and I was a little stunned, and a little suspicious.

He was never this nice to me and I couldn't help thinking that maybe Blake had gone against his word to me and told Cade I was his mate. But then I thought about it. If he knew, he would be going all territorial on me. I knew him well enough to know he was the possessive type.

"Thanks," I said as I took the cereal box back to my seat. I popped a handful of the chocolate cereal into my mouth.

"How are you feeling?" he asked as he leaned against the counter.

"A little sore, but I'll survive," I answered when I'd finished my mouthful of cereal. My head felt fine. It was only my ribs that still ached a bit, but I was sure by tomorrow it would be totally healed.

This caring and almost easygoing Cade was a little disconcerting. I was used to him being domineering and telling me what to do, so I wasn't sure how to handle him at the moment.

"I see you found a shirt," I babbled, feeling a little nervous around him. I hated the way he turned me into a nervous, hormonal teenage girl.

"Yeah," he answered with a smirk. The shirt was tight and hugged his body in all the right places. He was built beautifully. I mentally told myself to stop perving over him.

Get a grip, girl!

"We've finished making plans for tomorrow so I came to ask you if you wanted to see the compound?" he asked, closing the bottle of water and setting it down on the counter.

I was relieved I wouldn't have to spend another day confined to his property, so I wasn't going to ask what the plans entailed. Sometimes ignorance was bliss. I was too curious about the compound to turn him down even if it meant being in his company.

"Sure," I said, closing the cereal box. Other than briefly

this morning, I hadn't seen Gary.

"Where is Gary?" I asked as I put the cereal box on the kitchen counter. I had to mentally remind myself not to try and put it away.

"He is at the compound having a look around with Blake," he answered. At the mention of Blake, I couldn't help the guilt that washed over me. It was only for a couple of days, I reminded myself. What was two days, anyway?

"Come on, let me show you around," he said as he led the way out of the kitchen.

He was being so nice to me, and it made me feel a little guilty for keeping the fact that he was my mate from him. Despite how I felt, I kept my mouth shut and followed him.

He led me past a dining area and through a lounge to two double doors that opened toward the back of the property. The doors opened up on a beautiful swimming pool with water so clear it sparkled.

I took a deep breath of the clean, outside air. It had been one of my reasons for moving here. I wanted a place that I could spend more time outdoors. Now I knew why I'd felt like that. Quietly, I walked with Cade to the bottom of his property where the compound was.

The garden was well looked after and the boundary walls on either side were lined with tall dark-green trees. I wondered if they were there for added privacy. It wasn't like he needed it; there weren't any neighbors. Instead, there were open fields on either side of the property and beyond the compound I could see a forest. The compound itself was massive. It was a two-level building.

"It's like an apartment building," I said out loud to Cade as we stopped in front of it.

"Yeah, it gives the werewolves in the pack some privacy," he explained.

There was enough space on this property that they could

build a couple more of these. To the right of the apartment building were two smaller buildings, a tenth of the size, which also had two levels side by side.

"What are those buildings for?" I asked, pointing to the two smaller buildings.

"The one is a gym and the other is the dining area."

"How many werewolves live here?" I asked, a little stunned at the whole setup.

"About a hundred," he answered. "There are also some werewolves that belong to our pack but live outside the property."

I assumed that when he found out we were mates he would insist I join his pack and it would entail moving into his property. I wasn't sure that was something I was willing to do yet. If he allowed other members of his pack to live off the property, maybe I could do the same. I held onto that little bit of hope.

As we entered the front of the apartment building, I stumbled and Cade reached out to steady me, but I pulled away from him. Luckily, I'd caught myself on the railing; otherwise, I would have looked like a complete idiot lying face down on the ground.

"What's with you?" he said angrily. "I was just trying to help you."

And the aggressive asshole was back. I was already missing the easygoing and thoughtful Cade. I couldn't really blame him for being angry with me. He didn't understand why I didn't want him to touch me and he'd jumped to a conclusion that had made him angry.

Keeping my secret was going to be harder than I thought.

When I looked to the entrance of the apartment block, I noticed Blake standing with Gary.

"Hey, how are you feeling?" asked Gary as he stepped

forward, oblivious to the strained tension between Cade and me. Blake picked up on it because his gaze flickered between the two of us.

"Better," I answered with a forced smile. I could feel the anger still radiating off Cade who was still standing beside me.

"Cade said he was going to go and check on you," Gary said, surprising me. So Cade had come to check on me. I snuck a side-glance at him as he walked to Blake.

"He offered to show me the compound," I told Gary.

"They really have a good setup here," Gary commented as he walked me inside the front door of the apartment block to where Blake and Cade were waiting for us.

Cade's jaw tightened when his eyes fell on me. He was still angry. I looked to Blake and he smiled at me, a knowing smile. Yeah, I bet he was enjoying this.

This whole werewolf thing was becoming more complicated by the day. Then another thought occurred to me. I wondered how Gary would feel about finding out Cade was my mate. He might not be blood related, but he considered me a surrogate daughter so I couldn't see him being happy about it. It would be another hurdle I'd have to overcome when the time came.

I spent the next hour getting shown around the compound. I had to agree with Gary's comment about it being a good setup because it was. There were various-sized apartments that ranged from one to three bedrooms and, although there was an eating area, each apartment had a small kitchen.

It was like a whole self-sufficient little community hidden on Cade's huge property. Most of the younger werewolves were still at school so it was only the older werewolves that were busy with their day-to-day tasks when we passed by.

The apartment building formed a U-shape that faced a

set of iron gates leading directly into the thick forest at the back of the property. I studied the forest for a moment while the guys talked about what type of training the werewolves did.

I couldn't help feeling curious about how it would feel to be able to shift into a werewolf and to run free in the forest. I closed my eyes for a moment to imagine it. I'd have to be patient; I wasn't ready for sex yet, but I looked forward to being able to shift into a werewolf. I wondered if it hurt.

When Cade and Blake shifted, it didn't seem to hurt them. Maybe that was because they'd been shifting for a while already.

"Does it hurt to shift?" My question cut across the conversation.

"Only the first time and a couple of shifts afterward," Cade answered. His eyes met mine and I felt my butterflies flutter in response at his attention being on me. Damn those hormones! It was like when he looked at me, nothing around us existed.

"How bad does it hurt?" I carried on with my questioning and Cade kept his eyes on me.

"I'm not going to sugar-coat it. It hurts like a bitch," he told me. "Some of the older female werewolves compared their first shift to childbirth."

The first time I'd seen a TV program where the mother had screamed while she had given birth had traumatized me. It was the day I swore I'd never have kids. I wasn't the type of person to be scared of anything, but that scared me, just a little bit.

Cade waited for my reaction.

"That sucks," I said, trying to cover up how scared I was.

Gary looked at me with concern. He wasn't happy about that little bit of information either. No parent wanted their children to get hurt. It was another thing to go under the reasons why being a werewolf sucked.

For most of my visit to the compound, I walked with an alpha on each side and Gary tagging along behind us. To make sure there were no accidental touches with Cade, I gravitated closer to Blake.

A couple of times I caught Cade glaring at Blake and Blake would give him a helpless look. Was it possible Cade was getting jealous? Did he think I had a thing for Blake? The more important question was, why was he jealous? He didn't know we were mates. Did he feel the same attraction I felt for him without knowing we were mates?

Curtis greeted me when we walked into the medical office. It was a small building built behind the apartment block to the one side of the gate.

"How are you feeling?" he asked me with a friendly smile.

"Much better, thank you," I answered, matching his smile. Cade glared at him.

Like everything else in the compound, it was a good setup. It was one big room with a big central desk with computers. There were about ten beds with curtains in-between to give patients privacy. It looked like what you'd see in any hospital.

The thought that this was a necessity in the compound made me feel nervous. Did they get hurt a lot? Did they get attacked regularly? This whole tour of the compound was opening my eyes up to the new world I belonged to.

The only time I got really excited on the tour was when we walked into the building that housed the gym. On the top floor, they had state-of-the-art gym equipment and a few guys were working out as we looked around.

I noticed there weren't any female werewolves working out. I wasn't going to be happy if I heard only the guys trained and the girls were expected to cook and clean.

I trained hard so I was able to protect myself and not expect some guy to swoop in and save the day. Although at the moment I was relying on Blake and Cade to keep me safe and it wasn't sitting well with me. Once they trained me, I wouldn't need their protection; I would be able to protect myself. Downstairs was a sparring area similar to the one I had at home, except it was bigger.

A massive bulky-built guy walked out of a small office to the side. His legs were the size of tree trunks and he was the same height as Cade. But where Cade was well defined and etched, this guy was bulging with muscles. Just the sight of him was a little scary. He was the type of guy you wouldn't want to meet in a dark alley.

"This is Hank," Cade said as introduction to the guy.

Hank the tank. It was so fitting because that is what he reminded me of—a tank, indestructible. I had to suppress a laugh and all the guys looked at me a little strangely.

"Nice to meet you, Hank," I said as I held out my hand. He studied me for a moment before he smiled and shook my hand. In that instant, I decided I liked him. Cade introduced him to Gary.

"This is where everyone trains together," Cade said. "And Hank oversees the training."

It was no wonder he was built the way he was if he spent all day and every day in the gym. Personally I didn't like guys that built up; I preferred guys that were nicely built but not bulky.

"Good to hear the girls get to train as well," I quipped, letting my eyes drift around the room.

"Girls can train, but only the guys fight," stated Cade.

Oh, hell no! My eyes shot to Cade as I felt my temper rise.

"Why can't girls fight?" I asked, digging my fingers into the palms of my hands as I tried to rein in my temper. I knew the answer before I even asked the question, but I wanted him to say it out loud.

"Female werewolves are physically weaker than their male counterparts," said Cade.

Don't slap him, I said over and over. *If you slap him he'll find out you're his mate.* It took everything in me not to give in to the urge. *Sexist asshole.*

"Just because guys are physically stronger than girls doesn't mean we can't hold our own in a fight," I bit back, standing up for all the female werewolves. It was also hard to believe that they allowed themselves to be dictated to like that.

The truth was I'd never had to fight off anyone, never mind a powerful werewolf. But I refused to believe it wasn't something I could accomplish with the right training.

"Besides, it would be hard for a male werewolf to concentrate on a fight if he has to worry about his mate," said Blake.

I swung my gaze to him. I was in the presence of two sexist assholes, but this one I could slap.

CHAPTER ELEVEN

SCARLETT

Something in my eyes must have told Blake what I wanted to do to him because he took a step backward and he was out of my reach.

Clever boy. I glared at him.

"You might not be happy with the way things work in the pack, but these have been the way things have worked for centuries and it isn't going to change," Cade informed me with a steely glare.

I swung my gaze to glare back at him.

"We'll see," I challenged.

Unable to stand being around the two idiots any longer, I stalked out of the gym. There was no way I would allow this to continue if I had to join Cade's pack. I was not going to sit back and be a helpless female that needed males to protect her.

I remembered from some stories that members of a pack couldn't go against what the alpha said. I needed to get some more information from Blake. It made me more hesitant to give up my freedom and join Cade's pack.

I didn't want to talk to Blake, but I had to if I was going to get answers to my questions.

It didn't take long for Blake, Cade and Gary to exit the gym. Gary gave me a look that said he was on my side, but unfortunately he wasn't in charge—dumb and dumber were.

I completely ignored Cade and walked beside Blake back to the main house. Cade trailed behind us with Gary. The heat of Cade's glare on the two of us as we walked couldn't be ignored and a glance at Blake told me he felt it too.

As much as I was dying to ask Blake some questions, I didn't dare do it within earshot of Cade. I didn't want him becoming suspicious of why I wanted to know about mates and stuff like that. I'd have to try and talk to Blake another time when Cade wasn't around.

My stomach was growling by the time I entered the kitchen.

Lunch was strained. The four of us sat at the dining room table. There were various sandwiches and salads spread out.

"Who made all the food?" I asked Cade. He'd been a little preoccupied and he was acting jealous.

"One of the ladies from our pack likes to cook so I let her have free reign in the kitchen," he replied tightly. He was still angry, but he was trying to be polite.

By the end of lunch, I decided to retreat back to my room for a while. I needed space and time to try and figure out how I was going to deal with Cade finding out I was his mate. I had just over one day left before I had to come clean.

That night I slept well despite all the things weighing down on me and I was relieved I was going back to school.

Cade was nowhere to be seen when I went down to the kitchen after getting ready for school.

"Hi, how are you feeling?" Gary asked. He was always up

early.

"I'm good," I replied as I went to get some coffee.

Cade walked in and I felt the flutter in my stomach at the sight of him.

"Morning," he greeted as he grabbed a cup of coffee.

"Morning," I greeted, trying to keep myself from perving over him. He was gorgeous.

"You ready to leave for school?" he asked as he took a sip of coffee.

"Yes," I answered. The truth was I hadn't eaten yet but I wasn't going to make him wait while I had breakfast.

"Come on, let's go."

The car ride was quiet. I kept my gaze fixed on the scenery passing us by, trying to keep the flutter of excitement that came alive whenever he was close to me under control. I felt Cade's eyes on me a couple of times but I refused to look at him.

By the time he pulled into the school parking lot, I was frazzled and nervous. Quickly, I got out of the car and walked inside the school, leaving Cade behind.

I felt safe within the school. There were enough werewolves to keep me safe. Cade and Blake had gone through my classes and scheduled specific werewolves to keep an eye on me in each class. It was like a rotation of bodyguards.

I was at my locker getting a book when I turned to see Keri beside me.

"You're back," she said.

"Yeah, I was sick yesterday." The lie rolled off my tongue.

"I spotted you getting dropped off by Cade Presley," she informed me with a knowing smile.

"It's a long story and I don't really want to get into it right now," I said. I hadn't expected the question so I didn't have a suitable lie.

"Are you guys dating?" she asked, wide-eyed with excitement.

"No way," I answered, slamming my locker closed. I spotted Blake walking past us.

"I need to ask Blake something," I told her. "I'll see you at lunchtime."

"Sure, see you then," she said and walked away.

I caught up with Blake. He smiled at me when I grabbed his arm to stop him.

"Hey," I greeted, a little out of breath.

"Hi," he said. "You okay?"

"Yeah, I'm fine, I just wanted to ask you some questions," I told him.

"Okay," he replied and started to walk to the parking lot so we had some privacy, away from busy hallways.

"Does the pack have to do what the alpha says?" I asked Blake as he walked beside me.

"Yes, all except the alpha's mate," he answered.

Yes!

I wouldn't have to do what Cade said and it was the best news I'd heard since I'd found out I was a werewolf.

We'd just exited the school and were walking to the parking lot when I saw something that I hadn't seen coming.

The moment I saw Cade sitting on a bench with some blond girl straddling him, it felt like someone had hit me in the chest. It fucking hurt! I was dazed for a moment, trying to get a handle on my emotions, but nothing could stop the tidal wave of anger that rushed through me.

I'd thought he'd been attracted to me, but I must have been wrong.

"You okay?" Blake asked softly from beside me. He was the only one who understood why I was angry and upset.

I couldn't pull my gaze away from them. Cade smiled at the slut and I felt like someone punched me again.

"Yes," I said with determination, but I couldn't stop the anger and hurt from overwhelming me.

"Hold this," I instructed him, giving him my school bag.

"Don't do anything stupid," he warned as he took the bag.

I ignored his warning. I was way beyond thinking before I acted and there was no way I was going to stand by and do nothing. It wasn't logical thinking that propelled me forward —it was the raw emotions flowing through me that made me throw caution to the wind and stalk over to the couple.

"Get off him," I demanded to the girl as I stood in front of them with my hands on my hips. Her skinny jeans were so tight they looked like another layer of skin and the dark red halter-top barely contained her massive boobs.

"What the hell?!" said the girl as she turned to face me.

Cade's surprised gaze found mine as the girl shifted off him. She gave me a confused look, but the look I gave her told her not to mess with me and she took a step back in fear.

I'd kick her ass if I needed to and at that moment I really had a need to hit someone.

"Get lost," I told her as I shifted my eyes to Cade. She hesitated for a moment before she turned and walked off in a huff.

Students around us began to watch the unfolding drama with interest.

"What is your problem?" Cade demanded as he stood up.

I knew he was trying to intimidate me with his height but it didn't work. The fact that he didn't know he was my mate and that it was something I'd kept from him didn't let him off the hook.

"You're my problem," I bit back angrily, struggling to contain my temper.

He was my mate, and he was about to play tonsil hockey

with some random girl. That was a big problem. Before I could even stop myself, I stepped forward and I slapped him.

The instant my hand touched his face, I felt a bolt of electricity shoot through me. And in that moment I felt a rush of emotion for the boy in front of me and I saw my emotions mirrored in his eyes.

He knew.

This hadn't been the plan, but it was too late. He knew and I couldn't take it back.

Ah, crap! What had I done?

A red handprint began to form on his cheek as he glared at me. He was so angry he was shaking. I remained rooted to the spot in shock at the rush of emotions still coursing through me.

"Fuck," Blake said from next to me. A little dazed and confused, I turned to look at him. It was the first time I'd realized he'd followed me. He yanked me back from a stunned and angry Cade, and shoved me behind him so he stood protectively between my mate and me.

Is this what Blake had meant when he'd said not to do something stupid? Was he scared that Cade was so angry he might lash out at me and hurt me in the process?

Maybe slapping him had been a bad idea. I don't know whether it was because we'd connected or if it was because I'd calmed down slightly, but I regretted it.

"Get your hand off her," warned Cade in a deadly tone while fisting his hands at his sides. I could feel the anger radiating off Cade in waves. It was so powerful that I could only stand in awe of him. All the fear I'd felt before vanished even though he looked like he was about to tear into Blake.

Blake released my wrist and held his hands up in front of Cade to show him that he wasn't touching me. With his eyes still on me, he took a step toward me but Blake refused to move, remaining protectively in front of me. Was he really scared that Cade would hurt me?

"Calm down and I'll get out of your way," Blake tried to reason with the angry alpha and his best friend.

Cade closed his eyes for a moment and took a shaky breath to try and control the anger building up inside.

"I won't hurt her," he whispered hoarsely as he opened his eyes and fixed them on me.

I could see the possessiveness evident in his eyes. I was his whether I wanted to be or not. Before touching him I would have fought against it but it was too strong to deny. I wanted him and he was mine.

"Get out of my way," Cade warned Blake, not moving his eyes from me. "You're keeping me from what is mine."

I couldn't stop the flutter of butterflies in my stomach at the possessiveness in his words.

Blake didn't budge. I understood he was worried about me, but I knew Cade wouldn't hurt me. Don't ask me how, I just did. Blake was making things worse by keeping me from him.

"He won't hurt me," I assured Blake as I stepped around him. Blake grabbed my arm. Cade growled at Blake again and he let go of me.

I took one tentative step toward Cade. His intense gaze held mine and I took another step. Blake stood behind me, ready to spring into action if Cade lost it.

One more step put me so close to Cade that we were only inches apart. I stood in front of him unafraid but a little nervous. With one touch, things had changed. I liked to be in control of situations, but I had no control now, something bigger than the two of us connected us together.

His hand lifted to my face and he trailed his knuckles down my cheek. I closed my eyes at the feel of his touch. With one touch I felt the emotions that had stirred inside me resurface. The nervousness and anxiousness I'd been feeling evaporated and I felt content, complete. It was the stuff that soul mates were made of.

He was my soul mate.

I opened my eyes and tilted my face to gaze up to his. My thoughts were mirrored in his. I was his soul mate and he felt complete and at peace like I did when we touched.

His hands threaded through my hair as he pulled me closer. His eyes flickered to my lips and he leaned closer. He was going to kiss me and I wanted him to. I couldn't fight it even if I wanted to.

The moment his lips touched mine I felt something inside me come alive and overwhelm me. I gripped his arms to hold myself up as my knees weakened and I struggled to keep myself up.

Blake and the crowd of people were forgotten as he tilted my face up to his to get better access while his lips moved against mine. His tongue swept across my bottom lip. I held on tighter to his arms as I opened my mouth and he deepened the kiss.

I wanted more and I held him closer as his tongue tangled with mine. All thoughts vanished and all that mattered was his kiss. I groaned when he pulled away and I tried to get my breath back.

He rested his forehead against mine. Both of us were breathless.

"We need to get out of here," he whispered to me. Normally I would fight against anything I didn't have complete control over, but this time I didn't fight. Instead, I said, "Yes."

It was only when Cade turned to Blake did I notice the crowd of people that had been watching our show. I'd just slapped him and then the next moment we were kissing. The werewolves watching would understand but the humans would think we were crazy.

"We need time," Cade said to Blake who was smiling as he watched Cade take my hand in his. "I'll be in touch later."

"Sure," said Blake with a nod.

Cade walked me to his car and opened the passenger side and he helped me in and then closed the door. He walked around the front of his car and got into the driver's side.

He started up the car and as we pulled out of the parking space, he took my hand in his.

Normally, I'd ask where we were going, but I was content to just hold his hand and revel in the calm I felt when I was with him. It was different from before when we'd been at each other's throats. I couldn't help thinking it was because we'd been attracted to each other.

He drove to a part of town I'd never been to before. It was more secluded, with tall trees lining the dirt road that led to a house surrounded by more tall trees. He parked in front of the house.

I opened the door and got out. It was beautiful and I couldn't help but take a deep breath of the wilderness. Cade took my hand in his and led me to the door of the house. He reached behind a potted plant beside the front door and pulled out a key. It was such a typical hiding place for a key.

He opened the door and stepped inside.

"It's not much, but I like to come here when I need to be alone," he said as I entered the house.

I looked around. It was a small house. The lounge had a sofa facing a fireplace with a simple wooden coffee table in between. It was nothing compared to what I was used to, but I liked it. It felt homey. The massive houses that I'd lived in my whole life had been cold and empty.

There was a small kitchen in the corner of the lounge. It had a stove and a small fridge.

"I like it," I said honestly as he watched me for a response.

"I thought it would be better to talk here than at the house where there are too many distractions."

I nodded my head.

Gary was at his house. He was right, we needed time to talk about what had just happened and we didn't need other distractions. Like how Gary was going to take the news that Cade was my mate.

Besides, I knew that our talk was going to get heated. Irrespective of how he made me feel and how right it felt being with him, I wasn't prepared to just drop my life to be with him.

"But before we talk I need to do this again," he said before he reached for me and pulled me closer. His hands cupped my face and tilted it upward as his lips covered mine. His seductive touch sent a shiver of awareness through me.

I wished we didn't have to stop kissing. Once the kissing stopped and the talking started, things were going to get heated and we'd be back to fighting.

CHAPTER TWELVE

CADE

I'll never forget how I felt the first time I saw her.

I'd missed the first day back at school because I'd been out with a couple of members from my pack trying to track down a rogue that had shown up a few days before.

We'd managed to track him to the town's border but then his tracks had just vanished. It was never a good thing to have a rogue roaming in your territory. I had to up the patrols and security around my property.

The only reason I'd been waiting outside the school was to talk to Blake. I was leaning against my car with a couple of girls keeping me company when the smell of wild daisies hit me and I looked to the source standing at the entrance of the school.

It wasn't her outer beauty that kept my eyes glued to her. There was something about her—maybe it was the confident air about her or the defiant way her eyes had clashed with mine.

When I'd watched her walk over to the beautiful Maserati I'd raced the day before, my interest in her had gone up a level. The thought of a girl being able to drive a car like that made her sexier than before.

She was so different from the girls I was used to. She was like a breath of fresh air and I couldn't dispute the fact that I wanted her.

When I'd found out from Blake that she didn't know what a pack meant and he was convinced she had no idea she was one of us, I'd felt protective of her. That protectiveness had made me watch over her that night from the boundary wall of her property.

When I'd managed to get her to come to my house so Blake and I could reveal the truth to her, she'd lost her cool and left.

The fear that had hit me when she'd hit the rogue with her car had scared me. I was in charge, so there were plenty of lives I was responsible for, but I felt something very different when Scarlett had been injured.

But it didn't matter that I was attracted to her or that I cared. She couldn't stand the sight of me.

And it seemed the more time I spent with her, the more she disliked me and the more she gravitated to Blake. I usually never got jealous, but for the first time I wanted to hit my best friend because he'd seemed to have caught her interest. Watching it unfold in front of me was more than I could handle.

I looked forward to seeing Scarlett as I made my way downstairs.

When I walked into the kitchen and spotted her sipping her coffee, I felt the attraction I had for her come alive. Even though she'd spent most of the day before so close to Blake, it didn't stop how I felt about her.

I'd never felt jealous before and it took all my self-control not to beat the crap out of him.

"Morning," I greeted her as I grabbed a cup of coffee.

"Morning," she greeted back, holding her cup to her lips to take another sip.

"Are you ready to leave for school?" I asked.

"Yes," she answered as she set her still-full cup of coffee down on the counter.

"Come on, let's go."

Scarlett was quiet as she gazed out of the window. I couldn't help sneaking a few glances at her. She was an enigma that I couldn't figure out.

I had lots of experience with girls. Being an alpha, I never had a shortage of girls wanting my attention, but Scarlett made me feel things I'd never felt before. Maybe I felt this way because she refused to fall down at my feet like the rest of the girls did.

As soon as I parked in front of the school, she got out of the car and disappeared into the school. I felt anger and frustration at the fact that the girl I liked couldn't get away from me fast enough.

I'd never been in this predicament before, wanting someone who wasn't interested in me, and I didn't know how to handle it.

Feeling unsettled, I got out of my Jeep and slammed the door closed. I wanted to go into the school, but the thought of seeing Scarlett getting closer to Blake was too much to handle. So instead, I sat down on the bench outside the school contemplating whether I should skip school for the day to see if I could track the rogue that was after Scarlett.

I didn't like the idea of someone out there being hell-bent on hurting her.

"Cade," I heard the seductive voice say to me.

I looked up to see Nancy standing in front of me. She was a werewolf from Blake's pack. She wore skin-tight jeans and a halter-top that struggled to contain her big tits.

"Hi," I greeted her, giving her a smile.

Then it occurred to me. Maybe the best way to deal with what I was feeling for Scarlett was to get another girl to take my mind off her.

"I thought I'd come and keep you company," Nancy cooed and I smiled. She was definitely game.

"Sure," I said, running my eyes appreciatively over her figure.

I expected her to sit down on the bench next to me but she surprised me when she stepped closer and straddled me. My hands reached for her waist as she smiled at me seductively.

I smiled at her, thinking that she was exactly what I needed to work Scarlett out of my system.

"Get off him," a female voice demanded. Why would anyone care that Nancy was straddling me and getting a little friendly?

"What the hell?" said Nancy as she turned to look at the girl who'd issued the demand. I was shocked when Nancy shifted off me and I saw Scarlett, angry as hell, with her hands on her hips.

What the hell?

What surprised me even more was the look she gave Nancy. Nancy was about to argue, but the look Scarlett gave her made her bite her tongue.

"Get lost," Scarlett told her as her eyes shifted to mine. Nancy hesitated for a moment before she turned and walked off in a huff.

I was trying to figure out why Scarlett was acting the way she was. Why would she have a problem with what I did with another girl? It made no sense. Students around us began to watch the unfolding drama with interest.

"What is your problem?" I demanded as I stood up.

Most people would have been intimidated, but not Scarlett. She stood her ground.

She was acting like she was jealous. She'd been getting closer to Blake yesterday so I couldn't understand why suddenly she was standing in front of me acting like a jealous girlfriend.

"You're my problem," she snapped angrily. Why would I be her problem? She wasn't making any sense. She looked so angry and I was trying to figure out why. It was like trying to do a puzzle with half of the pieces missing.

She took a step forward and I felt her hand connect with my face.

Stunned, I stood rooted to the spot. The instant her hand touched my face, I felt a bolt of electricity shoot through me. And in that moment I felt a rush of emotions for the girl in front of me and I saw the emotion for me mirrored in her eyes.

She was my mate.

I was still stunned by the slap and the realization that I'd found my mate. Scarlett stood unmoving as I watched her struggle with the emotions coursing through her.

My cheek hurt. As small as she was compared to me, she'd slapped me hard. Anger flowed in me and I struggled to keep it under control. Slapping an alpha was never a good idea. We had tempers and that type of action would set us off without thinking.

"Fuck," Blake said and I noticed him standing beside Scarlett. He grabbed her wrist and yanked her behind him.

Even though logically I knew he was protecting her from me, I couldn't stop the jealousy that stirred in me at the sight of his hand on her wrist. A possessiveness I'd never felt before took over and I wanted to rip his hand off of her. She was mine.

"Get your hand off her," I warned in a deadly tone,

fisting my hands to stop myself from attacking my best friend for touching my mate. He was my best friend, but she was my mate. She outranked him—hell, she outranked everyone. To me she was the most important person.

Knowing I was about to lose it, Blake released her wrist and held up his hand to show me that he wasn't touching her.

I watched as Scarlett stared back at me. She was mine and I needed to touch her again. With my eyes still on her, I took a step toward her, but Blake refused to move.

"Calm down and I'll get out of your way," Blake tried to reason with me, but he didn't understand. It was the fact that he was in my way that angered me.

I closed my eyes for a moment and took a shaky breath to try and control the anger building up inside.

"I won't hurt her," I whispered, meaning every word I said. I opened my eyes and fixed them on Scarlett.

She was mine and he couldn't keep her from me. I wanted to reach for her and pull her close. I wanted to touch her so bad that I felt a physical pain at not being able to. She looked at me the same way I looked at her. I was hers and she was mine. We belonged to each other.

"Get out of my way," I warned Blake, not moving my eyes from Scarlett. "You're keeping me from what is mine."

But Blake didn't move. He had no right to keep me from her.

"He won't hurt me," Scarlett assured him as she stepped around him, but Blake grabbed her arm to stop her. Seeing him touch her made the rage grow inside of me again. No one was to touch her. I growled at Blake again to warn him and he released her. If he touched her again I was going to go ballistic.

I watched Scarlett take a tentative step toward me. Her eyes held mine as she took another step closer. With every step closer I felt the anticipation of touching her grow.

Blake remained behind her ready to spring into action if I lost it. He hadn't found his mate yet so he didn't understand the connection I'd just formed with Scarlett. There was no way I could hurt her, she was a piece of me. Hurting her would be like hurting myself.

She took one more step and she stopped. We were so close. I could see the uncertainty in her eyes. She was used to being in control and I could see something deeper than she understood pulled her to me.

My hand lifted to her face and I trailed my knuckles down her cheek. Her skin was so soft. She closed her eyes at the feel of my touch. I felt the anger begin to disappear and I felt complete. She was the other half of me and when I touched her, I felt at peace. Nothing I'd ever experienced was even close to what I felt at that moment.

My eyes drank her in. *She is mine.*

She is my soul mate.

She opened her eyes and tilted her face to gaze up at me. I could see she felt the same as I did, complete. I wanted to feel her skin against mine.

Slowly I threaded my hands through her soft, silky hair as I pulled her closer. My eyes flickered to her lips and I leaned closer. The smell of wild daisies was intoxicating. I'd wanted to kiss her since the first time I'd met her.

The moment my lips touched hers, I felt an overwhelming desire to hold her close and never let her go. She gripped my arms as I moved my lips against hers.

No one else existed as I tilted Scarlett's face up to mine to get better access while my lips moved against hers. I needed to taste her. My tongue swept across her bottom lip; her lips were so soft. Her grip on my arms tightened and she opened her mouth.

The first taste of her as I touched my tongue to hers was addictive. I twirled my tongue against hers and I felt her pull me closer. I wanted to keep kissing her and touching her, but then I remembered we were kissing each other with an audience that included Blake.

She groaned when I pulled away, ending our first kiss. She was breathless as she still held onto my arms. I liked that I had this effect on her.

I rested my forehead against hers as I struggled to catch my breath.

"We need to get out of here," I whispered to her. We'd just found out we were mates and we needed time by ourselves to figure things out. I half expected her to say no, but she surprised me by saying, "Yes."

I turned to Blake who was still watching us from the sidelines with a smile.

"We need time," I said to Blake who was still smiling as he watched me put Scarlett's hand in mine. "I'll be in touch later."

I knew we were skipping school, but what had just happened between the two of us was more important.

"Sure," said Blake with a nod.

Not wanting to waste another moment, I walked Scarlett to my car and opened the passenger side. I helped her into the seat before I closed the door. I walked around the front of the car and got into the driver's side.

As I started up the car and pulled out of the parking lot, I reached for her hand and held it. Just touching her made me feel calm. I liked it.

The ride was quiet. She seemed as content as I was to just be together with our hands touching.

I wanted to take her somewhere where we could talk without distractions or interruptions, so taking her back to my house wasn't an option. I decided to take her to a place I didn't tell many people about, a small house I'd inherited from my grandmother.

It wasn't flashy or anything like that. I could have renovated it but I liked the way it was—small and lived in. It reminded me of my grandmother and it was a place that I went to when I needed time alone or to think.

I'd never brought a girl there before.

The house was secluded, with tall trees lining the dirt road that led to a house surrounded by more tall trees. I parked outside the front of the house.

I watched Scarlett look around and take a deep breath. I was feeling nervous, unsure if she'd like it here. She was used to a certain standard of living that this house didn't live up to.

I reached for her hand and led her to the door of the house. I reached for the key in its usual hiding place behind a potted plant beside the front door and unlocked the door and stepped inside.

"It's not much, but I like to come here when I need to be alone," I said as I entered the house. Normally, I was the only one who came here other than the cleaning lady once a week. She stepped inside after me and looked around the small house. I waited while she scanned the house.

"I like it," she said, surprising me.

"I thought it would be better to talk here than at the house where there are too many distractions."

She nodded her head in agreement

I knew her well enough to know that our talk was going to get heated. She was my mate, but she was no pushover. It was something that I liked about her, but I knew there were going to be times that same independence was going to drive me nuts.

I don't know if it was the way she looked at me or just the fact that I needed to touch her, but I wanted to kiss her again before the fighting started.

"But before we talk, I need to do this again," I said before I reached for her and pulled her closer. My hands cupped her face and tilted it upward as my lips touched hers.

The urge to move my lips to her neck and mark her as my own was nearly impossible to fight, but I knew she wasn't ready for that yet and there was no way I'd mark her without her consent. I fought against the urge as I continued to kiss her.

I lost myself in the moment, moving my lips against hers. The thought that she was mine made me so damn happy.

CHAPTER THIRTEEN

SCARLETT

It was time to talk but I didn't want to stop kissing him. I'd never felt so alive before and it was hard to break away from him and take a step back. Breathlessly, I gazed up at him, still holding onto his arms to keep me up on weakened legs.

Knowing we were mates was one thing, but touching him and making that connection with him was something so different.

I'd felt attracted to him before but now it was so much more. I cared about him in a way I'd never felt before. It wasn't an instant love but I wanted to be with him and protect him and I knew he felt the same; it was written in his eyes.

"We need to talk," I insisted, trying to get my heart to slow down, but standing so close to him just made me want to shut up and keep kissing him. I released my hold on his arms and stepped back.

"Yes… we need to talk," he agreed, remaining where he was.

I needed to sit down so I took a seat on the comfortable sofa.

"Where do we start?" I asked as I clasped my hands together. This whole experience was so weird. It wasn't just like I was a girl who liked a guy and we kinda dated to see where it would lead. No, we were mates and we were destined to be together. We had to sit down and figure out what that meant, or at least I did.

I gazed at him as he took a step closer to me. We both knew this conversation wasn't going to be easy.

"How about we start with why you slapped me?" he asked as he cocked his head slightly to the side.

The answer was going to anger him. I knew he wasn't going to be happy that I'd hidden the fact that I knew he was my mate from him. I took a deep breath and released it.

"I was jealous," I admitted as I held his gaze. His self-assured smile widened.

"Jealous?" he asked. He was so enjoying this.

I narrowed my eyes.

"I didn't want some other girl with her hands all over my *mate*,"

The smirk disappeared and his forehead creased.

"You knew I was your mate? How?" he asked in a calm voice. It was way too calm, if you asked me. I kept watching him, waiting for him to explode with anger, but he remained calm. Then I noticed his hands had tightened at his sides. He wasn't calm at all.

I stood up and showed him the birthmark on my hip. He walked over to me and his fingers traced over the two teardrops.

"You saw mine when you came to my room to get pain pills," he murmured more to himself than to me. I sat back down on the sofa as he took a step backward.

It was like the silence before the storm.

"Why didn't you say anything?" he asked as he crossed his arms. His voice remained calm, but I could see the hurt in his eyes.

"I wanted a chance to get used to the idea," I explained. He might not like the answer, but it was the truth.

"How long were you planning on keeping it to yourself?" he asked softly as his jaw tensed.

"A couple of days," I answered.

"Why a couple of days?" he questioned, looking a little perplexed.

"Blake saw it. He told me I had two days to tell you and if I didn't, he would."

"Blake knew you were my mate!" he exploded. The storm had hit.

"He saw my birthmark," I tried to explain as I stood up, but I didn't take a step closer to him. He was furious. Normally, I didn't feel intimated by him, but it was hard to hold my ground when I could feel the anger emanating from him.

"He saw your birthmark," he repeated in a deadly tone as I watched him try and control the anger flowing through him. "How did he see it?"

He closed his eyes for a moment; it was like he was convinced the answer was going to upset him even more. I gave him a confused look and then I realized why he'd asked the question.

"He saw it yesterday morning when I was reaching for cereal," I explained to him, a bit of exasperation creeping into my voice. Trust him to jump to the conclusion that Blake and I'd been getting better acquainted, and that's how he saw it.

I was the virgin, he was the alpha of a pack with all the

girls falling left, right and center for him. And he had the audacity to get angry because he thought I was fooling around with Blake?

"So you and he didn't..." he said, unable to say the words. His anger began to disappear as he realized he'd overreacted.

"No, I'm not like you," I stated as I crossed my arms and glared at him.

"How are you not like me?" he asked, not sure what I was getting at.

"Not even an hour ago you were getting mauled by another girl," I said, trying to contain the jealously that I felt as I remembered how he'd enjoyed the attention. "And if I hadn't slapped you, you'd probably be screwing her already."

"I thought you had a thing for Blake," he tried to explain as he held the back of his neck. "You spent most of yesterday treating me like a leper."

"I don't have thing for Blake, I was just trying to make sure I didn't touch you by mistake."

He was silent for a few moments and then he let out a sigh.

"Let's forget about what happened before. All that matters is that we found each other," he said.

"Fine," I agreed as I nodded. "As long as I don't have to worry about your conquests coming out of the woodwork."

"I'm not going to lie to you, Scar, there have been plenty before, but now there is only you," he softly declared.

I wanted to stay angry with him, but it was difficult when he was so damn sweet. And I couldn't help the flutter inside my stomach when he called me Scar. There was something intimate about the way he said it that did crazy things to me.

"It's hard for me to think you've been with other guys, but there is nothing I can do about it," he said. Little did he know I had an empty past when it came to boys; I'd never had a boyfriend. I'd been kissed before, but that had been the sum total of my experience.

One moment of silence turned into another as I contemplated what I was going to tell him.

"Have you had... many?" He asked the question he didn't really want the answer to. *Hell no!* There was no way I was going to tell him there hadn't been anybody. He didn't get to have the clear mind of knowing that he would be my first when I knew for a fact that I wasn't his. He'd probably had so many that he couldn't even count them.

I hated the fact that when a girl slept around everyone called her a slut, but if a guy did the same thing he was called a stud. It was so unfair.

He would find out the truth when we mated but until then I would allow him to think that there had been others. If I had to think about all the previous girls he'd screwed, I'd occupy his mind with my imaginary guys. Fair was fair.

"A few," I lied.

His fists tightened and then he released them. He didn't like that one bit. *Welcome to my club.* I didn't like to think about all the girls he'd entertained before me.

He paced for a little while before he turned to face me.

"I know this whole werewolf thing is new to you and most people in your shoes would be freaking out," he began to say. I knew where this conversation was headed.

"And if your life wasn't in serious danger at the moment, I'd give you the time to get used to all of it, but I can't."

I pressed my lips together as he sat down beside me and took my hands in his. I knew he was going to insist I join his pack and mate with him so he'd be able to protect me better.

I knew he was doing it because he cared about me and wanted to keep me safe; I understood that, but there were just some things I wouldn't be forced into and I had to stand my ground.

"I want you to join my pack," he said as he watched me for a reaction.

It wasn't a surprise. I waited for him to continue.

"It will help me keep you safe. Like Blake explained to you, if you join my pack we will be able to communicate via the mind-link," he explained calmly, still holding my hands in his.

I could read in his eyes that he was expecting me to fight him on it. Before we'd connected as mates I would have fought him on it but now I understood his need to protect me because I felt that need for him as well. Above all else, I wanted to keep him safe.

Just the thought of something happening to him nearly had me hyperventilating.

"Okay," I said with a nod to emphasize I was agreeing to it. His mouth dropped open slightly in shock. Yeah, he hadn't seen that coming.

"I kinda expected you to fight me on that," he told me as he flashed a lethal smile that should come with a warning, like 'panties will melt'. I had an urge to reach for his face and press his lips to mine. The constant urge to touch him and have him touch me was very distracting.

"I understand you want to protect me, I really do and that's why I'm not going to fight you on *this*," I explained. I squeezed his hands in mine.

I wondered if he realized my wording meant that although I wasn't going to fight him on this, I was going to stand my ground on some other things. I'd conceded on this point and I hoped he'd be able to concede on the other ones I wasn't going to back down on.

"I'll miss the fact that you won't smell of wild daisies anymore," he murmured to me as he tucked a piece of hair behind my ear. He leaned closer and took a deep breath and sighed as he released it. He liked the way I smelled and I couldn't stop the flutter in my stomach at the thought.

I loved the smell of fresh rain, so I didn't mind.

"So is joining your pack going to hurt?" I asked as I looked nervously at him.

It just seemed like everything that was connected to the werewolf thing had to hurt: the biting to mate, and the first few shifts when I started shifting into a werewolf.

Was it too much to hope that it wouldn't hurt?

"A little," he answered, taking my hand gently into his. He opened my hand and my palm faced upward. "We make a small cut on your hand and I do the same on mine. Once we mix the blood, you become a member of my pack."

"Can this be done with just any member of your pack?" I asked.

"No, only I can allow a new member into the pack."

It made logical sense.

"Even you becoming a part of my pack will not be enough to keep you safe. We will need to mate," he told me. I let out a sigh.

Here comes the fight.

"No," I said as I pulled my hands from his. "I can't, at least not yet."

His jaw tightened and I could see the anger start to build inside of him. Although I understood his reason behind wanting to mate with me, it was something I wasn't ready to do just yet. I'd join his pack, but I wouldn't mate with him.

Because of my little lie, he wouldn't realize that it was inexperience that made me hesitate to do that with him. And although he was my mate and I cared for him, I wasn't going to take that step yet. I didn't even know him that well.

I had no idea how long it would take for me to decide I was ready. It might be a week or two.

"You're making it difficult to protect you!" he began to

argue in a raised voice, but I held my hand up to him, signaling him to stop talking. He took a deep breath to calm his anger, but it didn't seem to be working.

"Put yourself in my shoes for a moment," I explained to him as I stood up. "I haven't had a lot of time to get used to the fact that I'm a werewolf and now my life is going in an entirely different direction to what I'd originally planned."

He watched me pace back and forth in front of him.

"I'm not saying I never want to mate with you," I assured him. "I just need time to get to know you a little bit and get used to the idea."

It was my own fault my jealousy had put me in this predicament. I couldn't tell him the truth that I was a virgin and I'd never done anything more than kiss a guy. We were mates and destined to be together, but I was scared that his experience would make me feel inept.

What if I wasn't any good at it? I was always strong and confident, but how could I be confident in something I'd never done? Besides, I'd held onto my virginity for a while and I wasn't going to just give it up after only knowing him a few days.

I heard him let out a frustrated sigh as he stood up and faced me.

"You're my mate and I have to do everything within my power to keep you safe, do you understand that?" he said angrily.

I nodded my head at him. No matter what reasoning he came up with to try to persuade me, nothing was going to change my mind. I wouldn't be forced into taking a step I wasn't ready for.

"Yes, I do understand that, but I'm still not going to do it," I said, putting my foot down.

"I'll never be able to forgive myself if something happens to you, you know that," he said desperately. I could see the fear in his eyes.

"Answer a question for me," I said as I stepped closer to him. I wanted to reach out and hold him to ease his fear, but I couldn't, so I kept my arms at my sides. Besides, if I touched him it would distract us.

"Even if we mated, something could still happen to me?" I asked softly as my eyes held his.

He remained silent.

"Mating with you doesn't guarantee that nothing will happen to me," I repeated, watching his face for his reaction.

"No... but it will help," he finally answered, realizing where I was headed with all of this. I'd made my point. A few minutes of silence and I felt his anger begin to ease.

"Fine," he relented as he reached for me.

I smiled at him as I allowed him to pull me close.

"But if you won't mate with me, then I'll need to be with you all the time to protect you. It means I'll share your room and I'll drive you to school and back. You can't go anywhere after school without me."

Geez, he's not kidding! He was really going into over-protective mode now. The only thing that made me a little apprehensive was the fact that he was going to share a room with me, but I was happy I'd won this round.

"Okay."

This whole talk had gone a lot more smoothly than I'd anticipated, but I was glad we hadn't been at each other's throats and somehow we'd both compromised.

Now that that was sorted, we could go back to kissing. He pulled me closer and I raised my hand to brush across his cheek.

"I might snore," I teased him as he leaned forward and his lips were nearly touching mine.

"I can live with that," he said as he smiled.

His lips touched mine so gently that I felt a tingle run

through my body. I wasn't sure if it was part of the whole mate thing or if it was my body's reaction to his.

I groaned as his lips moved against mine and my hands snaked around his neck, pulling him closer to me. I opened my mouth and his tongue swept inside and danced with mine. The flutter in my stomach intensified.

By the time he broke free, I was breathless and so aware of his body against mine.

"So when are we going to do the blood thing for me to join your pack?" I asked, feeling a little nervous about it.

"When we get back to my house," he answered.

Soon, I would be a part of his pack.

CHAPTER FOURTEEN

SCARLETT

When we arrived back at Cade's house, Blake was waiting in the kitchen with Gary. I was surprised to see him because I thought he'd gone to school. It was another couple of hours before school ended for the day. I walked in first and Cade followed behind.

"What are you doing here?" I asked Blake.

"I thought I'd skip as well to make sure everything ran smoothly while you guys had your talk."

I hadn't even thought about it. It was then that I realized the responsibility that Cade had on his shoulders.

Blake began to stand up and Cade walked over to him and before I even realized what he was going to do, he hit him in the face. Blake took the hit and didn't even attempt to defend himself or try and hit Cade back. It was like he'd expected it.

"What the hell?" I gasped, taken by surprise as I rushed over to Blake. His lip was cut and bloodied.

"That's for being a shitty friend," explained Cade calmly and then he turned and walked over to the kitchen sink.

"I deserved that," Blake said to me. He didn't deserve it. He'd kept my secret because I'd asked him to. I would never understand guys.

"No, you didn't," I weighed in as I threw a glare at my mate.

"Yes, he did," stated Cade as he rinsed blood from his hand.

"We good?" Blake said, wiping the blood from his lip.

"Yeah, we're good," confirmed Cade as he walked over to the fridge and got out a bottle of water.

The slate was wiped clean. Men were so confusing. If they were girls, they wouldn't talk to each other for a couple of weeks. Gary looked from Blake to Cade and shook his head.

"What are you doing out of school?" Gary asked when he realized I was home early.

"Cade and I had some stuff to sort through," I began to explain. I sat down in-between Gary and Blake.

"Remember what Blake and Cade told you about mates and stuff like that?" I asked.

"Sure, I remember," he answered as he nodded.

"Well, Cade is my mate," I stated. Gary's gaze flickered from me to Cade and then it settled back on me. Cade leaned against the kitchen counter, keeping his distance as Gary took in the information.

"Wow," he mumbled as he pushed away from the table and turned to face me.

"How are you feeling about it?" he asked. It was so like Gary to worry about me.

"It's going to take some getting used to," I replied with a shrug. It was inevitable and it had to happen sometime, I just wanted to wait for a time when I would be ready.

It wasn't like I wasn't physically attracted to him, because I was. There was no denying it, but I wasn't sure if I was prepared for the emotional side of what would happen.

"I've decided I'm going to join Cade's pack," I revealed to Gary and Blake. Blake smiled and shot a look at Cade, but my eyes were focused on Gary's reaction.

His eyes widened in surprise and then he reached for my hand and gave it a squeeze.

"You know what you're doing," he said. "You've always had a good head on your shoulders. You've never needed me to point you in the right direction or tell you what to do. There is a reason I never fought you when you wanted to take control of your inheritance. You were responsible enough then and you are responsible enough now to make your own decisions."

My throat thickened at his words.

"Thank you," I whispered as I leaned forward to give him a hug.

A soft growl emanated from behind me as Gary's arms wrapped around me and hugged me. I released Gary and turned to see Cade growling at him.

"Down, boy," I told him as I shot him a glare.

I knew Cade was the possessive type, but I wasn't going to let him make a big deal out of nothing. Although technically Gary wasn't blood related, he was my family and I wasn't going to stop giving him hugs or showing him affection just because Cade got jealous.

"I don't like it when any guy touches you," he said through gritted teeth as he glared at Gary. Gary shifted back slightly, feeling intimidated by the power emanating from Cade.

"Like I said before, this is going to be fun to watch," Blake murmured to me as he leaned back in his chair and crossed his arms over his chest. I shot him a glare and I was tempted to wipe that smug look off his face. But the fact that he'd taken a hit for keeping my secret for me softened me up a bit. I'd let that one comment slide.

"Enough," I said to Cade as I stood up and walked to him.

"I don't want any guy to touch you," he said softly to me. His anger began to ease now that I was standing in front of him.

"You're going to have to get used to it because I can't have you overreacting every time a guy comes near me. Gary is my family," I explained to him as he reached for me and pulled me into his arms.

With the first touch, I was distracted and I was lost when his lips brushed against mine.

"I'll try," he whispered.

It took me a minute to remember what we'd been talking about. I pulled away from him because I couldn't think properly with him so close.

"So are you ready to join my pack?" he asked, letting me have my space.

"Yes," I said with a nod, sounding calmer than I felt.

Blake got up and got a knife from one of the drawers.

"I'll do it," insisted Cade. Was it too much to see someone else hurt me? Blake didn't argue and he handed the knife to Cade.

"This will hurt a bit," Cade told me as he took my hand in his. The knife was sharp and he made a small cut. I grimaced with pain and I felt my knees wobble a bit at the sight of blood.

It made me queasy, but I bit down on my lip and ignored it. I didn't want them to see me as weak. Cade made a small cut in the palm of his hand then he took my hand and gently pressed it to his.

His eyes held mine as our blood mixed and Blake and

Gary watched. At first there was nothing.

Then I heard it. *I can't believe she is mine.*

It was Cade and I smiled at him.

"I heard that," I revealed as he released my hand and pulled me into his arms.

"It worked," he murmured as his lips feathered a kiss to my forehead. I couldn't help but smile.

If I don't hurry, I'm going to be late.

I pulled away from Cade and looked up at him.

"Was that you?" I asked. He shook his head as he watched me carefully.

I wonder if this is going to be enough food for lunch.

The next time he swings, I'll duck and swing with my right fist.

I need to finish repairing this before lunch.

One thought after another hit me and my head began to pound. It was like I was standing in a room full of people, all talking to me at the same time. I raised my hand and touched my forehead as I squeezed my eyes shut, trying to shut out the flow of thoughts into my mind.

"What's wrong?" Cade asked with concern.

"I don't know," I muttered as more and more thoughts flooded into my mind. I couldn't think because of the jumble of thoughts. The pounding in my head began to get worse and I stumbled forward.

Arms reached out to steady me, then I felt someone lift me up and carry me.

"Say something, Scar?" Cade said as he laid me down. I opened one eye to see I was lying on the couch. Gary and Blake were standing behind a kneeling Cade, watching with concern.

"I don't know what's happening," I said as more thoughts flitted through my head. I closed my eyes again to try and push the unwanted thoughts from my head but it only got worse.

The pain started to become unbearable. It felt like my head was going to explode from the overflow of thoughts. I cried out.

"Scar!" I heard Cade say desperately from beside me.

The pain became so unbearable that when the darkness came, I gave in to it.

When I woke up, my head was still sore but the invading thoughts were gone. I rubbed my forehead and opened my eyes. Even though the room was dark, I recognized it as my own. I spotted the tall, lean form of my mate beside me in a chair.

"You're awake," said Cade. I heard the relief in his voice.

I reached for the lamp on my side table and switched it on. It took a few minutes for my eyes to adjust to the light. I tried to figure out what had happened and what I was doing in my room. Cade watched me silently as I began to piece everything together.

I'd joined Cade's pack and then thoughts from the members of his pack had begun to overload me. And then I'd passed out.

"How are you feeling?" he asked softly as he reached for my hand and held it in his.

"I'm okay," I answered while trying to sit up. Immediately, Cade was standing and he helped me to sit. Once I was comfortable, he sat back down beside me in the chair.

"What happened?" I asked, still feeling a little disorientated.

"We think you got overloaded with thoughts from my pack," he explained. "I'm sorry—I had no idea that would happen."

"Why do you think it happened?" I asked, rubbing my temple. If he hadn't seen it coming, then it wasn't something normal.

"I think it's because you haven't grown up in a pack. Most werewolves have and we learn from an early age how to cope with thoughts from the other pack members. It almost becomes second nature for us."

It made sense.

"So because I haven't been raised in a pack, I didn't know how to cope with all the thoughts?" I asked.

"Yes, pretty much," he answered. "I've never had anyone join my pack that hadn't been brought up in a pack before, so they knew how to control the mind-link."

"Why has it stopped?" I asked, because I couldn't hear a single thought. Not even his.

"I've got everyone in my pack keeping their thoughts to themselves at the moment, at least until you get used to it. They're only allowed to contact me if there is an emergency," he explained as he caressed my hand in his.

"You guys can control what thoughts are projected to the rest of the pack?" I asked.

"Yes."

It was probably a good thing because it would be weird for other people in the pack to hear private thoughts that didn't concern them. I'd definitely have to learn how to do that.

I glanced down at our hands. I loved the way my hand fit in his.

"And you brought me to my house," I said.

"Yeah, I didn't want to take any chances so we brought you here. The farther away we are from the pack, the less intense the thoughts are, so if someone slips up it won't be as traumatic for you," he explained.

This whole werewolf thing was going to be more difficult to get a handle on than I'd previously thought, but I was up for the challenge.

"If I'd had any idea..." he started. I could see he felt responsible for what had happened, but I didn't blame him. I was okay and there were no lasting effects.

"I'm fine," I assured him. "You didn't know it would happen."

"But it's my job to take care of you," he said softly, like he'd failed me in some way. I reached out and caressed his cheek. I couldn't help the intense flutter I got in my stomach at the thought that I meant so much to him. It made me happy and possessive of him.

"I'm big enough to take care of myself, you know," I chipped back. It was still hard trying to balance this intense connection we had as mates and my need for my independence. I understood his need to keep me safe, because I felt that same need for him.

But I didn't want to turn into one of those girls who couldn't be without a man. To me there was a big difference between wanting and needing someone. I wanted Cade in my life but I didn't need him and I wanted to keep it that way.

"Yeah, I know," he said, glancing down at our connected hands.

"What time is it?" I asked.

"Late, you've been out for a while," he said. "I was so worried I even brought Curtis with me so he could keep an eye on you. I also brought a few others to help protect you."

"It's fine," I said, waving off his concerns.

"I hope you don't mind, but they've all kinda moved in until you can manage the mind-link. Once you're able to manage, we'll move back to my house," he said.

"It's fine."

I was glad to be home, even if he and some members of his pack had invaded it. Everything had happened so quickly that I hadn't really thought about packing up again and moving in with him. At least now I had time to get used to the idea.

"You know, I need to learn how to protect myself," I mumbled to him.

"Yeah, I know. That's why I dragged Hank along," he revealed with a smile, knowing it would make me happy.

"Really?" I asked, a little surprised, but the corners of my lips were already tugging upward in a smile.

"Yes, really. You need to learn how to protect yourself. With the rogue after you, I can't take the chance of leaving you defenseless. I'm going to make sure you won't need to use it, but it will make me sleep better at night knowing that you can."

"Thank you," I said as I leaned forward and pressed a kiss to his lips. The feel of his lips against mine kick-started the butterflies in my stomach. Touching him, in a way, was comforting and volatile at the same time.

He pulled his lips from mine and held my face.

"The training is just to help you defend yourself; it doesn't mean I'll allow you to fight," he spelled out.

I could feel my temper rise.

'Allow me'? Who the hell does he think he is?

"Allow me?" I repeated, because I couldn't believe he'd actually said that to me. I pulled free of him.

"Listen—"

"No, you listen to me," I warned angrily. "You don't get to tell me what I can and can't do, do you understand?"

He rolled his eyes at me. I slipped off the bed as he rose up out of the chair he'd been sitting in. I hated the fact that I had to tilt my head up to his to glare at him.

"There is no need to be dramatic." He sighed as he ran a hand through his hair. My anger began to grow because now he was treating me like I was a child.

"I'm not being dramatic," I assured him, balling my hands into fists so I wouldn't be tempted to slap him again.

"Just because you're my mate doesn't mean you get to tell me what to do."

"Take it however you want to. You're not fighting," he stated firmly, standing in front of me with his arms crossed over his chest. It was like he was a parent calmly dealing with a child who was throwing a tantrum.

The urge to slap him was so strong that I nearly gave in but I remembered how he'd battled to control himself the last time I'd given in to the urge.

"Get out!" I shouted at him. My temper was in full force now. I wanted him out of my sight before I really lost my temper and slapped him.

"Scar, don't overreact," he said, shaking his head at me.

"I said get out!" I repeated and pointed to my bedroom door.

"Fine, I'll be back when you calm down." He sighed and turned to leave. I watched him walk out of my room and close the door.

I took a deep breath as I tried to calm down. I was still so angry I wanted to throw something.

Was it so wrong that I wanted to be treated as an equal? I didn't want him to look at me and see a weak mate that he had to protect. I wanted him to look at me and see a mate who was ready to fight alongside him to protect him and our pack.

CHAPTER FIFTEEN

SCARLETT

When I managed to calm down, I went downstairs. I was hungry and I needed food. As I made my way downstairs, I couldn't help looking for Cade as I walked to the kitchen.

I hadn't seen nor heard from him since our argument a couple of hours before. He was probably giving me time to cool off, which had probably been a good idea. Conflicting emotions raced through me at the thought of Cade; I'd never wanted to kiss and slap someone at the same time before.

Gary was sitting at the kitchen table and, at the sight of me, his eyes brightened and he smiled. He stood up and walked over to me.

"I'm so glad you're feeling better," he said as he pulled me into a hug and I hugged him back. I had to remember that as hard as it was for me to adjust to this new world, Gary had to adjust as well and it had to be pretty scary for him.

"I'm fine," I assured him as he released me and scanned my face.

"Are you sure?" he asked, still looking concerned.

"Yes. No more thoughts invading my mind," I assured him as I went over to the food spread across the kitchen counter.

"Where are Cade and the rest of his guys?" I asked, pretending to be interested in the food I was looking at, but I was dying to know where Cade was.

"He went out with them a little while ago. He said something about checking to make sure the surrounding area is safe," he explained as he went to sit back down at the kitchen table.

It was a reminder that my life was still in danger. Also, the thought of Cade actively searching for the rogue that had tried to kill me made me worry about his safety. As much as he wanted to keep me safe, I wanted to do the same for him.

"He said he wouldn't be long," Gary offered.

I tried to act relaxed as I sat down to have something to eat, but I couldn't help the growing worry that settled in my stomach. Eventually, halfway through my meal, I pushed my plate away. I was too wound up to eat.

"I'm going to have an early night," I informed Gary as I got up to leave. Getting an early night was probably a good thing because I had school tomorrow.

"Sure," he said as he watched me leave.

Upstairs in my room, I tried to keep myself busy with the task of getting ready for bed. I still had no idea where Cade was going to sleep. He had told me that he would be sleeping in my room, but I wasn't sure if he would be sleeping on the sofa or in my bed. I couldn't help the flutter of apprehension in my stomach at the thought of sharing the same bed as him.

My attraction to him was undeniable and when my eyes settled on my bed, I couldn't help but think about Cade without his shirt on and how I wanted to run my hands across his well-defined chest.

I bit my bottom lip as I let my fantasy continue. I wondered if his skin felt as soft as it looked, as soft as his lips were. Just remembering what his lips did to me was enough for my teenage hormones to go into overdrive.

I shook my head, trying to dislodge the thoughts of Cade.

I glanced at my beside clock and it was nine in the evening already. I had no idea how long Cade had been gone for and I wondered when he would be coming back.

I'd showered and changed into my pajamas. My room was slightly darkened, with only my side lamp lighting the room.

"Did you miss me?" Cade asked with a smug grin as he strolled into my room an hour later like he owned it. I narrowed my gaze to glare at him, signaling I hadn't forgotten about our earlier disagreement or the fact that he'd been out for hours and I'd been worrying about him.

"No." I issued the lie with a straight face, but his grin just widened.

"You do realize that when you became a member of my pack, I can hear your thoughts," he revealed smugly.

Ah, crap! I'd forgotten about that. Besides, even if I was aware of it, I had no idea how to stop my thoughts from filtering to him.

His smile widened as he stood with his arms crossed, watching me realize that he'd heard my thoughts all day. I couldn't stop the red tinge to my cheeks when I remembered some of my thoughts about my attraction to him.

I could glare at him all I wanted, but he knew exactly what I was thinking. It was so annoying.

If the werewolves in his pack could block their thoughts from me, then I should be able to block my thoughts from him.

"You're right," he confirmed.

"Will you teach me how?" I reluctantly asked. I wanted my thoughts to be private, so at least then I could decide what thoughts he would hear and which ones he wouldn't.

"I thought you were mad at me," he reminded as he watched me squirm. I was tempted to switch off my bedroom light and ignore him, but the need to keep my thoughts private made me soften my glare slightly.

"I still am, but I'm asking you nicely to teach me how to block my thoughts from other members of the pack," I said, and I may have fluttered my eyes a little. All was fair in love and war, wasn't it?

"You know I'll do anything you ask," he said as he walked over to the bed. I was already tucked into my side of my double bed and he sat down beside me.

"Anything?" I asked, thinking back to our argument over his unwillingness to allow me to fight.

"Anything but that," he said as his eyes held mine. He wasn't backing down, but I was stubborn enough to keep at it until he compromised.

"Fine," I stated with a sigh and crossed my arms.

"I'll teach you how to block your thoughts," he offered in consolation. I studied him for a moment before I relented and smiled at him.

"Okay," I said.

It was disconcerting that he was able to know what I was thinking without me saying the thoughts out loud. Maybe it wouldn't feel so weird if I could at least hear his thoughts, but just remembering the pain I'd gone through when I'd overloaded on the thoughts from the pack was enough for me to hesitate.

"Think of something," he instructed.

Trying to keep my thoughts clear of Cade, I thought about my car that had been totaled.

"We'll get it replaced," he assured me as he caressed my cheek. I knew it was replaceable but it would take time and I wasn't the most patient person.

"The next time you think about it, imagine a wall around the thought," he instructed as he dropped his hand from my face so I could concentrate. His touch was always so distracting.

Naked chest.

He gave me a smug, knowing smile. Annoyed with myself, I pushed the thought from my mind and thought about my car again. But like he instructed, I imagined a tall wall that protected my thought from prying eyes.

He watched me for a few moments and I got distracted and my wall around my thought disappeared.

"You need to hold the wall because otherwise I know exactly what you're thinking," he said.

"Okay, let's try again," I said, determined not to let him distract me. It was going to be a lot harder to hide my thoughts around him because he had a way of making me think of nothing else but him.

I repeated the exercise and watched as his forehead creased and then he smiled.

"And?" I asked, waiting to find out if I'd managed to succeed.

"I don't know what you're thinking," he revealed. Not entirely convinced, I thought about the two of us on my bed, making out, and I watched him for the smug smile that never appeared.

He had no idea what I was thinking.

"That is awesome," I said, excited at the fact that now he wouldn't be able to tell what I was thinking.

"I think I preferred to know what you were thinking," he said as he trailed his knuckles down my cheek.

I closed my eyes as I enjoyed the feel of his skin against

mine. He took me by surprise when his lips covered mine and pulled me against him. Enjoying the thrilling touch, I complied and let him kiss me.

I got up and straddled him, running my hands through his silky midnight-black hair as his lips moved against mine with more intensity. He grabbed my ass as his tongue slipped into my mouth and tangled with mine.

I groaned as I pressed my body against his.

He growled against my lips and next I felt the softness of my bed underneath my back as he pressed against me from above.

I slid my hands underneath his shirt to feel his soft skin under my fingertips. He felt so good. He pushed harder against me as our kiss intensified and I wrapped my legs around his waist.

I didn't think, I just acted instinctively. He pulled his lips from mine and rested his forehead against me as he breathed hard.

"We need to stop, otherwise I won't be able to," he warned hoarsely.

I was breathing hard and struggling to rein in my out-of-control hormones.

"Okay," I managed to say as I unwrapped my legs from his waist and he rolled off of me.

As much as I wanted to make out with him and feel him against me, I wasn't ready to take it as far as he wanted and it wasn't fair to expect him to be able to hold his control.

"I'm sorry," I mumbled.

He turned and faced me.

"Don't be sorry, I know you're not ready. I can wait," he assured me.

I gave him a nod. It was this caring and sensitive Cade that was my weakness. It was easy to keep the hard and domineering Cade in his place, but it was harder to fight the caring and sensitive Cade who looked at me with those soft, adoring eyes.

I swallowed the emotion down as he gave me a reassuring smile.

"I need to shower," he told me as he got off the bed. He walked over to the sofa and picked up a duffel bag and, with one more lingering look at me, he disappeared into my bathroom.

I let out a sigh.

I might not have been ready to take that step with him right then, but I knew it wouldn't be long before I would want to go all the way with him.

Still preoccupied with thoughts of Cade and mating, it was a good thing I'd learned to block my thoughts. I tucked myself into my bed and waited for Cade to come out of the bathroom.

There was no chance of me falling asleep. My nerves bounced around my stomach and kept me wide awake. I'd never shared a bed with anyone, and I wasn't sure how much sleep I was going to get if he slept right next to me.

It wasn't long before the bathroom door opened and he appeared with wet hair and only wearing black sweat pants that hung low around his hips. He didn't have a shirt on. How was I supposed to control my raging hormones if he pranced around half-naked?

He switched off the bathroom light and dropped his duffel bag beside the sofa as he walked over to the bed.

I quietly watched as he lifted my bedcovers and slipped into my bed beside me.

Yeah, I won't be getting any sleep tonight.

"Come here," he whispered to me as he held his arms open.

Unsure of myself, I scooted over and he wrapped his arms around me. I laid my head against his chest.

"Go to sleep, Scar," he instructed gently. I loved it when he called me that.

Despite my nervousness at sleeping in the same bed as him, I drifted off into a peaceful sleep.

The next morning I woke up and discovered I was lying across him with my legs tangled with his and my arm wrapped around his waist. I blushed slightly as I tried to shift away from him without waking him.

He looked much younger as he slept, and I took a moment to watch him in that peaceful state.

"You getting all stalkerish on me?" he mumbled with his eyes closed. Trust him to open his mouth and ruin the moment.

"You're my mate, I can stalk all I like," I stated to him as I got out of the bed.

"True," he said with a grin as he watched me disappear into my walk-in closet and select some clothes before I went into my bathroom and closed the door.

I got changed into a pair of black skinny jeans and a red top. I brushed my hair and teeth before I put some lip-gloss on. Cade was still lying in my bed, watching me, when I exited the bathroom.

"Those jeans are too tight," he said as he sat up. I rolled my eyes at him.

"They are fine. They are skinny jeans, they're supposed to look like this," I argued, but he didn't look happy.

"I don't want you to wear them," he insisted as he got out of the bed and walked over to me. "I don't want other guys looking at you like they are going to look at you if you go to school in those jeans."

"You don't have to be jealous," I insisted as I pressed a kiss to his lips. I wasn't interested in getting any attention from anyone else; he was the only one that I wanted.

"I still don't want you to wear the jeans," he continued

to argue, but I shook my head.

"I'm going to wear what I want to wear. I don't tell you what you can and can't wear, so you don't get to do that to me," I warned him gently. We'd had such a peaceful night together and the last thing I wanted to do was start another fight, but I didn't want to be one of those girls who was told what I could or couldn't wear.

He let out a sigh as he held me.

"Fine, you can wear them, but you'll be responsible for all fights I'll be getting into today because of the guys checking you out," he teased as he dropped another kiss to my lips.

It was hard to pull away from him, but if we carried on we wouldn't be going anywhere. I went downstairs to the kitchen while Cade stayed upstairs to change for school.

I heard a rowdy noise coming from the kitchen as I descended the stairs. Hank, Jake and a few other werewolves I'd seen before at school were seated at the kitchen table with Gary.

"Morning," I greeted them and they greeted me back.

I got myself a cup of coffee and joined them at the kitchen table. It wasn't hard to work out that Jake was Cade's beta. Cade entered the kitchen not long after that. When I looked at him, I couldn't stop feeling the satisfied possessiveness that he was mine.

Hank stayed behind with Gary while the rest of us left to go to school. I rode with Cade, and the rest of them climbed into the Jeep that Jake drove behind us.

Once we got to school, everyone watched as I got out of the car with Cade. He held my hand as we walked side by side into the school. At my locker, he pressed his lips to mine, leaving me breathless and weak-kneed as he walked off with a smug smile. There was no denying he'd stamped his ownership all over me.

He didn't get into any fights because the werewolves knew I belonged to him and the human boys were too scared of him to even look in my direction.

"I want all the details," said a voice behind me. I turned to see Keri giving me a knowing smile.

I smiled back.

"Yeah," I said back. My brain was already sorting through my existing thoughts, trying to come up with plausible lies that I could tell her because there was no way I could tell her the truth—that we were werewolves and mates.

"Spill," she instructed as I opened up my locker and got some of my books out.

"He likes me and I like him," I explained vaguely as I closed my locker and spun the combination

"Those are definitely not enough details. He is the player of the school and then a couple of days after you arrive he is suddenly holding your hand and looking all loved-up," she said, watching me for a response.

"You do realize I've never seen him hold hands with a girl ever," she added.

"It just kind of happened. He isn't the shy type and he told me that he liked me and I'm attracted to him—any girl would be—so we are dating," I lied with a shrug. We were way more than dating; we were forever.

CHAPTER SIXTEEN

SCARLETT

Keri tried to pump me for as many details as she could but I tried to keep things vague. I wasn't used to keeping the whole 'I'm a werewolf' secret so I thought it was best to keep my lies simple so I'd remember them.

"I bet you his kisses are hot," she said as we'd walked to my first class of the morning.

I remained quiet but the smile on my face confirmed what she suspected and she shook her head at me.

Keeping my thoughts to myself was exhausting. I knew with time it would probably get easier but, because it was a new thing, half the time I forgot and I would get a knowing smile from a couple of the students who passed me in the hallway.

It didn't help that the thoughts that I kept forgetting to keep to myself were the ones of Cade. It was disconcerting that other people had access to those thoughts of him.

I didn't see much of him in the morning because he wasn't in any of my classes.

I was glad he didn't feel the need to crowd me. I didn't want to become one of those couples that were joined at the hip and couldn't do anything without the other.

For me, being with someone was about balance. It was nice to spend time with them and to do things with them, but I also wanted to be able to do things without him.

When the lunchtime bell went off, I made my way to the cafeteria.

When I walked into the cafeteria, he wasn't sitting at the table with his pack. Blake was sitting at his usual table with his pack when he spotted me. He gave me a smile and I smiled back at him.

Although I belonged to Cade's pack, I didn't feel comfortable sitting with them without him and besides, I spotted Keri sitting at our usual table and I refused to leave her sitting on her own so I walked over to her.

I got a few looks from my pack as I sat down across from Keri, but I ignored them.

"You're not going to sit with lover-boy?" said Keri as she glanced to Cade's usual table.

"No. I'm going to sit with my friend," I stated as I opened my soda and took a tentative sip.

A few minutes later I looked up to see Cade strolling into the cafeteria. He stopped for a moment when our eyes met and he noticed I wasn't sitting at his table.

Honestly, I wasn't sure if he was going to get angry or not, but I was determined to sit with Keri whether he liked it or not. It would just make things easier if he wasn't upset.

I couldn't pull my eyes away from him as he walked toward me. I studied his expression, but it was blank.

When he got closer, he gave Jake a nod as he passed his usual table and came to stop by mine. Nervousness stirred in the pit of my stomach as I looked up at him.

He took me totally by surprise when he smiled as he sat

down next to me. He pressed a gentle kiss to my lips and then he put his arm around me.

It took me a few minutes to recover from the slight shock. I introduced Cade and Keri.

"Nice to meet you," he said to Keri and flashed her a smile. I appreciated the fact that he was making an effort to be friendly to my only friend in the school.

"You, too," Keri said.

"Can I join, too?"

I looked up to see Blake standing beside the empty seat next to Keri.

"Sure," I said, taken by surprise.

He sat down next to her.

It should have been awkward, but somehow it wasn't. The conversation flowed easily and a comfortable atmosphere settled over us.

I caught a few looks from Blake's usual table. They looked as confused as I was, but I wasn't going to question why Blake had suddenly felt the need to join our table.

By the end of lunch, I walked out of the cafeteria with Cade holding my hand. Butterflies fluttered in my stomach as he stopped and turned to face me. He kissed me and I felt my knees weaken.

"I'll see you later," he said softly as he turned to leave me standing in front of my next class.

I was still trying to stand on my slightly weakened knees when I saw him turn and smile at me before he disappeared into the crowd of students.

Thoughts of him kept occupying my mind as I tried to concentrate on the rest of my classes. By the end of school, I was looking forward to seeing him again. I walked to my locker and put some books away.

Cade was leaning against his car, talking to Jake and Blake when I walked out of the school. When Cade noticed me, he stepped away from his friends and walked to meet me.

"Hey," he said, dropping a quick kiss on my lips. It wasn't a passionate kiss, but it still sent a tingle right through me.

"Hi," I replied as I handed him my school bag to his outstretched hand. He walked me back to his car.

Suddenly a smell hit me and I stopped. It was so strong and overwhelming—liked burned wood. It was another werewolf.

Cade tensed beside me and then I felt him put his arms around me protectively. Blake and Jake looked alert as they all began to scan the forest beside the school.

Something was wrong.

"Get her back to my house," Cade instructed Jake as he released me and threw his car keys at him.

"Cade?" I questioned. I felt fear grip me as I held onto his arm.

"You need to go with Jake, now," he instructed firmly.

"But—" I tried to argue back.

"Don't argue. Go with Jake, I need you to be safe," he demanded as he opened the passenger door and put me inside his car.

I didn't want to leave him. Jake got into the driver's seat and started up the car.

"Keep her safe," Cade instructed to Jake as he closed the passenger door.

Jake pulled out of the parking lot and I turned to see members from both packs begin to pour out of the school as they followed Cade and Blake into the forest.

By the time we made it to Cade's house, I was a nervous wreck. Jake had driven as fast as he could and I'd been too worked up to say anything. As soon as we stopped in front of the house, Jake switched off the car and jogged around to open the door for me.

He steered me firmly into the house.

Safe inside Cade's house, I began to pace back and forth in front of the window in the formal lounge.

I'd asked Jake what was happening, but all he'd said was that rogues had crossed over into our territory. Cade and the other werewolves were tracking them.

Jake was quiet and tense as he watched me from the doorway of the lounge.

I was so worried about Cade and Blake. A few times I'd tried to close my eyes and hear thoughts from Cade or any of the other members of my pack so that I would know what was going on, but I heard nothing.

"You won't hear anything," Jake informed me.

"Why?" I asked.

"Because when they are tracking, they keep their thoughts from us. It allows them to concentrate," he explained.

Even though Cade was experienced, I couldn't help the worry that kept me pacing back and forth. I didn't know what I would do if anything happened to him.

Images of two massive wolves tearing into each other made me sit down on the sofa as my legs trembled with fear. I closed my eyes and dropped my head into my hands.

"He'll be okay, he knows what he's doing," Jake said, trying to soothe me, but I wouldn't believe he was safe until I saw it with my own eyes.

Fear grew inside of me. I couldn't contemplate the thought that something could happen to him while I was sitting safe and sound in his house, oblivious.

Half an hour later, I heard the sound of a car engine and rushed to the window to peer outside.

Any hope that I had that it was Cade vanished when I saw Hank and a few other guys, along with Gary, get out of the car.

I rushed to the front door with Jake fc
me.

"Have you heard anything?" I asked anxiou .
entered first.

"No," he answered as he shook his head.

"How are you doing?" Gary said as he entered the house behind Hank. I gave him a look that revealed the panic that was rising up inside of me. He walked over to me and pulled me into a hug.

Still being tightly hugged by Gary, I noticed Jake stiffen for a moment and then he dashed through the formal lounge. I pulled myself out of the hug as I saw Jake disappear out the patio doors toward the compound.

My heart began to hammer inside my chest as fear began to overflow inside of me. I watched Hank hurry to try and catch up with Jake. Something was up.

I followed them to the compound, where there was flurry of activity. The air was filled with a nervous energy.

Just as the gates at the bottom of the property came into view, I saw a couple of injured guys lying on the ground. Curtis leaned over one of the injured people. It was only seconds, but time seemed to slow down as I looked down to the faces of the people who had been injured, my feet leading me to them.

Blake. He grimaced in pain as Curtis put his hand on a wound bleeding on his stomach. Horror filled me when I saw a deep gash through a tear in his shirt. There was so much blood.

Oh. Dear. God.

My head began to spin as I came to a stop a couple of feet away from him. I couldn't pass out; I needed to know where Cade was. I took a deep and struggled breath to stop the dizziness. My mind fought with my body to stay upright and in control.

In the back of my mind, I couldn't stop the thoughts that something bad had happened to Cade. He and Blake were inseparable and Blake looked seriously injured. Had Cade been injured as well?

I don't know how, but when I opened my eyes again, the sight of blood didn't make me feel sick.

Cade.

I needed to know that he was okay, because if he wasn't... it wasn't something I could think about without feeling like someone ripped my heart from my chest.

I wanted to help Blake. I knew I'd just get in the way, though, so I stood nearby, just a couple of feet away as I watched them load him onto a stretcher and carry him to the medical center.

Where was Cade?

Frantically, I scanned the area for Jake. He would know, but I couldn't find him in the crowd of people that had built up around the gate. I spotted Hank standing guard at the gates with a few others watching into the forest. Were they waiting for Cade?

Panic gripped me, but I pushed forward in Hank's direction. Even though I was petrified of the answer, I needed to know where Cade was.

As I reached Hank, he glanced at me.

"He's on his way back," Hank informed me with a soft expression when he saw the state I was in. I clutched his arm. Relief flooded through me and I felt my knees weaken. The array of emotions that had gripped me from the time this had all started had exhausted me. It felt like I'd been stuck on a roller coaster for the last hour.

"He's okay," Hank reassured me as he studied me for a moment. "They got ambushed."

I stood beside Hank, waiting for Cade and holding my breath. Even though I knew he was okay, I wasn't going to relax until I could see him for myself.

I heard the sounds coming from the forest before I spotted the massive black wolf that I knew was Cade being followed by a dozen other werewolves, none of them as big as Cade.

The crowd parted as the wolves ran onto the property. As I turned to see Cade and the rest of the werewolves shift back into human form, I heard the large gates behind me close with the sound of metal against metal. I recognized one of the werewolves as Jake. He'd left the compound to join Cade.

I rushed over to Cade, who had spotted me and was already walking toward me. He held his arms open as I rushed to hold him.

"I'm okay, Scar," he assured me as he hugged me, lifting me off my feet.

"I was so scared something would happen to you," I spoke against his shirt, loving the feel of him warm and alive under my hands.

"I'm fine," he reassured me as he settled me back down on my feet and pulled away. With his finger to my chin, he lifted my gaze to his. My eyes glistened with unshed tears. "I need you to keep it together for me."

I nodded my head and took a deep breath. He pressed a feathered kiss to my forehead.

"Go back to the house and wait for me. I need to check on Blake and the other wounded werewolves," he explained gently as he released me. Then I remembered the massive wound across Blake's stomach and all the blood.

"Will he be okay?" I asked. If Blake had been human, I was pretty sure he would have died already.

"Yeah, he'll be okay," he assured me. "Remember we heal quickly."

"Okay," I said as I pulled myself together. He gave me one last lingering look before he turned and hurried to the medical center.

I wanted to go with Cade. I didn't want to be in the way, though, so I turned and headed back to the house with Hank following behind me. It was then that I remembered that the rogues that had ambushed Cade and Blake were the same rogues that were after me and I felt a shiver of fear run up my spine.

Seeing the remains of the attack had made the threat all that more real in my eyes and I had to admit I was scared.

Inside the guest room I'd used before, I sat down on the bed. I felt exhausted. The panic and fear had faded, but I was still struggling to work through what had happened from the time I'd been bundled into the car with Jake.

It had also been one of the first times I'd seen Cade in his alpha role, in charge and giving orders. He'd earned a newfound respect from me. I'd never actually thought before about the responsibility that he held on his broad shoulders. Being responsible for the safety of an entire pack wasn't an easy job and he seemed to pull it off effortlessly. He'd been born to lead.

I wasn't sure I was capable of the same. Even though the attack had scared me, I was more determined to fight alongside Cade. I didn't want to be left behind, wondering what was going to happen, I would never forgive myself if something had happened to him today while I'd been safely guarded in his house.

An hour later, Cade walked into the room.

My eyes lit up at the sight of him. I'd been sitting on the bed, quietly contemplating my thoughts.

He hesitated for a moment a couple of feet away from the bed. I stood up and walked over to him. As I reached him, his hand reached for me and he pulled me close.

"It's been a long day," he sighed as he held me in his strong arms.

"What happened?" I asked, leaning my head against his chest as I held him tight.

"We walked straight into a trap," he began to explain as he rested his chin on my head. "Normally, rogues don't work together, but for some reason these guys did. We didn't see it coming."

"How many rogues were there?" I asked.

"There were about twenty of them."

"I was so worried about you," I let out. I usually wasn't one to talk so openly, but I needed him to know that he meant a lot to me and that what happened today had scared me.

"It's one of the reasons we train so hard, to make sure we are prepared for anything. You can also feel my heightened emotions like fear through the link so if I'm ever in any real danger you will feel it," he said. I lifted my eyes to his.

I'd forgotten about that.

"I don't think I can let you go alone if it happens again," I revealed. I wanted to be honest with him even though he probably didn't want to hear it.

"And I don't think I can let that happen," he sighed as his lips pressed to mine.

We both wanted to protect each other, but we both had different ideas of how to accomplish that.

CHAPTER SEVENTEEN

SCARLETT

A couple of hours later, I went with Cade to check on Blake.

He looked much better, sitting on one of the beds in the medical room. He had sweats on but no shirt and a large bandage covering his stomach. The pale and pained face was gone and he looked a healthy color again. He smiled when he saw us approach.

"How are you feeling?" Cade asked him as he stopped beside the bed.

"Much better," he answered. "Another day and I'll be as good as new."

It was hard to believe he had healed so dramatically in just a few hours.

"Next time you want your ass kicked, I'll do it," I offered in a teasing tone as I rocked on the balls of my feet with my hands shoved into the front pockets of my jeans.

He chuckled. Easygoing Blake was so different from Cade. It was sometimes hard to see him as an alpha of his own pack.

"As if," he scoffed as he gave me a playful look.

The reality was he'd probably kick my butt. I needed to start training with Hank. The sooner I started, the sooner I'd be able to protect myself. I wasn't going to be seen as a weak girl who couldn't protect herself.

I wanted to be Cade's equal. I wondered what type of training they did and how hectic it was; it was probably a lot more intense than anything I'd covered with Gary.

A sound behind me made me turn to see a young woman in a nurse's outfit. The outfit looked a little tight, I observed, and I couldn't help but wonder if she was dressed like that to help with the scenery in the sterile environment.

"Probably," Cade confirmed with a grin when I pulled my gaze back to Blake.

Ah, crap!

I was still getting the hang of keeping my thoughts to myself. There were times when I wasn't concentrating and some of my thoughts would be open for others to hear.

I playfully glared at Cade like it was his fault for invading my thoughts.

"Hey, it's not my fault you can't keep your thoughts to yourself," he defended as he raised his hands to ward off my glare.

"Still endless entertainment," commented Blake as he watched the two of us at it. I turned my glare to him as I put my hand on my hip.

He looked from me to Cade before he shook his head and grinned. Half an hour later, we left Blake so he could rest.

Cade and I were both unusually quiet as we walked back to the main house hand-in-hand. I think we were both too busy, still processing the events from the day to try and make small-talk.

By the time we made it back to the house, dinner was ready. When we entered the dining room, Gary, Jake, Hank and a few others were already seated at the table.

As soon as the food was on our plates and we were seated, I watched as Cade began to discuss the events of the day with our pack members. Gary listened intently as I did.

"It just doesn't make any sense," Jake muttered as he shook his head.

We were discussing the attack and trying to figure out how the rogues had worked together to attack us, since according to Cade this wasn't normal behavior for rogues.

He'd said that rogues were normally loners, although they did sometimes meet up with other rogues. The most rogues he'd ever seen together had been a handful and nothing like the twenty-strong rogues that had attacked them earlier.

"Only twenty attacked us today, but what if there are more?" asked Hank with a grim look.

"We have no way of knowing if they have more than that," said Cade as he put his knife and fork down and pushed his food away.

I tried to eat but the nervous knot in my stomach was making it difficult, so I did the same with my plate.

"We need to face the possibility that there might be more," stated Jake as he ran a hand through his hair. He voiced what everyone was thinking but didn't want to say out loud.

"What happens if there are more of them?" I asked Cade. I'd seen their training setup and I was impressed, but then again, I didn't know a lot about werewolf fighting.

"We normally only get attacked by a couple of rogues at a time. Everyone is trained so they are able to defend themselves, but we have dedicated fighters who are trained to fight rogues. Rogues don't normally work together because they don't like authority. What we experienced today is worrying because we have no idea how someone was able to group together and organize the rogues that attacked us today."

"Do we have any idea who it could be?" I asked. It was still puzzling why all of these rogues were hell-bent on trying to attack me. I couldn't think of a single reason why anyone would want to hurt me.

"No," Cade said as he reached for my hand. This new piece of information about the attack had made him nervous and he seemed to relax as his fingers covered mine. It was a comforting peacefulness that came over us when our skin connected.

The rest of dinner was spent trying to strategize a defense to a hypothetical attack by rogues with larger numbers.

"What about letting the girls fight?" I suggested. Conversation stopped mid-sentence and all eyes swung to me. All but Cade looked at me like I was talking a different language. Cade shook his head at me.

"No way," he stated vehemently. His eyes warned me off the subject.

"You can't expect us to just sit here and do nothing while you guys go to fight a battle you might lose because you're outnumbered."

I was arguing on behalf of all the girls in the pack, whether they wanted me to or not. Exasperation and anger entered my voice as I argued with them.

"There are other options," was Cade's stern reply.

"And what is that?" I asked as I glared at him. Trust him to come up with an alternative to letting girls from the pack fight.

"We could join packs with Blake," he suggested as he scanned our pack members for their reaction.

Jake seemed to mull the idea over for a moment before

he announced, "That could work."

I was so angry that I'd just been dismissed so easily, I wanted to scream, but instead I said, "Are you guys for real?"

Silence descended as the pack members looked to Cade.

"Like I've told you before, it will never happen," he stated. His eyes darkened with anger as he tightened his hold on my hand.

Trying to discuss it with Cade and our pack members was a waste of time and effort. I'd have to come up with another way to get them to consider it. There had to be a way.

"And like I told you before, I can't let you go out to fight without me," I reminded him as I held his angry gaze.

He was the first to pull his gaze away from me and then he began to discuss the effects of joining a pack. It was like he ignored everything I'd just said and carried on with their conversation.

Angry and annoyed, I pulled my hand from his and pushed my chair back. Cade's eyes swung to mine. I gave him the angriest look I could muster before I turned and stalked out of the dining room before I did something I regretted, like slapping someone and the closest person to me had been Cade.

I'd slapped him once already that week.

On my way upstairs, I hesitated for a moment. I knew Cade would probably want me in his room tonight, but I was so angry I couldn't be in the same room with him until I calmed down. Instead, I headed to the guest bedroom I'd previously used.

Once I entered the room, I slammed the door closed. There was a key in the door and I locked it. It would give Cade the clear message that he wasn't welcome in my room.

With that thought, I leaned against the door and let out a frustrated sigh.

One thing that had been nagging me at the back of my

mind was the fact that if I mated with Cade, then I would be able to shift and I'd be able to heal more quickly. It would make me stronger and I'd be in a better position to fight.

On one hand, I wanted to be ready before I took that step with him—I didn't just want to do it just to be able to fight. It wasn't like I wasn't attracted to him, I was. He made my heart race and he made my knees weak with just a few kisses. I could just imagine what effect he would have on me with more.

I cared for him and I knew he cared for me. So I had to ask the question: What was keeping me from mating with Cade? Was it the fact that I didn't want to be pushed into it by outside influences? That I wanted to make the decision on my own?

I let out a sigh when I thought about the whole fighting thing. As determined as I was, Cade seemed to be just as determined to stand his ground on the subject. It was like I was pushing against a brick wall.

If I put my mind to it, the only way he was going to be able to stop me was to keep me physically locked up and, knowing Cade, he wouldn't hesitate to lock me up if it would keep me from fighting.

I wasn't sure how long I was asleep for before the banging on the bedroom door vibrated through the room. I lifted my head and scanned the dark room, trying to figure out what was going on as I rubbed my eyes.

Then the banging was accompanied by yelling.

"Goddammit, Scar, open the fucking door!" Cade yelled from the other side of the locked door.

I sat up and glared at the door. I crossed my arms and remained in the bed, refusing to budge.

"If you don't open the fucking door, I'm going to break it down," he warned in a deadly tone.

For a few seconds, there was silence, and I got out of the

bed and stood up. He wouldn't really break the door down, would he?

I'd just completed the thought when—with a loud crash and bang—the door gave way and cracked into two, falling with a thud to the floor.

Fuck! He'd broken the door down.

Shocked that he'd actually broken the door down, my eyes met his and our gazes clashed. His eyes narrowed and he glared at me as his chest rose and fell with the anger coursing through him. I took a step backward. To say he was angry would have been the understatement of the year. He was livid.

As much as I wanted to take another step backward, I held my ground stubbornly. I wasn't going to show him that he intimidated me. It was a good thing I'd remembered to block my thoughts from him, otherwise it would have been a waste of time.

He took a menacing step into the room, his eyes fixed on me as I watched him take another step toward me. Instinct told me to run, but I held firm. His hands clenched into fists at his sides.

"Why did you lock me out?" he asked angrily. I could see that he was trying to control his temper.

"Because you're being a sexist ass," I told him truthfully, but my response just seemed to ignite his anger again as he glared at me. He took the few remaining steps between us.

He grabbed my arms and even though he was still so angry with me, the hold around my arms was firm but not painful.

"What are you playing at?" he asked as he searched my face for answers.

"Nothing," I replied as I tried to pull my arms from his grasp, but he wouldn't let go. "I just don't want to be around someone who believes I'm weak because I'm a girl."

His anger wavered for a moment as his eyes softened.

"It's not that I believe you're weak, Scar," he began to explain to me. "I'm just scared something will happen to you and I wouldn't be able to concentrate on fighting if I had to worry about you in the fight as well. I just found you and I can't afford to lose you."

"And it never crossed your mind that maybe that's how I feel about you? Maybe the reason I want to be able to fight alongside you is so I can try and protect you, too?"

He was surprised and he stilled for a moment before he pulled me into a hug and kissed my forehead. I relaxed against him despite my anger.

It was just one of those arguments that neither one of us was going to back down from. Arguing about it was only going to lead us around in circles, getting us nowhere.

I glanced down at the broken door lying on the floor. It was still hard to believe he'd actually broken the door.

"Did you have to break the door down?" I asked, feeling my anger begin to rise at the fact that he'd forced his way into the room.

"Well, I had to do something. You wouldn't let me in," he explained stiffly as he noticed the angry tone in my voice.

"You didn't have to go all barbaric."

"Enough fighting. I'm exhausted, I've had a rough day," he said as he released me, his eyes softening for a moment. It was then that I noticed the visible signs of tiredness in his face.

"Next time don't break down the door; instead, try apologizing for being an ass," I suggested.

He let out a sigh and shook his head.

Before I knew what was happening, he had picked me up and carried me out of the room.

"Where are you taking me?" I asked, hating the fact that he was manhandling me.

"To my room," he informed me as he walked to his bedroom. There was no point in struggling because he was stronger than I was. Once he entered his room, he walked over to his bed and dropped me on it. I landed with a bounce and I made a move to climb back off.

"If you move one foot off the bed, I'll tie you to it," he threatened as he glared at me.

He'd broken down a door already and I had no doubt that if I tried to move off the bed he would tie me down, so I stayed where I was.

He gave me one last look before he disappeared into the bathroom. I slumped back against the pillows. It would be pointless to try and leave his room because I knew he would just find me and haul me back.

At times he could be so annoying.

He returned dressed in sweats and I glared at him even though the half-naked sight of him made my stomach flip. He ignored my glare and got in the bed on the opposite side.

He pulled me down and into his arms.

"Enough, Scar," he whispered softly when I struggled against him.

As annoyed as I was, I couldn't help feeling a little bad that I was fighting with him after everything that had happened earlier. As strong as he was, I could tell he'd taken strain.

So for the moment I decided to ease up and instead snuggled into his arms. He pressed a kiss to my forehead and held me close.

Despite the fact that I was angry with him, I couldn't help being super aware of how his body molded to mine and I felt an awareness in my body that I'd never felt before.

Ah, crap!

I realized it was going to be harder to keep myself from succumbing to his kisses because my body had a mind of its own. It didn't matter that I was still angry, because no matter what my mind said, my hormones reveled in the feel of him against me.

I was tired. Instead of sleeping, though, I lay beside him, listening to his steady breath while I fought with my body's reaction to his. Every brush of skin against skin made me hold my breath.

It was only going to be a matter of time before I gave in to my female urges and had my way with him. I closed my eyes as an image of the two of us getting hot and heavy flashed into my mind. There was no doubt that he knew how to please a girl.

It must have been hours later that I finally drifted off to sleep. But I knew in the morning I'd have to face the problems I'd been wrestling with.

And tomorrow we could argue about the fighting thing again.

CHAPTER EIGHTEEN

SCARLETT

The next morning when I awoke, I didn't feel Cade's warmth. I opened an eye and scanned the room. The sun shone through a gap in the curtains as I sat up and rubbed my eyes.

I was alone.

We'd only known each other for a short space of time, but I already didn't like waking up without him in the bed.

With renewed determination, I slid off the bed. I wanted to go and have a shower, but I didn't have any clothes to change into.

It was then that I noticed a set of folded female clothes on the side table with a new toothbrush. The clothes were a black shirt and a pair of gray sweats and, although they were a size too big, I wasn't going to complain because at least they were clean.

After a quick shower, I brushed my teeth and got dressed.

I walked down the hallway and when I heard some activity inside Gary's room, I knocked briefly on the door.

"Come in," Gary instructed.

I opened the door and found him sitting at the desk, typing away on a laptop. Where had he gotten it? Since the scare at school, we hadn't managed to get any clothes or other stuff from the house.

"Hi," he greeted briefly before he turned his concentration back to what he was doing.

I leaned over his shoulder, trying to figure out what he was doing.

"What are you doing?" I asked.

"I'm trying to find all the information that I can about your parents," he explained absentmindedly as he scanned the web page that came up. I wasn't quite sure why on earth he would be doing that. He'd known my parents better than anybody else.

"Why?" I asked, unsure of what that information would yield.

He stopped and spun around to face me as I took a step backward.

"Cade had hoped that once you joined his pack that the rogues would leave you alone, but they haven't. This confirms that they were after you for more than just the fact that you were a rogue. Blake and Cade are even more convinced the reason behind the rogue attacks is tied to your parents," he began to explain. "So I'm trying to find out all the information that I can."

He rubbed his temple. It was a sure sign that he was stressed. I couldn't blame him. The fact that the rogues were working together to get me had me concerned, too. It wasn't like I didn't believe that Cade would fight to the death to keep me safe; the problem was that I didn't want it to come to that.

As strongly as he cared for me, I cared for him.

"I met your parents when your mom was in the early stages of pregnancy with you," he reminded me. "I was your dad's best friend, but even I have no idea where they'd come from. They didn't like to talk about their life before I met them and I respected that."

He let out a deep sigh as his eyes met mine.

"But I can't just stand by and do nothing while rogues plot to get you," he said. "I love you like you were my own daughter."

My heart squeezed at his words and I leaned down to hug him.

"And I love you like a second father," I assured him in a whisper.

He might not be blood-related, but to me he was family. I kissed his cheek as I released him.

"We all believe that these attacks have something to do with the life your parents left behind," he added.

"It sounds like you're on the right track," I said.

There had to be a reason behind the attacks and the only logical reasoning was that it had something to do with my parents. It was also very possible that my parents were murdered by werewolves and those same werewolves were after me for a reason I didn't know.

"Have you seen Cade this morning?" I asked as he swung around to face the laptop.

"He was going to meet up with Blake this morning," he said.

"Is Blake already up and about?" I asked, a little surprised he had healed that fast.

"Yes." Gary looked at me over his shoulder. "It's quite astounding how fast werewolves can heal".

Holy crap, that was fast.

"Okay, see you later," I said as I left the room to search

for Cade.

It took me a while to find him. I thought he'd be in the compound somewhere but, after asking a few people, I discovered he was with Blake in his study at the house.

The door was closed so I knocked.

"Come in," Cade instructed and I opened the door.

Blake, Hank, Jake and Ross looked up at me as I entered the room. Ross was Blake's beta. They were standing around a medium-sized square table that looked like a table meant for meetings. There was a map open on it.

At the sight of me walking into the study, Cade walked forward to meet me.

"Morning," he said as he pressed a kiss to my lips.

"Hi," I greeted him. I pulled away from him and greeted the rest of the guys who were watching us with smiles.

"Are you ready to start your training?" Cade asked me.

"Yes," I replied. I was surprised he was thinking about the same thing I had. I'd been blocking my thoughts so there was no way he could have known what I was thinking.

"The sooner you get trained up, the better," he said as he looked to Hank. "Don't be too rough with her."

I gave Cade an annoyed look. I wasn't that weak and I hated the implication that I was. When Cade caught my look he sighed and cupped my face.

"I just don't like the thought of you getting hurt, even if it's for training," he said as he kissed me again.

"I'll be okay," I assured him as I pulled away.

I knew that Cade allowed everyone, including women, to train, but was it too much to hope that he'd changed his mind and he was going to allow me to fight?

He could read my thoughts because he shook his head at me.

"I still won't allow you to fight," he told me. "This training is to ensure you are able to protect yourself."

Would we ever be able to agree on this subject?

I followed Hank out of the study and to the compound gym. On the way there he asked questions about the type of training I'd been doing with Gary.

"This training will be different and, in conjunction, you will need to do some weight-training to build muscle," he informed me.

"Okay," I said, following him into the gym.

"Even though you're stronger than most humans, you are no match against a male werewolf," he told me as he walked me to the weight machines.

"By building up your muscle, we can increase your strength slightly," he began to explain.

"It still won't be enough for you to take on a male werewolf, but that's why our training will concentrate on speeding up your reactions. The faster you can get away, the better." He gave me a serious look.

I could see he also wasn't keen on the idea of me fighting the rogues alongside them. I wasn't going to try and argue with him because Cade's mind was the one that needed changing, not Hank's.

Four hours later, or what honestly felt like forever, I landed with a thud on the gym mat. Winded and in agony, I rolled onto my side, trying to keep from screaming out in pain.

"Have you had enough yet?" Hank asked as he bounced on his feet, waiting for me to get back up. I looked like I'd been at it for hours but Hank had barely broken a sweat.

He was brutal and ruthless with his training. I'd trained on the weights until I couldn't feel my arms or legs anymore. Then he'd proceeded to kick my ass on the gym mat for the last couple of hours.

I squeezed my eyes closed for a moment to try and wrestle with the aching limbs. I wanted to get back up and fight again but my body had other ideas. Every muscle screamed out in pain.

Breathing hard with the sweat dripping from my face, my clothes drenched in sweat, I lay on the ground unable to get back up.

"I think we are finished for the day," Hank said as he bent down beside me. It was hard not to show how defeated I felt at that moment. There was no point in arguing with him. I was done for the day.

"What the fuck!" I heard Cade shout as I turned to watch him hurry to me. He was very angry. When he reached me he dropped to his knees beside me and looked over me with concern.

"I told you to go easy on her," he said angrily as his eyes lifted to clash with Hank's and he growled at him. Hank leaned back from fear of his alpha.

"I know, but she wanted to keep going," Hank replied, lifting his hands to show Cade that he wasn't to blame for the state I was in.

"You've been at this for four hours?" Cade directed the question at me in disbelief. He closed his eyes for a moment and took a deep breath. I watched as he tried to control the anger trembling through him.

"It's okay," I said as I gently reached for his hand and squeezed it.

His eyes opened as he looked down at me.

"No, it isn't."

His jaw tightened as he stood up and bent down to pick me up. My muscles ached in protest at the sudden movement.

Honestly, I was too tired and sore to argue so I lay my head against his chest. With me firmly in his arms, he strode out of the gym and toward the house.

It wasn't long before he entered his bedroom and laid me

gently on the bed. The softness was so inviting that I was determined never to move again.

Yep, I'll just stay here, all sore and sweaty.

Cade disappeared into the bathroom and I heard him turn the water on. Five minutes later the sound of water stopped and he walked into the bedroom.

"I've run you a bath so you can soak," he instructed as he stood beside the bed. I looked up at him like he was crazy if he thought I was going to move anywhere.

"Come on, you will feel better," he encouraged.

"Fine," I relented, knowing he wasn't going to back down and he did have a point. A nice warm soak in a bath would ease some of the aching in my muscles.

He helped me into the bathroom.

"Shout if you need anything," he told me before he turned and left me alone in his bathroom.

Slowly, I stripped down and eased my body into the bath with a sigh. It felt so good as the warmth from the water began to make me better.

That night, Cade was over-protective and kept checking on me when I went to lie down after my bath. He brought me my food to the room so I didn't have to try and get to the kitchen.

Gary popped in a little later that evening to check on me.

"I heard you took a beating today," he said with a teasing smile as he sat down on the bed.

"Yeah, werewolf training is a lot harder," I told him. It was true. The training that Gary and I had been doing was a walk in the park compared to what Hank had put me through.

"But you're still going to do more training tomorrow," he said. He knew me so well.

"Of course," I added with a weak smile.

"I know you're determined, but I think I've finally met

someone with more determination than you," he revealed.

"Who?" I asked, arching an eyebrow.

"Cade," he answered. "I don't think he is going to allow you continue with the training."

"What makes you say that?" I asked.

"That's what I heard him say to Hank before he hit him."

My jaw dropped open in surprise.

"Cade hit him?"

Gary nodded his head at me.

"Why?" I asked, not able to understand how Cade thought Hank was at fault.

"He said he should have known better."

"I'll talk to him," I said. I'd overdone it today but that hadn't been Hank's fault, it had been mine.

"You find out anything yet?" I asked while fiddling with the edge of the blanket where a thread had come loose.

"No, not yet, but I'm still looking," he assured me. I don't know if it was the look or the tone of his voice, but something made me lean forward to hug him.

He was scared for me and I loved him for it.

The next morning I changed in to my gym clothes. My body was still sore and stiff, but I felt much better than the day before. I was glad Gary had gone to get some of our clothes and stuff yesterday. There was no way I was going to school dressed in sweats and a shirt that belonged to someone else.

"Where exactly do you think you're going?" I heard Cade ask from behind me.

I turned to see him standing with legs slightly apart and his arms crossed over his chest.

"I'm going to train," I said like it was nothing important as I sat down on the bed and shoved my feet into sneakers.

"No, you're not," he told me in a firm and unyielding

voice as he stood blocking the only exit out of the room.

"Look, I admit I overdid it yesterday and I promise I won't make the same mistake again," I tried to reason with him. He was concerned about me and, while I appreciated it, I didn't want him to feel that I should stop training.

I needed to train like they did in order to be able to fight alongside them and that was never going to happen if I didn't persevere with the training and show that I was capable of doing what they were.

His jaw twitched as he studied me for a moment.

"Fine, but I'm going to be there," he relented with a frustrated sigh.

I smiled for a moment. He was learning to back down on certain things and I appreciated it.

I stood up and walked over to him. My hands touched his chest as I raised myself up onto my tiptoes to press a kiss to his mouth. He tilted his head down to mine as his arms encircled me and held me as we kissed.

It was a good thing I was a werewolf and could heal quicker than humans, otherwise I wouldn't be able to train again today.

A look of surprise appeared on Hank's slightly bruised face as I stepped into the gym with Cade following behind me.

"You're back for more?" he asked, not quite believing I was going to punish myself further.

"Yes, I am," I said as I stood with my hands on my hips. Although any movement still hurt slightly I wasn't going to show it. I didn't want them to look at me as if I was weak. If I had any chance to fight, I had to show them that I was determined and capable.

Hank looked to Cade and I saw Cade nod his head.

"All right, let's get started," instructed Hank as he walked over onto the sparring mat.

Cade leaned against the wall, watching Hank and I spar. Every time my body hit the mat, Cade closed his eyes and rubbed his temple. He was struggling with having to watch me get hurt in any way.

Luckily, the sparring had helped my body warm up and my muscles no longer hurt as much.

It was pure determination that got me through the next hour. Like Hank had said previously, I would never match his strength, and he was right. Even with increased weight training, it still wouldn't increase my strength to that of a male werewolf. If I had any hope in being able to hold my own, I needed to learn to increase the speed of my reactions to defend myself.

Sweat dripped down my forehead as I waited for Hank to make his next move. I hit the mat a few more times, but I was starting to get quicker. I felt my confidence starting to grow.

Cade watched anxiously from the sidelines.

As Hank moved forward to try and grab me, I moved out of his way. His fingers didn't reach me and I pushed him using his momentum to lose his footing and land on the mat with a thud.

I'd done it and I couldn't wipe the grin off my face when I saw the look of disbelief on Hank's face as he rolled onto his back to look up at me.

I turned to look at Cade. He smiled at me and looked at me with a look of pride that made my heart feel like it was going burst with feeling.

I could do this. I knew I could.

Hank got back onto his feet, but this time when he looked at me there was a little respect in his gaze.

CHAPTER NINETEEN

SCARLETT

The next week went by with everyone on edge and expecting another attack from the rogues, but it never happened. It was like the rogues had backed off totally, which had confused Cade and Blake. It wasn't normal rogue behavior apparently, but then again we already knew that these rogues weren't behaving like normal rogues.

If they'd been acting like normal rogues it would have been easier to try and figure out what their next move was going to be. The fact that they weren't predictable made them more dangerous. We had no idea what they would do next.

Cade became more protective, which was a little hard to handle. I was so used to being able to do what I wanted, when I wanted it and never having to take another person into consideration. It was taking some getting used to and a few times I'd lost my temper with him.

I'd started getting better at handling thoughts, although I was only linked to Cade. There were times when I was training with Hank that he would allow me to hear his thoughts and I did the same with him.

It was getting easier, but I was in no way ready to handle all the thoughts of the entire pack just yet. Just remembering what happened the last time I'd heard everyone in my head was enough for me to take it slowly.

The couple of times Keri had tried to arrange to go out, I'd had to make up some excuse not to go. Also the fact that I was training for at least two hours after school every day with Cade watching was a good excuse as well.

Slowly but surely my body's strength increased. I was also learning to react more quickly due to all the sparring. So far, under the proud gaze of Cade, I had been able to land Hank on his back three times.

Unlike human bodies, mine adjusted to the exercise pretty quickly and the pain from the training lessened each day.

Blake had totally recovered from his injury and was back to his normal self. He annoyed me every chance he got, but I had to admit I was happy he was okay.

Cade and Blake joined Keri and I for lunch every day at our table. Cade would sit beside me and Blake would sit beside Keri. From an outsiders' point of view it looked like Blake had a thing for Keri and I was pretty convinced with the fluttering of Keri's eyelids that the feeling was mutual. I was starting to suspect that they liked each other.

I didn't know enough about the whole mating thing to know whether if what I suspected was happening between Blake and Keri was even allowed.

I kept meaning to ask Cade about it, but it kept slipping my mind.

It was dark and I was lying in Cade's arms in his bed. It was late and I was tired. It had been a long day of school and training. I could tell from Cade's breathing that he wasn't sleeping so I decided to finally ask what I'd been curious about for so long.

"Where are your parents?" I asked softly. I felt him shift slightly underneath me as he pulled me closer.

"They are dead," he answered.

His answer took me by surprise. I'm not sure why it hadn't crossed my mind. The heaviness in his voice revealed that it still affected him deeply so I hugged him closer.

"They were killed about a year ago by rogues," he revealed softly.

I remained silent.

"There had been a couple of rogues in and out of territory a couple of months before, but by the time we discovered that two rogues had entered our territory it had been too late."

He let out a deep sigh and rubbed his forehead.

"I'm sorry," I said. There was nothing that you could really say that would help with that type of loss, I understood that, but I needed some way to tell him that hearing the loss in his voice had affected me, too. I didn't like the idea of anything hurting him.

He feathered a kiss to the top my head.

So many things began to fall into place. That bit of information gave me a better understanding of him and his fear for my safety against the rogues that were after me.

This had to be bringing up the memories of what had happened to his parents and I couldn't help feeling a little bad that I'd been pushing so hard against him when all he was trying to do was to make sure that what happened to his parents didn't also happen to me.

I felt like a complete bitch. I promised myself that I'd be more understanding in the future.

My thoughts drifted to Blake and Keri.

"Blake seems to like Keri," I started as I ran my hand across his bare chest.

"Yeah, I think you're right," he replied, confirming my suspicion.

"Is that type of thing allowed?" I asked.

"What type of thing?" he asked.

"You know, a werewolf together with a human," I clarified.

"There are no rules that say it isn't allowed but it doesn't normally happen unless the wolf has lost their mate," he explained.

"Blake hasn't found his mate yet, has he?" I asked, already being pretty sure he hadn't.

"No," he answered.

"How often does it happen that a werewolf doesn't find their mate?" I asked, wanting to know more.

"Not very often. Fate has a way of making sure their paths cross."

Well, that made it very complicated for Blake and Keri. There was no disputing it; Keri was human, and Blake hadn't found his mate yet.

It meant that despite how they felt about each other, there was no point in doing anything about it because when Blake found his mate, he would end up hurting Keri.

I kind of felt for them.

"There is no point in getting emotionally involved with someone until you find your mate because you'd have to walk away from them."

I understood why. There was no way anyone else— human or not—could compete with what I felt for Cade.

In that moment, I felt a wave of emotion for him and I hugged him tighter.

"I'm glad I found you," I revealed softly.

I felt him move and he shifted beside me so he was lying on his side, facing me, when he leaned forward and kissed me. I reveled in the feel of excitement that tingled through me at the contact of his lips against mine.

"I'm glad I found you, too," he whispered. In the darkness, I couldn't see him properly. I felt the heat of his gaze on me, though, which made my stomach flip.

It was astounding how with one simple touch he could make me feel so much.

Through the last week, it had become harder and harder to stop at just kissing. I hadn't been quite ready to go further, although my hormones that were running wild in my body disputed that.

I cared for him more than I ever had for a boy and I was sure that I was already starting to fall in love with him. But I wasn't ready to say those words to him just yet and he hadn't said them to me, either.

We'd come a long way from our first meeting.

He was so much more than the arrogant and self-assured player that I thought he was when I'd first met him. In the short time we'd been together, I'd learned that he was compassionate and caring while still being strong and in control. He was also extremely possessive and over-protective as well.

No matter what I was going through or feeling, just a small touch from him settled me into a peacefulness that only he could give me.

"What's going through your mind, Scar?" he asked softly.

In the darkness, I put my hand on his cheek and caressed it as I leaned forward and touched my lips to his.

He let me lead him into the kiss as my tongue tentatively slid into his mouth and touched his. His arms slid around me and pulled me closer as I deepened the kiss tentatively. Normally he always instigated it and I simply followed his lead.

I loved being in charge for a change.

I pulled away and looked at him in the darkness for a moment before I leaned toward him again and kissed him harder.

And in that moment, I'd made my decision. Even though the thought made me nervous and I had no idea how I was going to explain my little white lie, I was ready.

His tongue tangled with mine and he groaned against my lips. Our kiss intensified and I was getting lost in the new reactions to him when he pulled away.

"We need to stop," he whispered breathlessly, rolling onto his back away from me.

For a moment, I felt nervous; I had no idea what I was doing, but I sat up and faced him.

"I don't want to stop," I whispered.

He didn't move.

"I don't want you to feel pressured to do something you're not ready to do," he told me.

I hadn't expected him to say that. I'd actually expected him to take me in his arms and kiss me. Did he not want me? A little surprised and hurt, I sat quietly, unsure of what to say or do, so I said what I was thinking.

"Don't you want me?" I said, trying not to sound as hurt as I felt.

He sat up quickly and faced me.

"Of course I want you, Scar," he said. "From the moment I saw you, before I even found out you were my mate, I wanted you."

Butterflies began to flutter in my stomach at his words. He wanted me.

"I just don't want you to feel pressured to do this," he explained as he reached for my hand in the darkness and I felt his fingers thread with mine.

"I don't," I assured him as I leaned closer and touched my lips to his.

He remained still as his lips moved against mine tentatively. It was like he was holding back.

"I want you," I whispered as I pulled my lips from his.

"Are you sure?" he asked hoarsely. I could feel his control was hanging on by a thread.

"Yes."

He reached for me and pulled me over him. His strong arms positioned me above him and I straddled him as his lips crushed against mine. He kissed me urgently like he was letting his need and want for me take control.

I let him take the lead as I felt my body come alive against his. I wanted this, but I couldn't help the nervousness that was building up inside of me. Our bodies fit perfectly together and I felt his need for me. I was scared I'd be bad at this and I was scared it would hurt.

I snaked my arms around his neck and threaded my hands through his hair as he kissed me like I was a life source keeping him alive. Moments later he stopped kissing me and I was breathing hard in anticipation of what was to come.

"I can't tell you how many times I thought and dreamed about this moment," he whispered to me as he lifted me up off his lap and lay me down on the bed.

Instead of lying down with me, he shifted off the bed. I lifted up with my elbows.

"What are you doing?" I asked hoarsely as light flooded into the room.

"I've been waiting for this moment and I'm not going to miss a thing," he stated as he walked back over to the bed. "I want to see all of you."

Feeling a bundle of nerves knot in my stomach, I licked my lips and his eyes narrowed at the gesture as he knelt on the bed with one knee. I lay down flat and he moved onto the bed. His body covered mine carefully and he kept the majority of his body weight off me by holding himself up on his elbows on either side of me.

He kissed me tenderly before I felt him settle his body between my legs. He ran a hand from my thigh to my knee softly as he guided it around his waist.

"God, you feel so good," he whispered against my lips as he ground his body against mine.

As good as it felt and as much as I wanted to give in to the new feelings of wanting him in a physical way, I was scared. I debated whether to come clean or just hold my tongue and pretend. It only took me a moment to decide it was best to come clean.

Feeling him against me, I felt a wave of panic at the thought of what was going to happen and I stiffened.

Cade stopped.

"What's wrong?" he asked as he lifted his lips from mine and searched my face.

"I lied," I blurted before I could chicken out, letting my hands fall from him.

His forehead creased in confusion as he pulled away from me and sat up beside me. The worrying thing was that he'd put space between us and I felt the loss of his warmth.

"What did you lie about?" he asked, sounding confused and strained at the same time.

I took a deep breath and let it out. The reality was that I was scared he was going to be angry with me.

"I lied about being with other guys," I confessed nervously while watching him for his response.

For a moment he just stared at me and then he surprised me by smiling. I expected him to be angry so the fact that he wasn't threw me off guard.

"You've never been with another guy?" he asked with that stupid grin on his face. He wasn't angry.

"Never," I answered, shaking my head, confirming that I was a virgin.

"Why did you lie about it?" he asked with curiosity as he cocked his head to the side and watched me twist my hands in my lap.

"It was hard thinking about you with all the other girls you've been with…and I wanted you to know what that felt like," I replied truthfully. I dropped my gaze, unable to face him. "Even though I knew you'd find out the truth when we mated."

"Scar," he said as he reached for and lifted my chin. "I wished you hadn't lied to me."

Had I read him wrong? Was he still angry with me?

"I haven't been able to stop thinking about you being with other guys and to be honest…it was hard," he admitted in a serious tone. His smile had faded.

"I understand why you did it. But I want you to understand that from the time I first met you, all the girls before you ceased to exist. You are all I want and need," he declared softly, taking both my hands in his.

Everything inside of me turned to mush at his beautiful words.

"Do you understand that?"

I nodded my head, unable to form a response.

"Come here so I can show you how much I want you," he instructed gently, but I could see a hunger in his eyes. Still mesmerized by his words, I moved closer to him and he pulled me onto his lap as my legs wrapped around him.

"I don't want you to be scared," he whispered as he feathered a gentle kiss to my lips.

"I'll take it slow, okay?" he said against my throat as he feathered another kiss. Any coherent thoughts I had were fleeing out of my mind at the feel of his lips trailing down my throat and I arched my neck to give him better access.

"You need to understand that I'm also going to have to mark you with a bite to complete the mating," he said, pulling his lips from my neck and cradling my face in his hands.

"Where?" I asked.

His fingers trailed from my neck to the place where my neck curved into my shoulder. At that point he said, "Here."

"Okay."

And with that one word I gave him my consent to take my virginity and mark me as his.

That night he brought me to life with his body and just before we reached our peaks together, he brought his mouth to the point that he'd shown where he would mark me and I felt him press a kiss to the spot.

Then he opened his mouth and I felt the gentle graze of his teeth against the sensitive skin before he sank his teeth into me. I bit down on my lip from the pain.

I was still breathing hard when he rested his forehead against mine. His bite still throbbed, but it didn't hurt as bad as I thought it would.

"I'm sorry, Scar," he whispered to me. My heart fluttered at the remorse he felt for hurting me.

"It's okay," I whispered back and kissed him.

No matter how strongly I'd felt for him before, there was no disputing the feelings that now were bursting from my heart for my mate. I loved him and I would do whatever I had to in order to keep him safe.

I saw my intense feelings mirrored in his eyes. He felt the same.

CHAPTER TWENTY

SCARLETT

I stretched across the bed when I woke up. I was alone, but I couldn't help smiling when I remembered what had happened last night. I still ached in some places, but I couldn't wait to do it again. After the initial mating, we'd done it again and—unbelievably—it had been even better.

I'd also found out that unless I was in heat it was impossible for me to fall pregnant.

A blush tinged my cheeks at the naughty memories. All I could say was wow. I'd heard people talk about it before, but I had no idea it could be that good—and Cade, he was so good at it.

I pushed the reason he was probably so good at it from my mind. Like he'd said, the girls before me ceased to exist. I was addicted and, like an addict, I needed more. My plans to keep him in the bedroom for the day were spoiled.

I wondered where Cade was, but I wasn't going to get up yet. It was still too early so I lay on my stomach, hugging a pillow, about to doze off again when I heard the door open.

I opened my eyes to see Cade dressed in a pair of sweats, carrying breakfast on a tray.

"Hi," he greeted as he carried the tray over to the bed. I sat up, pulling up the covers to cover up my nakedness. It wasn't like he hadn't seen all of it before, and he'd studied me well, but I didn't feel comfortable sitting naked in front of him.

"Hi," I greeted as he set the tray over my lap. "What's this for?"

"I wanted to make sure you got something to eat," he said, and then added with a grin, "Especially after last night."

My grin matched his and I felt a little shy all of a sudden. It was going to take a little time to get used to knowing him in that way without feeling shy about it.

His smiled broadened at my shyness.

"Eat," he instructed. "I'm going for a shower."

While he was busy in the shower, I was trying to decide if I was going to join him in there. The rumble of my stomach pulled me out of those thoughts, though, and back to the food in front of me.

I was starving.

He was so thoughtful. He'd brought me breakfast in bed. No one had ever done that for me. There was no denying that the more time I spent with him, the more I was growing to love him.

I'd eaten most of the food by the time he walked out of the bathroom with wet hair and a towel wrapped around his waist.

It took all my self-control not to push him down onto the bed again. Both times that night he'd been in control and I wanted to have my turn at being in charge.

"Don't give me those eyes," he said, shaking his head as he headed into his wardrobe.

"What eyes?" I asked innocently while fluttering my

eyelashes.

"The 'come to bed' eyes," he said as he reappeared wearing a pair of jeans and pulling a shirt over his head.

"And why can't I look at you like that?" I asked, watching him.

He sighed and turned to face me.

"I'd like nothing better than to keep you in bed all day, but you need to take it easy," he explained. I was a little achy, but other than that I felt fine.

"Why?" I asked.

"Did you forget?" he asked.

"Forget what?" I asked, having no clue what he was talking about.

"You will shift for the first time today," he revealed.

First shift. Oh, crap!

I'd forgotten about that. Then I remembered it was supposed to be very painful. That really put a damper on my nice and warm fuzzy feeling I'd been experiencing since last night.

I'd been so deep in my thoughts that I hadn't noticed Cade was sitting in front of me on the bed.

"Don't be scared, Scar. I'll be there every step of the way," he assured me as he tilted my chin up so I was looking at him.

I gave him a brief nod.

"I just need to go and do a couple of things, but I'll be back soon," he informed me.

He saw the fear in my eyes.

"Don't worry, it shouldn't happen for another few hours and I'll be with you."

I swallowed my fear at his reassurance and gave him a tentative nod.

"Mind-link me if you need me sooner, okay?" he told me.

"Okay."

He gave me a feathered kiss to my forehead before he headed out of the room, leaving me alone.

I would be lying if I said I wasn't scared. Some of the women had compared it to childbirth. No matter how brave I thought I was, I had to admit that scared me. The bonus was that I would be able to shift into my wolf form and run free. It was something I'd been looking forward to since I'd discovered I was a werewolf.

I spent the next hour holed up in Cade's study, trying to get some stuff done on my laptop. I'd managed to move across some of my stuff so I could still do what I needed to. It was only a temporary arrangement, but we had yet to talk about a permanent one.

Usually I'd be in the gym training, but I was taking it easy. I didn't want to tire my body out before my first shift. If I thought for a second that Cade had suggested I take it easy because he was feeling overprotective, I would be in the gym.

I couldn't help wondering when I was going to be able to feel Cade's emotions as well. Blake had said that when two werewolves mate, the link between them strengthens and they can feel emotions as well as hear each other's thoughts. It was hard at times keeping a handle on my own emotions, so the thought of feeling two sets of emotions was going to be difficult.

But I wasn't one to back down from anything. With time and perseverance, I would master what I needed to embrace my new life.

My fingers touched my temple, trying to ease a slight headache that set in as I studied the document on my laptop. It was starting to get warmer so I opened a window and hoped that would ease the heat in the room.

But after about ten minutes, the heat in the room was stifling and I decided to go to the kitchen to get something cold to drink. My throat was feeling so dry it was becoming increasingly uncomfortable.

I closed my laptop and left it on the desk. By the time I made it into the kitchen, I felt the sweat beading on my forehead. It was then that I realized that it was my internal heat that had increased as I brushed the sweat from my forehead.

Then it occurred to me that I might be starting my first shift. I glanced at the clock hanging on the wall. Cade had said it would be a few hours, but it had only been an hour since I'd last seen him.

It was happening earlier than he expected.

Cade?

I waited for a response, but there was nothing. Closing my eyes again, I tried to concentrate harder.

Cade? I pushed the thought to him.

Suddenly, it was getting harder to breathe. It was like the heat inside of me was suffocating the air out of my lungs.

I clutched the kitchen counter as I tried to draw in small, desperate breaths. Trying to breathe was becoming more difficult as the fire inside of me felt like it was moving from the inside of me to the outside.

I gasped in pain as my grip on the counter loosened and I fell to my knees. I tried to draw a breath in as my body burned in pain. In my haze of pain and panic, I tried to call out to Cade again as I clutched my hands to my chest.

Cade!

I literally screamed in my mind.

Nothing. I slumped forward and lay on the kitchen floor, gasping, trying to ride out the pain that had my body gripped. It felt like my body was being ripped apart from the inside, like every cell was being ripped apart and slammed back together.

My scream that had built up inside of me came out as a

whimper. There was no one to hear me.

Scar?

It was Cade. Another rush of pain gripped me and I fisted my hands to try to stop a scream from escaping.

Help! I pushed the thought to Cade.

I'm coming!

I just had to hold on until he got here.

Another wave pain of sliced right through me and this time I let out the scream. I'd never experienced such intense pain before and I prayed that I never did again.

As much as I wanted to hold on until Cade got there, the pain and heat became too much. The darkness that would take away the pain beckoned to me and I closed my eyes and gave in.

I was drifting out of the darkness that had given me refuge from the pain. The more conscious I became, the worse the pain became. My body still felt like it was on fire, burning from the inside. Sweat was pouring off me. I opened my eyes and found myself upstairs in Cade's room. My body arched as pain sliced through me again and I screamed.

"I'm here, Scar." I heard Cade trying to soothe me as he held my hand. The wave of pain only eased for a second before my eyesight changed. Normal vibrant colors changed to various shades of amber.

"My eyes," I gasped in panic as I found Cade's concerned gaze above me.

"It's okay, it is part of the change," he assured me softly, holding my hand in both of his.

"I'm sorry I wasn't there when it started," he whispered to me. He felt guilty that I'd started it on my own with no one to help.

It was too much effort to talk and I felt so weak. I squeezed his hand so that he would know that I didn't blame him for it. I knew him well enough to know that he would have a good reason why he didn't answer me sooner.

I lost track of time and every moment of the burning pain felt like forever. Cade soothed me with words and a wet cloth dipped in cold water that he pressed to my forehead, easing the heat.

I groaned and gasped as I thrashed. My body was transforming, pushing the limits of my human shell. My bones ached; it felt like they'd been broken and put back together.

A good while later the heat began to ease, and along with it the pain. But I was exhausted and I could barely keep my eyes open.

"Sleep, Scar," soothed Cade with a feathered kiss to my forehead.

I heard the sound of a door opening.

"How's she doing?" I heard Blake ask.

"It's over, she's sleeping."

Cade let out a sigh.

"That was intense," Blake murmured.

"I know," Cade murmured. "Watching her in that much pain and being unable to do anything about it was torture."

"I know. Is there anything I can do to help?" Blake offered.

"Will you just let everyone know that it's over and she's sleeping?" Cade responded and let out a heavy sigh. "I don't want to leave her."

I heard the door close and then a few moments later I felt the bed dip. He didn't reach for me. Maybe it was because he wasn't sure how tender my body was, but I needed him.

Slowly, I turned and shifted slightly so my head rested on his chest.

"Sleep, baby," he soothed again as he held me close to his chest. The sound of his heart beating under my ear soothed me into an exhausted but peaceful sleep.

When I woke up, I yawned and stretched. I felt great.

"How are you feeling?" I heard Cade ask. I looked to see him sitting beside the bed, watching me.

"I feel fine," I replied. In fact I felt better than fine. I felt stronger. I sat up.

"Why are you not in bed with me?" I asked.

He ran a hand through his hair. He looked exhausted.

"I couldn't sleep and I kept tossing and turning so I got up. I didn't want to wake you," he explained.

"Why didn't you go and sleep in one of the guest bedrooms?" I asked.

"I wasn't going to leave you."

My heart squeezed at his words.

I shifted over and held the comforter open and patted the empty spot next to me. He smiled at me as he got up and got into the bed next to me. Still sitting up, he pulled me against his chest and hugged me. I reveled in the feel of him holding me so close. I closed my eyes for a moment and breathed him in.

For a few moments we sat in silence, both lost in our own thoughts.

"I need to get up and shower," I said as I pulled away and looked up to him.

"I'll start the shower for you," he offered as he pulled away from me and got out of the bed. He disappeared into the bathroom and a few moments later I could hear the water running.

It was then that I remembered what they'd said about the pain of the first shift.

Cade walked out of the bathroom.

"If that's what childbirth is like, you're getting fixed," I told him, crossing my arms over my chest as I glared at him. There was no way I was ever going through that type of pain willingly.

He actually laughed at me and I felt my temper rise. He pressed his lips together to smother any further laughter. It must have been my glare that made him mask any further amusement because he knew his life depended on it.

"No, childbirth is not that bad. Normally the first shift is painful, but it's not usually as bad as what you experienced."

"Why was mine that bad?" I asked, feeling it was a little unfair that mine was worse than what most werewolves experienced.

"Only werewolves with alpha-blood experience a first shift like you did," he explained.

Firstly, it physically made my heart hurt to think he'd experienced that pain and then a moment later I realized what he was saying.

"I've got alpha blood?" I asked, needing confirmation of my thought.

Cade held my gaze and nodded. I'd never even suspected that.

"What does that mean?" I asked.

"It means that your father or mother belonged to an alpha bloodline," he answered. My forehead creased as I began to process that thought.

"Come on, your shower is ready. We can talk about this when you're done," he said, pulling me out of the bed by my hands.

In the shower under the constant stream, I thought about the ordeal I'd just gone through. It had been the most intense thing I'd ever experienced and I was so relieved it was over.

I don't know if it was because I was thinking about my first shift or not, but I suddenly wanted to go into the forest and shift into my wolf for the first time. Or maybe it was something stronger that made me get out of the shower and dry myself off. I got changed quickly and then I strode out of the bathroom toward the door.

"Where are you going?" Cade asked from behind me. I'd been so focused on what I needed to do that I'd completely forgotten about him.

I stopped and turned.

"I need to...go outside," I tried to explain the need that was growing inside of me.

"Okay, Scar," he said and took my hand in his.

It took us a few minutes to get to the gates in front of the compound.

"Open the gates," he ordered to someone.

I wrestled with the growing need to shift into my wolf. Nothing else around me mattered.

The gates opened and I walked into the forest with Cade and a few others behind me. In the forest, with trees around me, I dropped to my knees. The need in me was so strong, but I had no idea how I was supposed to shift.

"Just let it happen," Cade whispered from beside me.

I closed my eyes and gave in to the need. It took a few moments, but then I felt my body change. It was painful, but I could handle it as my human form shifted into my wolf. The pain was nowhere near what I'd just experienced earlier.

This time when I opened my eyes, I was a wolf.

"You're beautiful," said Cade in awe as he stood in front of me.

I cocked my head at him and he smiled at me. My heart warmed at his words.

I looked down to my front legs and paws. I had soft midnight-black fur covering me.

In a moment, Cade changed into his wolf and he stood beside me, magnificently powerful. The color of his fur matched mine. He walked closer and nuzzled me with his wet snout. I loved the feeling of his fur against mine.

The two of us stood side-by-side, facing the forest.

I felt alive and I closed my eyes for a second to adjust to the intensity of my senses before I ran for the first time in my wolf form through the forest.

CHAPTER
TWENTY-ONE

SCARLETT

The feeling of running as a wolf through the forest was indescribable. Instinctively, I ran with Cade running protectively beside me. I pushed as hard as I could, feeling my powerful legs carry me through the forest so fast that the trees I was running alongside began to blur.

I felt a peacefulness settle over me as I enjoyed the feel of the air brushing past my face. The feel of the wind gliding through my fur was soothing. I ran as fast as I could, but Cade stuck beside me. I glanced to him and he looked at me briefly.

You are so beautiful, I heard him murmur to me. I felt like a giddy girl at his words. Every girl wanted to be told that they were beautiful, but the difference with Cade was that he didn't have to say the words because he made me feel beautiful.

The smell of something I couldn't place hit me and my running faltered for a moment as I tried to figure out what it was.

Stop, Scar! Cade shouted through the mind-link desperately. I dug my paws into the dirt and came to a stop.

I turned to look at Cade, but he was already standing protectively in front of me. He looked like he was braced to attack. I looked past him but couldn't see anything, despite the distinctive smell filling my nostrils.

Cade's eyes fixed on the row of trees in front of us.

What's going on? I asked him.

While I waited for Cade to answer, I saw the others move in front of me beside Cade. It almost looked like they were preparing for an attack.

Cade? I questioned again, feeling the initial feeling of fear.

It'll be okay, Scar, just stay where you are, he soothed as he kept his eyes on the threat ahead of us. A threat we still couldn't see.

Despite his words, I felt a sliver of fear creep up my spine. He might be saying one thing, but I could see from their actions that something wasn't right. What had been an innocent and carefree run in the forest had just turned into something unexpectedly deadly.

I kept my eyes fixed on the trees in front of us, but I couldn't see anything. The silence was deafening.

I sniffed the air. The initial smell that had hit me became stronger. It was then that I realized it was another wolf. Another whiff of the air told me the smell was too strong for only one wolf, there had to be more than one.

Oh. My. God.

There was more than one. That meant a group of wolves were about to attack us and we had no idea how many of them there were. I got a sinking feeling in my stomach that it might be the rogues. But the only thing that disputed that thought was the fact that this smell was different from the one I'd smelled before.

It couldn't be the rogues.

My eyes shot to the other wolves standing beside Cade. There were only about ten of us and we had no idea how many wolves were closing in on us. Just because it wasn't the rogues didn't make us any safer.

I didn't have sufficient training as a wolf and it worried me that I wouldn't be able to fight well alongside Cade. I looked to my mate and felt my heart squeeze in fear for a moment before I pulled myself together.

I wasn't one to back down from something that scared me and I wasn't about to start now.

There was no doubt in my mind that if Cade could, he'd send me back to the compound, but he couldn't take the risk that another wolf might get to me before I made it back there safely. He had no choice but to keep me with him while he faced off with the wolves about to attack us.

Anger began to seep into me and take over my fear. I couldn't be left alone long enough to enjoy my first run as a wolf? They had to ruin it and I could feel my anger begin to grow.

It wasn't fair.

I mimicked the attack position Cade and the rest were in. My head was lowered and my right leg was lifted off the ground and slightly bent. My back was straight and the hairs stood up straight in anticipation. My ears picked up on movement in front of us and as the sound got closer, I watched Cade and the others tense.

My eyes were glued to the first wolf that stepped out in front of us. Immediately you could see it was an alpha wolf because it the same size as Cade and it had an air of authority around him like Cade and Blake had. This wolf was also midnight black in color, with vibrant amber eyes. For most people it would be hard to tell the difference between this stranger and Cade, but I could tell them apart.

I'd expected the wolf to be threatening, but I could clearly see from its body language that it wasn't going to attack. Instead, it sat back on its haunches and scanned us, one by one.

This didn't seem to ease Cade's fears so he remained in the same position, tensed and ready to attack at any second. His eyes stayed on the alpha in front of him.

The moment the alpha's eyes settled on me, I felt a nervous tug in my stomach. A slow, menacing growl came from Cade at the fact that the alpha was looking at me. I tensed at the sound. He was being territorial and he was warning the other alpha off me. I was taken; I was his.

The alpha took his eyes off me and settled them back on Cade, which stopped the growling.

Another six wolves, all in various sizes and colors, stepped behind the alpha and it seemed to make Cade and his pack more tense and aggressive. But the wolves sat behind their alpha, back on their haunches. From their actions, they didn't seem to want to attack.

The alpha still had his eyes on Cade, but he bowed his head slightly. It signaled that he wasn't here to fight. Cade seemed to relax a little.

No matter what, Scar, you stay behind me, I heard him say to me.

Okay, I replied to him, trusting his judgment. I sat back on my haunches and watched the scene play out in front of me.

My eyes were still on the alpha when he shifted to his human form. In the massive wolf's place was a tall guy with black hair that hung across his forehead, ending just above his strong cheekbones. He was a good-looking guy and looked a couple of years older than us.

I was expecting him to have the same color eyes as Cade, but he didn't. He eyes were a dark gray color.

Cade shifted into his human form. With his legs slightly apart and his arms crossed over his chest, he looked formidable. I felt proud that he was mine. I'd never been one for being possessive, but that was until I met Cade.

"What are you doing here, Kyle?" Cade asked in a deadly tone. He was being openly hostile to the alpha.

"I'm looking for someone," he revealed. As powerful as Cade was, I could see that he didn't intimidate Kyle.

"Entering someone's territory without their permission is an act of war. You know the rules," Cade said. I could feel the anger coming off Cade. Kyle held up his hands in surrender.

There was no doubt that Cade was livid, but I think what made him angrier was the fact that I was with him. He wasn't happy something like this might be going down with me so close to it.

"I'm sorry, but it's urgent I find her," Kyle explained. He looked genuine. "There are rogues on the loose and I need to find her before they do."

I wondered if he was talking about the same rogues that had been after me. Maybe there was more than one group of rogues in the area.

"Who are you looking for?" Cade asked, looking at Kyle suspiciously. His anger had eased slightly, although it was still bubbling just under the surface.

Kyle paused for a moment. It was like he was trying to find the best way to say what he needed to.

"My sister," was his answer.

"I've known you nearly my whole life; you don't have a sister," replied Cade, still watching him suspiciously, his jaw tightened. I couldn't help but wonder how Cade knew him.

"She's been gone a long time," Kyle answered cryptically as he held Cade's gaze. They seemed to have a standoff for a few minutes before Cade relented.

"Fine, come back with us and we'll try and help you."

Kyle nodded his head in agreement and, within seconds, Kyle and Cade shifted back into their wolf forms.

The run home was more serious and my light-heartedness from earlier was forgotten as I thought about Kyle's sister.

I couldn't help that little bit of jealousy that I felt when I saw siblings together. A sibling was someone who grew up in the same circumstances and environment. They would know you better than anybody else—even your parents.

There had been more than a few moments in my childhood that I'd been so lonely that I'd wished for a brother or sister, but no matter how much I'd wished, it hadn't changed the fact that I was an only child.

Cade ran beside me the whole way back to the compound, with Kyle and his pack following behind us

The gates were open and there were a few people waiting for us as we entered the compound. Cade stopped beside me and shifted back to human form. I'd managed to transform into a wolf, but I wasn't sure how to shift back.

Take our visitors into my study. Tell them I'll be with them in a few minutes, Cade instructed Jake.

When I didn't shift back, Cade dropped to a knee in front of me.

You having troubling shifting back?

I nodded my head.

Close your eyes and see yourself in your human form.

He was so thoughtful, I leaned forward and licked his cheek. He laughed and wiped his cheek. It was nice to see him in the carefree state; it didn't happen often.

I closed my eyes and did what he said. Sure enough, I felt my body change. But unlike when I shifted into a wolf, I felt pain shoot through my body. When the shift finished, I was on my knees with my hands grasping the sand as I breathed through the pain.

"It's okay," Cade soothed as I felt him pick me up. He tucked me closer to his chest as he carried me to the house. I was glad that Kyle and his pack had been directed to Cade's study so that they wouldn't see me like this.

I heard the murmur of voices coming from the study as Cade climbed the stairs. Once inside his bedroom, he laid me gently on the bed.

How are you feeling?

"A little achy, but I'll survive," I answered him out loud. It was still more comfortable to talk aloud than to talk to him through the mind-link. He sat down beside me and tucked a stray piece of hair behind my ear.

"I'd stay but I have to talk to Kyle," he said as he pressed a kiss to my lips.

"It's fine, go do what you need to."

He gave me one last lingering look before he left.

I lay on the bed for about fifteen minutes before I felt the ache ease from my limbs. I wondered if it would be this painful every time I shifted back to human form, but then I remembered Cade saying something about it only hurting a few times after the first shift.

Thank goodness.

I wandered downstairs in search of Cade. I knew he was in the study with Kyle. Most people would have left them alone to talk, but I wanted to know what was going on.

The door was closed, but I didn't knock. I opened the study and walked in. Cade turned to look at me. I wasn't sure if I expected him to be mad that I'd barged in, but he smiled.

"Hi," he greeted as he stepped forward.

"Hi," I replied.

I heard a gasp and I turned to see Kyle standing a couple of feet away from me with his gaze fixed on me in surprise. His mouth was slightly open in shock.

It was like he'd seen a ghost.

"Eyes off her," warned Cade when he saw Kyle gaping at me. Cade took a menacing step toward him. Kyle was yanked back to reality as he shot a glare to Cade. This guy was really acting weird. Then, despite the warning from Cade, he turned to me. His eyes softened slightly as he searched my face.

"Scarlett?" he whispered.

Cade stopped mid-step. Confused, he looked from Kyle to me. I didn't know why Kyle was acting the way he was, but I stood firm.

"Yes, I'm Scarlett," I confirmed while holding his questioning gaze.

A few moments of deathly silence descended.

"I'm sorry, should I know you?" I asked, feeling a little impatient that I wasn't seeing the whole picture.

"Yes...you should know me," he replied cryptically. I racked my mind, but I'd never seen him before today. He didn't go to our school and he didn't live in our town so I wasn't sure how I was supposed to know him.

In the meantime, Cade looked deep in thought as he rubbed his chin and then it was like a light went off in his mind.

"Scarlett?" he said to Kyle. Kyle nodded his head gently, but his attention didn't move from me. I hated not knowing what was going on.

"Where am I supposed to know you from?" I asked, feeling a little impatient as I cocked my head to the side and studied him.

"You..." he began, "... are my sister."

My eyes narrowed for a moment as I considered the fact that he might be high on something. I looked to Cade but Cade's expression was blank as he watched my reaction. The fact that Cade wasn't laughing his ass off told me that he believed what Kyle had just said.

A brother.

It was unbelievable. I heard a rush of blood in my ears as the room suddenly became too hot. I took a deep breath and released it.

"Sit down," Cade instructed as he steered me to a chair and I sat down.

One thought after another ambushed me. More questions than answers flooded through my mind. How was it possible? I dropped my head into my hands for a moment to try and get a hold of myself.

"You okay, Scar?" Cade questioned with concern and I looked up to see him bent down on one knee in front of me as he searched my face.

A brother.

The thought resounded through my mind and my eyes went to Kyle's, who was watching me just as carefully as Cade was.

It was his eyes—they were gray, like mine. Could he really be?

I stood up and Cade shifted out of my way as I walked to Kyle. Everyone else in the room was forgotten about. I stopped just in front of him and he stood watching me as I studied his eyes. The more I looked at him, the more I saw glimpses of my dad's strong features and my mom's coloring.

Then it hit me. He was my brother and I felt a sob rip from inside of me.

I wasn't the emotional type, but in that moment I threw my arms around him and hugged him tightly. Another sob followed as I felt the tears start to run down my cheeks while I cried.

The parents I'd mourned since I was a little girl lived on in him and I held him close, feeling like I was connecting with my parents in some small way. The grief that I'd wrestled with began to break free at the thought that I had a brother I knew nothing about.

His strong arms wrapped around me and held me tightly against his chest. That small gesture made me sob even harder. I didn't know how it was possible, all that I knew was what I saw confirmed that he was my brother.

For the first time since I'd lost my parents, I didn't feel alone in the world.

I pulled back and brushed his cheek with my thumb and he smiled at me. Feeling vulnerable as my throat thickened with emotion, I took a step back.

"I'm sorry," I mumbled, averting my gaze. I felt embarrassed at my outburst.

"I needed that as much as you did."

My eyes went to his and I bit my lip to keep more tears from breaking free.

"I don't want you to take this the wrong way, but I need time to process this," I told him, brushing the tears from my cheeks.

"You take as long as you need."

It seemed to be enough that somehow he'd found me.

I turned to see Cade watching me. I tried to give him a reassuring smile, but he saw right through it. Overwhelmed, I turned and rushed out of the study.

CHAPTER
TWENTY-TWO

SCARLETT

Thankfully, I managed to get to the gym without running into anyone. By the time I made it inside, I was breathing hard and I felt like I was going to explode from the emotions tearing into me.

Tears stung my eyes as I tried to take a deep breath and expel it. A couple of tears slid free and I brushed them away angrily. I hated being so emotional; it made me feel vulnerable.

I stood in front of the punching bag. I swung my fist and hit the bag hard. I repeated the motion again. It was a way of expelling some of the anger building up inside of me.

If I had a brother, it meant that my parents had lied to me. The betrayal was too much to deal with. No matter how hard I hit the punching bag, it didn't ease the feeling of betrayal. Why had they kept it from me?

I hit the punching bag again and again, the sweat pouring down my face as I kept at it.

I closed my eyes and held the punching bag as I tried to imagine what Kyle's life was like without our parents. I swear I felt my heart break for him. I was getting upset over the fact that our parents lied to me, but what they did to him was far worse.

He'd grown up without a family.

The tears I'd managed to hold up to that point broke free and I began to sob. I didn't hear anyone come in, but I felt hands turn me around gently. Through my tears, I looked up to see Cade looking at me with concern and understanding.

Another sob trembled through me as he pulled me into his arms and held me close.

"It's okay, Scar," he soothed as he rubbed my back gently. I clung to him. He was like my anchor to Earth while everything spun out of control.

Slowly my sobs began to ease and finally the tears dried up. I rested my cheek against his chest as he continued to hold me. I felt like I'd cried so much and experienced so many emotions all at once. Now that I'd stopped crying, I felt emotionally exhausted.

Gently, Cade pulled back slightly and tilted my gaze to his with his finger under my chin. He brushed the tears from my cheeks as I closed my eyes.

He led me to Hank's small office and made me sit down in one of the chairs as he got me a drink of water. He handed me the cup and I took a sip. He sat down on a chair across from me and leaned forward with his elbows resting on his thighs.

"Talk to me, Scar," he pleaded gently. I couldn't even look at him at the moment so I dropped my gaze to the floor.

I took an emotion-filled breath and released it like it would help me let go of all the negative emotions I was feeling, but nothing eased them. One minute ticked into two. I don't know how much time passed as I sat there feeling like my whole life had been a lie.

They hadn't told me I was a werewolf. They hadn't told me I had a brother. What else had they kept from me?

I set the glass of water down on the table and stood up. I began to pace back and forth as I tried to come up with a reason why my parents had done what they did. But I couldn't come up with an acceptable excuse.

"Scar." Cade said my name and I turned to face him. I crossed my arms across my chest as I held his gaze. I didn't like people seeing me exposed and vulnerable like I felt at the moment.

"I hate feeling weak and emotional," I said to him.

He let out a sigh then he stood up and walked over to me as I held his gaze.

"It's okay to feel weak and emotional," he said as his eyes softened and I bit down on my lip to keep from crying again. "You don't always have to be strong and in control. You just found out that you have a brother you knew nothing about. I can't even imagine what you're going through."

He paused for a moment.

"I'm here to be strong for you when you need strength. So feel what you need to, fall apart if that's what it takes. I'll be there to pick up the pieces."

I pressed my hands to my mouth to stop another sob that was provoked by his beautiful words. He reached for me and pulled me against his chest. His words covered me like a blanket, making me feel safe and protected.

"I think you'll feel better when you've talked to Kyle and found out why your parents did what they did," he suggested. "Maybe they had a good reason."

He was right. I couldn't guess why they didn't tell me about Kyle. I needed to sit down with my brother and find out what he knew. Maybe somehow he knew why our parents had left their pack and covered their tracks so well that Gary hadn't been able to find out anything.

I hugged him for a moment before I pulled back.

"Come on, let's go and find my brother," I said. It still felt so strange saying that. *My brother.*

Cade held my hand as we walked back to the house.

"Where's Gary?" I asked Cade as we entered the house.

"I think he's upstairs," he answered.

"Please, would you get him to meet me in the study?" I asked.

"Sure," he said. He pressed his lips to mine and I savored the brief kiss.

While Cade hurried up the stairs, I turned to face the door of the study. It was time to get answers.

I opened the door to find Kyle alone, sitting in a chair with his hands clasped together. His eyes met mine and he stood up. He didn't strike me as the type to be nervous, but I could tell he was.

"Hi," I said. It felt inadequate, but it was the best I had.

"Hi," he replied, shoving his hands in his pockets.

"We need to talk." I stated the obvious.

He nodded his head in agreement as he sat back down and I sat down across from him. I felt nervous as Gary entered the study, looking a little confused.

I stood up and gave him a hug.

"How are you feeling?" he asked as he scanned my features. The last time I'd seen him was before I'd mated with Cade and shifted for the first time. It hadn't been that long ago, but it felt like a lifetime.

"I'm good," I lied. He was asking about my physical well-being, not my emotional state.

Kyle stood up as Gary turned to face him.

"Kyle, this is Gary, he was our dad's best friend and my guardian," I introduced.

"Gary, this is my...brother."

Gary took a moment before what I said sank in and he turned to me. It was like he wasn't sure he'd heard right.

"Yes, he is my brother," I confirmed.

Gary and Kyle shook hands briefly before Gary sank down in the only other empty chair. He looked shocked. I wondered if that was what I'd looked like the first time I'd heard the news.

"I don't understand," he mumbled.

"I'm hoping Kyle will be able to shed some light on it," I said as I sat down and faced Kyle. At that moment, the study door opened again and in walked Cade. I smiled at him as he came over to me and stood beside me.

"So how do you and Cade know each other?" I asked.

"I'm an alpha of a neighboring pack," Kyle answered. It made sense. That was how Cade and he knew each other so well.

A few questions raced through my mind at that snippet of information. Cade had said I had alpha blood. Did that mean that my father had been the alpha of the pack that Kyle now ran?

But to me there was a more important question than why my parents had done what they had.

"Who raised you?" I asked, bracing myself. It had affected me deeply that I had grown up—even if it was just for a short time—with our parents while he'd been alone.

"Our uncle, Nate, Dad's brother," he answered.

Just when I didn't think there was anything more that could shock me, I had an uncle—another family member. Somehow, I knew there would be a few more shocks before this conversation was over.

I rubbed my hands over my face as I contemplated that the man who was my father had a sibling I knew nothing about. I wondered if they looked similar.

"How old are you?" I asked.

"I'm twenty-two," he answered. I was still trying to get used to the idea that I had brother who was five years older than me.

"How old were you when they left?" I asked, feeling nervous and apprehensive about the answers I was about to get.

In my mind, they had always been good and loving parents, but that image would change if the reason they'd left Kyle hadn't been good enough. Even though he'd had our uncle to look after him, it still didn't make me feel any less sad that our parents had left him.

"I was four," he answered. Seeing my visible reaction to that, he pulled his chair closer and took my trembling hand in his. I hadn't been born yet. Was my mom pregnant with me when they left?

I still couldn't shake the feeling that the people I'd known as my parents felt more like strangers to me because of what little I really knew about them.

"I don't want you to feel sad that they left me behind," he began as he used his free hand to run it through his hair. "They did what they had to."

His words didn't make the sadness in me ease and I felt the sting of tears again. He squeezed my hand gently as I tried to keep it together.

"I can't understand how they were able to leave you behind. Why would they do that?" I whispered while struggling to hold my tears in again as an image appeared in my mind of Kyle as a little boy standing on his own as my parents walked away from him.

I felt Cade's hand rest gently on my shoulder.

"It was the only way to protect me," he answered. "Let me start at the beginning."

He had my undivided attention.

"Mom and Dad knew each other their whole lives.

They'd both been brought into the same pack and when they discovered they were mates, they were deliriously happy. They were in love and as soon as they were old enough, they mated."

Hearing that made me more emotional and I bit my lip to stop myself from crying like a baby.

"Dad was the next in line to be the alpha and when our grandfather died, Dad took over. Then Mom fell pregnant with me. They were so happy."

What on Earth could have happened to tear them away from their families and son? What had made them run and never look back?

"One day an alpha from another pack came to visit. His name was Victor."

Kyle glanced up to Cade and they shared a look.

"What has he got to do with this?" I asked, growing impatient.

"Victor is an alpha of one of the most powerful packs in the country. He is ruthless and unpredictable, which makes him a very formidable opponent."

I didn't like the sound of this guy already and I hadn't even heard the full story yet.

"He was mate-less. His mate died just after they met. He didn't take the death well and started to become emotionally unstable."

Ruthless and unpredictable added with emotionally unstable sounded really dangerous. But what did he have to do with my parents leaving?

"The day he arrived to meet with our father, he saw Mom for the first time," he began to explain and I could feel the dread beginning to grow inside of me.

"The fact that he wasn't her mate and that she was already mated to another alpha didn't matter to him. He was so taken with her that he had to have her no matter what. He swore he'd do everything in his power to get her."

Holy crap!

"At first they didn't think that he was serious about it. Then he tried to kidnap Mom, but thankfully he didn't succeed. They tried to reason with him, but nothing worked."

"But why would he want someone who wasn't interested in him?" I asked out loud.

"Just because we are werewolves doesn't mean that we aren't susceptible to being bad," explained Cade.

"I don't know what it was about Mom that made him want her so badly," Kyle said with a shrug.

"So they left?" I asked.

"They didn't want to put the rest of the pack's lives on the line trying to protect Mom. Victor was more powerful and his pack was double our size. If we'd gone to war, he would have won and in the process our pack would have been slaughtered," he explained. There wasn't a lot of emotion in his words.

"Why did they leave you?" I asked the question again. They could have taken him with them when they'd taken off.

"They didn't want to leave the pack without an alpha was what they told Nate, but honestly, I don't think they wanted to risk my life. Victor never knew about me so when they left it was easy to pretend I was Nate's son and not theirs. By doing that, they kept me safe from him."

I pulled my hand free from Kyle's and rubbed my face as I tried to understand what he was telling me.

My parents had given up a son that they'd loved in order to keep him safe. My heart broke at this thought. I didn't have kids of my own, but I knew it wouldn't be easy to walk away from your own child, even if it meant they would be safer.

Everyone quietly watched me as I stood up and began to pace. So they had left the safety of their pack and they'd left their son behind to keep them safe. I knew deep down that my parents wouldn't have abandoned him without a good reason.

They fell pregnant with me after they left so they kept me with them.

"Who killed them?" I asked the question bluntly. I knew the answer already, but I needed him to say it out loud for me.

I turned to look at Kyle and his eyes met mine.

"Victor."

I felt Cade's concerned gaze on me as I continued to look at my brother.

"He was livid when he found out that our parents left the pack and disappeared. He swore he'd hunt them down and kill them for it," explained Kyle.

It was hard to think that my parents had left what little safety that the pack provided to face Victor's wrath on their own and that they'd died for it. I put my hand to my forehead and tried to breathe.

Suddenly the room became too hot and I couldn't take in a breath. He'd murdered my mom and my dad. Their deaths had been hard on me, but knowing why and who had killed them was too much to handle.

"Sit down," Cade gently instructed. I felt his hands on my arms as he led me to my seat. I sat down as my knees gave way. It was at that point that the emotion I'd been able to keep a lid on finally bubbled to the surface and I felt the tears beginning to slide down my face.

"It's okay," Cade soothed.

I felt like I was mourning my parents all over again, but at least now I knew the truth behind their deaths. They hadn't done anything wrong; they died because some madman had seen my mom by chance and it had led to them having to run for their lives. But somehow he'd still found them.

If I'd been with them that night, I would have been murdered as well. My tears eased and I sniffled as I contemplated the new questions, and thoughts began to take hold inside my mind.

"I'm okay," I assured a worried-looking Cade.

"Is he still alive?" I asked, hoping that he wasn't.

"Yes," replied Kyle. It wasn't fair that he was still alive, because my parents had died at his hands.

Another thought occurred to me. If my parents had gone to such lengths to hide Kyle from Victor, what would Victor do if he knew about me?

Granted, it had been years, but would that matter to a guy that had been ruthless and determined enough to hunt my parents down nearly eleven years after they'd disappeared?

"Does he know about me?" I asked Kyle and I felt Cade stiffen beside me.

"We don't know," he answered and I could see the worry in his face.

CHAPTER
TWENTY-THREE

SCARLETT

I was silent as I processed all I'd just heard. Kyle and Gary watched me with concern and Cade bent down on one knee beside me as he covered my hands with his.

Feeling fear starting to build up in me again, I couldn't sit still anymore. I stood up and Cade let go of me. I brushed my hair out of my face as I walked over to the window. The silence continued as I tried to fit all the pieces together.

"How did you know about their deaths?"

Even now, years later, it was still hard to say it without the grief surfacing. I hugged my arms around my waist as I waited for Kyle's answer.

"Dad stayed in touch with Uncle Nate. Dad didn't want him to know too much in case Victor found out, so he would only tell Nate which area. He usually only called from a payphone."

He paused for a moment. It was like stuff out of spy movies.

"Then one day the phone calls just stopped."

I closed my eyes to keep the emotion from escaping me and I swallowed.

"Nate knew something was very wrong."

Our parents were dead.

"He found out our parents were murdered. To us, there was no mystery. They had been murdered by another werewolf."

I turned to face him. It was like each revelation brought new questions I needed to ask.

"Did he know about me?" I asked as I dropped my arms to my sides.

Kyle looked uncomfortable with the answer. He couldn't look at me. His eyes dropped to the floor.

"Yes."

I don't know why I felt hurt at his answer, but I was. It felt like my family abandoned me when I'd needed them the most.

Cade was watching everything play out, but the twitch in his jaw was a telltale sign he was angry as his eyes remained on Kyle. It was like he was debating whether to hit him or not.

Don't. His eyes shot to mine.

It's not his fault.

He studied me for a minute before he answered me via the mind-link. *Fine.*

He unclenched his hands by his sides and I couldn't help loving his protectiveness over me. Kyle's eyes were on me. As hard as I tried to stay unaffected by what he'd said to me, he could read the hurt on my face.

"He didn't want to leave you. He saw that our parents had picked a good guardian for you and he decided that you were safer with him. You hadn't turned sixteen so another werewolf couldn't find you by your scent. It was for the best."

That explanation eased my hurt a little and I shot a weak

smile to Gary. I couldn't dispute that Gary had been the best person to look after me.

"If he had brought you back, there was always a chance that Victor would find out who you were and then you would have been in danger. Our pack isn't big enough to go up against him."

He stood up and walked over to me under the watchful eye of Cade. He came to a stop in front of me.

"I know you don't know us that well," he began as he ran a hand through his hair. "But that doesn't make you any less our family and that doesn't mean we love you any less."

I bit my lip as he held my gaze.

"Everything we've done up to now has been to keep you safe," he finished as his eyes implored mine to believe his words.

I was never the affectionate type, but I felt myself hugging my brother again. His arms wrapped around me and hugged me back. I rested my head against his chest for a moment and took a deep breath. Everything he was telling me was a lot to deal with, especially when it opened up the grief I'd kept bottled up.

After what I'd just found out, I'd remember my parents as heroes who sacrificed their lives to keep their children and pack safe. I pulled out of my brother's embrace and looked up at him.

"How did you know I was here?" I asked.

"We've been keeping tabs on you, watching you from the time you turned sixteen," he revealed softly. And there was that betrayed feeling again.

I rubbed my forehead slightly, trying to ease a headache that was starting to develop.

"It was hard keeping a closer eye on you when you were in another pack's territory," he said as he threw a look in Cade's direction.

"If you'd told me I would have allowed you into my territory," Cade threw back.

"I couldn't tell anyone the truth in case it got out. If Victor finds out about her..." He couldn't even finish his sentence as he held Cade's gaze. I was pretty sure I didn't want to hear what he couldn't say.

"Your sister is my mate and this is her pack as well so you are welcome onto our territory any time," Cade said to Kyle.

At his words, I touched the healed bite mark on my throat and blushed. My brother just smiled and shook his head.

"I'm glad you found your mate," he said as he wrapped one arm around my shoulders and gave me a squeeze.

"Me too," I said as I shot the lucky guy who was my mate a smile.

We'd been so wrapped up in the conversation that I'd totally forgotten about Gary, who'd been quiet the whole time. I glanced over to see him still sitting in the chair, watching us.

I smiled. He got up and walked over to stand beside Kyle.

"Thank you for taking such good care of her," said Kyle to Gary as they shook his hands.

"Your parents would be so proud to see you now," said Gary, still looking at Kyle like he was looking at a ghost.

"I hope so," he replied softly.

It was hard to say goodbye to my bother a little while later. I'd only let him go because he'd insisted that he needed to get back to tell Nate that I was safe.

"I'll be back in a couple of days," he'd reassured me before hugging me tightly. We stood by the open gates of the property that overlooked the forest.

"Okay," I muttered, not happy about letting him leave.

He shot me one more smile before he shifted into his

massive wolf. I watched with Cade beside me as Kyle and his pack disappeared into the forest.

You okay? I felt his fingers intertwine with mine.

Yeah, I'm just tired, I replied through the mind-link.

He gently tugged me forward and we walked hand-in-hand back to the house. Silently, we went up to our room.

I went straight for the bed and lay down on my back and rested my arm over my eyes. My headache was still pounding. I heard Cade walk across his room and then I felt the bed dip. I moved my arm to look up at him.

"Here, take these," he instructed as he gave me a glass of water and two headache tablets.

"Thanks," I mumbled as I did what he asked.

I handed him back the glass and lay back on the bed. A few moments later, I felt the bed dip again and I turned to see Cade lying next to me.

"Sometimes, you can be really awesome," I said, watching him look up at the ceiling.

He smiled and turned to face me.

"Only sometimes?" he asked playfully and my smile widened.

"Yeah, only sometimes." I stayed firm.

"I'll have to work at it."

Then I had a thought. I knew something that would make me forget the emotional day I'd had, and I knew for sure it would make me feel better. I got to my knees on the bed and leaned in to kiss Cade. He smiled against my lips.

"I thought you were tired," he said when I lifted my lips from his.

"I'm never too tired for this," I replied in the same playful tone.

"Are you sure, Scar?" he asked with a more serious tone as his eyes held mine.

"I need this," I admitted to him. He studied me for a

moment, then his arms snaked around me and brought my lips against his.

He moved his lips against mine and he gripped my waist as his tongue slipped into my mouth. I groaned and my stomach flipped at the intimate action.

It was exactly what I needed.

Afterward, I lay with his arm wrapped around me with my head against his chest.

"I think you're going to have to keep working at it," I teased. His chest rumbled with laughter.

A little later, after we'd both showered, we went downstairs to have dinner.

"Blake is joining us tonight," Cade informed me as we entered the dining room.

"Hey, look at you, all mated, shifted and everything," Blake teased as I walked in first. He was already seated.

I gave him a playful glare as I sat down across from him. Cade took the spare chair beside me and sat down as he laughed at the two of us.

We'd come a long way in a short span of time. It was hard to remember how much I'd disliked Blake and Cade when I'd first met them. I cared for Cade in a way I'd never cared for a guy, and I cared for Blake as family.

A few minutes later, Gary arrived and we started to eat.

"So, you said you had some stuff you needed to tell me?" Blake asked Cade.

"Scar and I had an eventful day," Cade began. "Kyle came onto our territory without permission."

"He can't be that stupid," Blake remarked, all humor and playfulness gone. He was all alpha.

"He was desperate to find his sister," Cade replied.

"He doesn't have a sister," scoffed Blake. I kept quiet as they talked about my brother. Before Cade continued, he glanced in my direction.

"What am I missing?" asked Blake as he witnessed the brief look.

"I have a brother," I revealed.

"You have a brother?" he repeated in disbelief. "But how?"

"I only found out about him today," I added, setting my fork down beside my plate.

"You have a brother you didn't know about and Kyle has a sister no one knew about. What are the odds," he said, shaking his head. It took him a few moments to put those two puzzle pieces together.

"Kyle is your brother." He gasped when he finally got it.

I nodded my head.

"But, I don't understand," he said, still looking bewildered at the shocking revelation.

"Remember the stories about Kyle's parents abandoning the pack?" Cade began to explain.

"Yeah, I remember the stories."

"Well, they didn't abandon the pack. They left Kyle and their pack to keep them safe," Cade explained further.

"Why?" Blake asked.

"Victor."

Blake's features changed from confused to angry. For the first time, I wondered how well they knew Victor.

"What did he do?" asked Blake. He clenched his jaw as he pushed his plate aside. Clearly the subject of Victor was enough to ruin his appetite.

"You remember the story of him losing his mate."

"Yeah," Blake confirmed.

"When he met Scar's mom, he wanted her as his mate despite the fact that she was already mated to an alpha," Cade explained.

"I can't say I'm surprised—the guy is a fucking lunatic," Blake replied.

"They couldn't reason with him. He even went as far as to try and kidnap Scar's mom," Cade explained. "They decided that it was best to leave the pack to keep them safe. Victor didn't know about Kyle so they thought it was best to leave him behind. Nate, their dad's brother, took Kyle and passed him off as his own son."

"Holy crap," Blake muttered as he shook his head in disbelief. When our eyes met, he gave me a sympathetic smile.

"Their parents ran and kept a low profile. But he found them ten years later and killed them," Cade said, emotion starting to creep into his voice. "He didn't know that they'd had a child at all, never mind two."

Cade paused for a moment as he shared a look with Blake. Blake looked somber as he ran a hand through his hair.

"Kyle said they managed to keep tabs on her. As long as she hadn't turned sixteen, she was still undetectable and they thought it was safer to leave her in Gary's guardianship than take the risk of bringing her back into the pack and Victor discovering who she really is."

Cade's hand reached for mine.

"Kyle panicked when he heard there were rogues on our territory and he was scared Scar would be unprotected against them," Cade finished.

"This shit is like something out of a soap opera, you know," muttered Blake.

Blake pushed back from the table and stood up. He was agitated as he began to pace up and down. Cade and I watched him silently.

Then he turned to face us.

"You do realize we are fucked if he finds out about her," Blake said, getting straight to the point.

Cade stood up, pushing his chair back.

"I'll talk to you in the study," he barked at Blake.

Without another word the two of them strode out of the dining room. Why wouldn't they talk in front of me? I glanced at Gary. He knew me too well because he shook his head gently.

"I would tell you not to, but I know you well enough to know that you aren't going to listen to a word I say."

He definitely knew me too well.

I got up and left the dining room. I snuck as quietly as I could to the study so I would be able to overhear what they were saying. It was at times like this that I appreciated the fact that Blake didn't belong to our pack so they couldn't communicate through the mind-link. They had to talk to be able to communicate.

I strained my ears.

"...I have a bad feeling about this." It was Blake and he sounded stressed. For the short time I'd known Blake, he was always so laid back, but there was no doubt he was seriously stressed.

"I know," sighed Cade.

There was silence.

"The rogues aren't a coincidence," said Blake. It wasn't a question; it was a statement. "They were planted by Victor to capture Scarlett."

It meant Victor knew about me.

"I know." It was Cade, his tone resigned.

I felt a little bit betrayed that he hadn't shared his suspicions with me. Was it his way of trying to protect me?

"We have to join our packs," said Blake.

Wow! I hadn't expected that. I wondered how complicated that would be.

"We can, but I don't think that's going to help," said Cade.

"You're like a brother to me and I'll do everything I can to keep you and Scarlett safe," Blake told him.

My heart squeezed at his words. They were closer than best friends; they were non-blood-related brothers.

"I know, I just don't think we stand a chance," Cade admitted. The heaviness in his voice pulled at my heart. It was the responsibility of every life in our pack that weighed on his shoulders.

"Even with the help of Kyle's pack it isn't going to be enough to defeat Victor and I can't lead so many innocent lives into a slaughter," admitted Cade.

"Running isn't going to help," said Blake. He knew his friend well enough to know that that was going to be the next thing he'd contemplate.

"I know that."

There were no other options. No matter which option we chose, someone was going to die. The option to run would be a better one because it would at least save the pack, but I couldn't live with an option that would end Cade's life.

Fear and desperation filled me as I began to realize the full effect of the situation we were in.

Having heard enough, I snuck upstairs into our bedroom.

I began to pace up and down. It was a good thing I was protecting my thoughts, otherwise Cade would know I'd heard what they'd said.

I rubbed my forehead as I tried to come up with an alternative option where less lives were sacrificed to keep me safe. Any life other than my own was too much to sacrifice.

My own!

Then it struck me. I had a third option I hadn't thought of. I could give myself over to Victor.

If I gave myself willingly to Victor, I'd be able to keep Cade and our pack safe. I'd also be keeping my brother and his pack safe as well. It was the only option that didn't cost lives. I swallowed hard as I tried not to think about what that choice would cost me. It didn't matter. It was the only option. I wouldn't contemplate another one.

Now that I'd made up my mind, I had no idea how to put it into effect. Kyle had told me that Victor's territory bordered his and Cade's so I knew exactly where to go.

My mind began to set up scenarios of how I could get away without anyone stopping me. I knew that if Cade even suspected what I was going to do, he would lock me up to stop me.

I only had one chance to do this and I couldn't fail.

My failure would cost lives, and I wasn't prepared to live with that.

CHAPTER TWENTY-FOUR

SCARLETT

Once I managed to make my decision, I felt a calmness settle over me. I still needed to work out how I was going to get away without Cade or anyone else noticing. That part of my plan might prove to be the most difficult. I took a deep breath and expelled it. I had to go downstairs and pretend everything was fine.

Cade and Blake were in the formal lounge with Gary, talking to one another when I found them.

"Are you okay?" Cade asked with concern as he noticed me in the doorway. I hesitated for a moment before I smiled at him. I needed to put my acting skills to the test.

"I'm fine," I assured him calmly. I felt bad for deceiving him.

I walked to him and he scanned my features as if he didn't quite believe me while I sat down in the empty seat beside him. I tried to look relaxed.

Gary watched me closely, but I refused to meet his eyes. He obviously knew there was something very wrong, but I couldn't tell him anything. He would try to stop me.

Jake appeared in the doorway. He looked nervously at Cade.

"I'll be back in a moment," Cade murmured as he left the room to see what Jake wanted.

"I need to go and do some stuff," Gary announced moments later as he stood up.

He bent down to give me a brief kiss on the cheek before he left me alone with Blake.

"Today must have been a shocker for you," Blake said. It was still sometimes hard to believe that Blake was an alpha like Cade. Where Cade was a force to be reckoned with, Blake seemed like a warm teddy bear. But I had no doubt that if he needed to be he could be as ruthless as Cade was.

"Yeah, it was," I replied. It was hard to believe that I'd shifted for the first time today. I'd discovered I wasn't alone in the world and I had two family members. I found out the truth about what happened to my parents. To say it had been a hectic day would be an understatement.

I'd never had the opportunity to talk to Blake alone, so I took full advantage of it.

"I know this is none of my business," I began. I don't know what possessed me to broach the subject with him but I just couldn't stop myself. Maybe it was curiosity. Perhaps it was the fact that I knew a long life wasn't guaranteed for any of us that made me want to ask him about this specific subject.

"Like that would stop you," he shot back with a grin. He knew me well and I couldn't help but smile back at him.

"True," I confirmed with a slight nod.

"What do you want to ask me?" he asked, looking a little curious.

"What's up with you and Keri?" I asked, watching his features. Initially he looked surprised—he must not have been expecting me to ask him about her—and then he masked his features. I knew my friend had a thing for him.

He watched me silently for a few moments as he contemplated my question.

"It can't be anything," was the only response I got. I felt a weird burning feeling in my chest, I felt hurt. It was weird.

"I know that," I replied, remembering what Cade had told me. The weird feeling in my chest eased. "It's just I've seen the way the two of you look at each other. You'd have to be blind not to be able to see there is something between the two of you."

He sighed.

"If I get involved with her and then I find my mate, all I'll end up doing is hurting her. I can't do that."

I felt sad for him but I understood. I wouldn't be able to fight how I felt about Cade and when Blake found his mate he wouldn't be able to either. Keri would get hurt.

"It is what it is."

Another silence settled over us as I began to think about getting away. I made sure I kept my thoughts blocked off from Cade.

"You look like you've got a lot on your mind," commented Blake.

"I'm okay. It was just a lot to take in today," I lied.

Cade would go crazy when he discovered I was gone and I didn't want him doing something stupid. Blake would need to make sure he didn't do anything to put himself at risk.

"Promise me that no matter what happens, you'll keep your friend safe," I said to Blake. "Cade won't allow me to fight with him so I need to know that when I'm not there you will keep him safe for me."

I added the last part so he wouldn't suspect what I was up to. Blake frowned at me for a moment.

"Of course I will. I'd do the same for you."

His words made my eyes sting with tears. I smiled to try and cover up the emotion I was feeling.

"Thanks," I replied, unsure of what to say to something like that.

At that moment Cade returned. He strode into the lounge to the seat beside me, and he shared a brief look with Blake before he looked to me. He smiled at me but the smile never reached his eyes. There was definitely something going on.

"Is everything okay?" I asked. I knew there was something going on and that he was trying to hide it from me.

Was he keeping it from me so that I wouldn't worry?

"Everything is fine," he assured me.

"I'd better get back," Blake said as he stood up.

I stood up and walked with Cade to see him out.

After we said goodbye to Blake, Cade and I walked silently to our room.

"Is everything okay?" I tried asking.

"Everything is fine, Scar," he said as he gave me a brief kiss to the mouth.

I didn't believe a word he said. I knew he was lying to me. There was something going on and he wasn't going to tell me.

There was an unexpected knock at our bedroom door while I was in the bathroom brushing my teeth. I couldn't hear anything because Cade was probably using the mind-link to communicate with whoever it was that had knocked.

By the time I finished, Cade was lying in the bed, his chest naked while he wore a pair of sweats. Even with everything going on around us I couldn't stop my hormones from kicking in at the half-naked sight of him.

"Who was that?" I asked as I climbed into the bed. He pulled me into his arms as he covered me with the blanket.

"It was Jake. I needed him to do some stuff for me and he was just reporting back," he replied as I settled into his arms. I closed my eyes for a moment and enjoyed the feel of his arms around me. I couldn't think about everything I was going to lose; I had to enjoy every second of what I still had until I could put my plan into action.

"I love you," Cade whispered as he pressed a kiss against my forehead. Shock filled me as I looked up to Cade. He'd never said those three little words to me before.

"I love you too." I did, there was no disputing it. I was going to sacrifice my life to keep him safe.

"You are everything I ever wanted," he murmured as he hugged me to his chest. I closed my eyes and reveled in the moment. Even if it was all I had, it was worth it.

I felt a painful prick in my back. My eyes flew open at the sudden pain.

"I'm sorry," was all he whispered. I tried to move but my limbs felt so heavy and my eyelids began to flutter closed.

I was still confused and shocked as I drifted into the darkness.

When I woke up I still felt drowsy. Panic set in when I realized I wasn't in Cade's room. It was hard to focus my eyes so I closed them for a moment before trying to open them again. This time they focused.

I gasped.

I was lying on a small bed in a room with white walls. I didn't recognize it. I turned over in the bed and looked around the room.

I rubbed my eyes again, hoping I was seeing things, because it didn't make any sense. But nothing changed when I opened my eyes again. I sat up and I felt a wave of dizziness hit me.

The room looked like an ordinary room except for bars that ran the length of the room a meter from the door.

What the hell?

To the one side of my prison was a door. I assumed it was some sort of bathroom or something.

Taking a few deep breaths I waited for the dizziness to pass before I tried to stand up. I heard the door open and I looked up to see Cade in the doorway.

He stepped into the room, facing me through the bars. My limbs still felt so heavy. I struggled to get them to obey my commands.

"Take it easy, the effects will take a few minutes to wear off," Cade said.

His features were tight and unreadable as he stood with his feet apart and his arms crossed over his chest, watching me.

Suddenly, I remembered that feeling. Horror filled me when pieces of what happened before I had blacked out began to surface in my mind again. I remembered the prick and then the pain.

My eyes flew to Cade as I realized he'd injected me with something. Why would he do that? I rubbed my forehead for a moment trying to figure out what I'd missed.

"I don't understand..." I began to say as I managed to walk to the bars that confined me. I was about to reach out to hold one.

"Don't touch the bars," Cade warned me, just in time for me to be able to pull my hand away from the object. My forehead creased at the warning.

"What's going on?" I asked. What was happening didn't fit with the fact that he was my mate and he loved me. If he cared about me, why on Earth was I caged up like an animal?

"The bars are covered in wolfsbane," he revealed. I had no idea what wolfsbane was.

"It will burn your skin if you touch it," he continued. "It's a security precaution we take to keep werewolves from escaping."

"I don't understand," I said. I felt the effects of whatever he'd injected me with begin to wear off. I couldn't help the feeling of betrayal at his actions and I still didn't fully understand why.

"After you came downstairs last night I knew there was something up, I just had no idea what. I went to talk to Jake and Gary came to me. He told me that you'd overheard what Blake and I had been talking about. I had this dreadful feeling that you were going do something stupid."

I remembered feeling that strange feeling in my chest when I'd been talking to Blake. Had I felt his emotions? He looked at me like he expected me to deny it but I didn't. I was angry that Gary had told Cade that I'd overhead his conversation with Blake.

"I began to understand why you were acting so strangely. I decided it was in your best interest to keep you confined so you wouldn't try and do something stupid. I knew you wouldn't be able to sit back and do nothing."

He paused for a moment and I saw his jaw tighten. Even though his voice and his features looked calm, I knew he was angry.

"It was only after I injected you with the sedative and I heard your jumbled thoughts that I realized how far you were prepared to go," his said, and his voice broke on the last word.

I couldn't deny it because it was the truth. He expected me to feel guilty for being prepared to go to extreme lengths to keep the people I loved safe, but I didn't feel that way.

"Do you have any idea what he might do to you?" he exploded when he didn't get a reaction out of me. "Do you have any idea what that would have done to me...your brother...or Gary?"

That made my heart crack.

"And you really thought that I'd just stand back and do nothing while you gave yourself over to a fucking lunatic!" he shouted. I tried my hardest not to flinch under his verbal attack.

"I would have started a war to get you back," he told me. Anger still visibly coursed through him as he ran a hand through his hair. He dropped his gaze to the floor—it was as if he couldn't stand the sight of me anymore. He struggled to contain his temper.

I'd remained quiet while he'd had his say, but it was my time to talk.

"Blake made a comment about the rogues not being a coincidence," I stated, watching his reaction. His features were veiled, and he remained quiet.

"How long was it going to take for you to tell me that you'd figured out that Victor was behind the rogue attacks?" I asked, feeling my anger rise at the fact that he'd kept that from me.

"It was only when Kyle told you about your parents and Victor that things started to make more sense. Jake confirmed it last night. A couple of the rogues were in our territory and Jake tracked them to the border of Victor's territory. He saw them talking to some of the pack members from Victor's pack. It explains how he was able to get the rogues to work together. He is an alpha," he said, shoving his hands into the front pockets of his jeans.

"So when were you going to tell me?" I asked in a calm voice, knowing the answer already. His silence answered my question.

"You weren't going to tell me, were you?" I asked with my hands on my hips. He'd planned on keeping that information from me.

"I didn't want to worry you," he replied.

"How could you keep that from me? I had a right to

know," I shouted, losing my temper.

"And when you found out? What did you decide to do?" he threw back at me with just as much anger.

"Do you really expect me to stand back and do nothing while the people I love are slaughtered trying to protect me?" I said, raising my voice even more. "I heard what you and Blake said. You'd be going into a fight that you would lose."

His gaze lifted to mine.

"You didn't even give me a chance to come up with a solution," he replied, sounding hurt. "Instead you decided you were going to go and hand yourself over to a monster."

I kept silent.

"You can't keep me locked up," I said.

His eyes met mine with a challenge.

"Yes, I can," he stated.

Damn it!

He was right, he could keep me locked up in this room for as long as he wanted to and there was nothing I could do about it.

"I'll hate you for it," I warned him.

"If hating me is the only way to keep you alive, I can live with it," he replied. "You can't hate me if you're dead."

Forgetting his earlier warning, I reached to grab a bar and I felt my skin sizzle against it. I screamed as the pain sliced through me and I let go. Cade tensed as he watched me, looking down at the red burn on my hand. He was clearly wrestling with the urge to rush to me and check my hand.

"I'll send Curtis to check on you," he said tightly.

"You told me you love me," I said, trying to figure out how someone that loved me could do this to me.

"I'm doing this because I love you."

He gave me one more piercing look before he turned and left me alone in my prison.

True to Cade's word, Curtis came in a little while later with some ointment to put on the burn on my hand. The guards wore gloves to be able to open the cell door.

I kept silent the entire time.

I'd discovered the little room inside my cell contained a toilet and a small shower. Later when someone brought me food I refused to touch it. I climbed onto the bed and lay with my face to the wall.

I ignored the next meal as well even though my stomach grumbled. My stubbornness made me refuse to give in. Later, I was still lying on the bed when I heard the door open. I didn't turn to see who it was.

"You have to eat," Cade said to me. I refused to acknowledge him.

"If you refuse to eat I'll have to get Curtis to sedate you and put you on a drip," he warned.

Silence hung in the air between us.

"You have till tomorrow morning, otherwise you leave me with no choice."

It was his final warning. I knew him well enough to know he meant what he said.

Once I heard the door close again, I rolled onto my back.

I felt like my life was spinning out of control and there was nothing I could do except hold on tight, hoping I wouldn't be swept away.

CHAPTER TWENTY-FIVE

SCARLETT

Later that evening when Gary made an appearance, my blood still boiled with the anger I felt at his betrayal. If he hadn't told Cade about me overhearing his conversation with Blake I would not be locked up.

At the sight of him, I turned over on the bed to ignore him.

"I know you're angry with me," he began and then cleared his throat nervously. "I did it because I love you."

I ignored him as the anger simmered inside of me. Because of him my hands were tied and there was nothing I could do.

"We are all doing this because we love you and we want to keep you safe," he argued further when he didn't get a response from me.

"You need to eat," he instructed. He'd been sent to try and get me to eat. That just made me more determined not to eat.

"If you don't, Cade will get Curtis to sedate you and put you on a drip," he said, repeating Cade's warning.

"Please, Scarlett," I heard him plead.

One moment's silence ticked into another.

"I brought you some clothes and toiletries," he offered but I continued to ignore him. I heard the door to the cell open and after a few moments I heard it close again.

"Cade has sent a couple of werewolves to watch over your house until this thing with Victor is resolved."

My silence hung in the air.

"I'm sorry that you're still angry with me," he said softly. "But one day you will thank me for what I did."

I wasn't sure I would be able to forgive any of them, including Cade. They had no right to do what they'd done. They'd taken away my right to choose.

He waited for a few more moments and then he let out a heavy sigh as I heard him leave. Once I was sure he was gone I turned to see he'd left some folded clothes next to my toiletry bag on the floor by the door of the cell.

That night, before going to bed, I had a shower and changed into new clothes. As I lay on the bed staring up at the dark ceiling I thought about the mess I was in. I couldn't believe how quickly my life had changed in such a short space of time.

Then I thought about Cade. My feelings were mixed. As angry as I was with him I still loved him. I'd told him I would hate him if he kept me locked up but the truth was I didn't. I was angry and upset with him but I didn't hate him.

For most of the night I tried to come up with ways to get us out of the situation that my past had landed us in. Sometime during the night I drifted off to sleep. My sleep was anything but peaceful so the next morning I felt exhausted.

I glanced around the room I was being held in. I'd

walked around it trying to find any weakness so I would be able to escape but there was nothing.

My anger was still going strong when Cade walked in. In his hand was a plate of food. I was sitting on the bed with my back leaning against the wall. My stomach rumbled at the sight of the food.

"Here is your breakfast," Cade said as he looked to me for a response.

I kept silent.

"Scar."

It was only one word but it took me back to a time when there wasn't this massive obstacle standing between the two of us, to a time where things had been simpler.

"I'm giving you an hour. If you haven't eaten anything I will follow through on my threat," he stated calmly. There was no emotion in his features. It was like I was looking at a stranger and not the boy that I loved.

I got off the bed and walked over to the bars in front of him.

"Let me out," I instructed in a firm tone. His eyes held mine in a challenge. I wasn't going to beg.

"No."

His answer was plain and simple. He wasn't going to back down and if I wanted to get out I was going to have to do something drastic. Then I bit my lip as I reached for the bar. I knew it was going to hurt but it was the only way I could think of to get Cade to let me out.

"Don't," he said just before I wrapped my hand around the bar. The pain sliced through me and my face contorted in pain as I gasped.

"Let go!" Cade yelled but I put all my strength in holding on. If he saw me in enough pain he would relent and let me out. I just had to hold on long enough. The pain worsened and it vibrated through every cell in my body.

"Stop it!" Cade screamed urgently but he didn't open the door to try to stop me.

Unable to hold on any longer I let go and dropped to the floor. I held the injured hand against my chest.

"Let me out," I requested, breathing hard through my pain.

I looked up to see Cade looking at me. He was livid and his jaw was clenched. Then he turned and threw the plate of food against the wall with such ferocity the plate shattered and fell to the floor.

He gave me an angry and hurt look before he turned and left. In that moment I knew I'd pushed him too far.

Minutes later Curtis along with two guys from our pack entered the room. I was still sitting on the floor hugging my burned hand to my chest.

I knew what he was going to do. I wanted to fight him but with my injured hand I wouldn't be able to. The one guy opened the door and Curtis entered. I saw him holding a bag in his hand.

They were going to sedate me.

I wished I hadn't injured my hand because I'd have a better chance of fighting them if it were healthy. My hand throbbed painfully as I eyed out the three guys in the room.

Curtis watched as the two guys approached me. I stood up and backed up. I struggled but the guys took hold of each of my arms and lifted me off the ground. They set me down onto the bed. They were firm but they made sure not to hurt me.

Once they got me onto the bed and restrained me, I watched as Curtis took a syringe out of his bag and filled it with some liquid. As he reached to inject me I began to wrestle. The two guys held my arm still so Curtis could inject me. There was a prick of pain and then I cried out in frustration when I watched the syringe push the liquid into my vein.

As soon as they were done they released me.

Suddenly the two guys with Curtis stood straight and alert. Curtis looked at them curiously and then both of them dashed out of the room.

Something was happening. I felt panicked but then I felt a calmness seep into me as I tried to sit up but couldn't. Whatever they'd given me was strong because as I lay on the bed unable to move, I felt my eyelids grow heavy.

The last thing I saw before the sedative took effect was Curtis standing beside me.

When I started to come around I felt disorientated and weak. My eyes fluttered open and I tried to focus. My throat was dry and I swallowed. I wasn't in the white room anymore. Had they moved me?

I looked down to my arm expecting there to be a drip but there wasn't one. Instead I saw two small Band-Aids. Had they taken the drip out already? How long had I been out for? My hand was tender and I saw that the red burn mark had healed slightly.

The last memories before I blacked out surfaced again. I remembered the guys running out of the room, leaving me alone in the room with Curtis. What had happened?

My thoughts went straight to Cade. I hoped that everything was okay.

I scanned the room and it looked like I was in another type of cell. This one was dark and cold. I glanced around and saw a door with an inlaid window with bars covering it. I didn't have a good feeling about this at all.

If Cade moved me anywhere I would be in the medical center with a drip in my arm. But I wasn't.

Something isn't right.

CADE

From the time Scarlett came downstairs, she'd been acting strangely. At first I'd put it down to the stress of discovering Kyle was her brother and finding out about Victor, the man who had murdered her parents.

I left the lounge to find out what Jake had to say. Earlier, some rogues had been spotted in our territory and I'd told Jake to track them without being detected. I needed to confirm my suspicions that Victor was behind the rogue attacks.

He'd just told me that the rogues had been tracked to the edge of Victor's territory. He'd even seen the rogues talking to some members of Victor's pack.

"There is something up with Scarlett," said Gary as he joined Jake and me. I turned to face him, giving him my full attention. Anything that had to do with her was always important, more important than anything else.

"What were you and Blake talking about?" asked Gary before I could say anything.

I kept silent. I wasn't sure I could trust him with the information and I didn't want to take the chance that he would share it with Scarlett.

"Fine, don't tell me. But know that she overheard you and she's been acting strange ever since," he revealed with worry.

Fuck!

Why the hell had she been eavesdropping? I ran an agitated hand through my hair as I tried to remember everything that had been said between Blake and me.

I remembered Blake had mentioned that we suspected Victor was behind the rogue attacks. We'd also talked about the fact that Victor was more powerful than we were. If she'd overheard our conversation she'd know that even if we combined our pack with Blake's and Kyle's, we still wouldn't have enough werewolves to defend ourselves if Victor attacked.

I rubbed my forehead. If she'd heard this, she was going to do something stupid, really stupid. Jake and Gary watched me as I wrestled with the few options I had to keep Scar safe. The problem was she wasn't going to be happy with any of the options I was considering.

I let out a sigh and turned to Jake.

"Tell Curtis I need a sedative, strong enough to knock out a female werewolf," I instructed. Gary's eyes widened at my request.

"What are you going to do?" he questioned as Jake left.

"Everything I can."

I kept hoping that she would mention that she'd overheard my conversation with Blake but the longer it went without her admitting it to me, my uneasiness increased. It cemented the fear that she was planning something.

I tried to act as normal as possible but Scarlett picked up that there was something wrong.

While Scarlett was brushing her teeth, Jake knocked on the bedroom door. He handed me the syringe as he gave me a sympathetic look.

I closed the door and before Scarlett came out of the bathroom I got into our bed and hid the syringe under her pillow. I felt a pang of guilt but I tried to ignore it. I kept questioning if I was doing the right thing but I knew that keeping her alive was all that counted.

"Who was that?" she asked as she climbed into the bed. I pulled her into my arms and held her close as my hand reached for the hidden syringe.

"It was Jake. I needed him to do some stuff for me and he was just reporting back," I lied.

She closed her eyes and I realized how far I was willing to

go to keep her safe—it made me realize that I loved her. I loved her more than the fate and destiny that joined us together.

"I love you," I whispered as I feathered a kiss against her forehead. She looked up at me, obviously surprised at my declaration.

"I love you too," she murmured. My happiness at the words she said was weighed down by the guilt that was building up inside of me.

"You are everything I ever wanted," I said quietly to her as she closed her eyes and I hugged her. At the same time I pushed the syringe into her back.

"I'm sorry," I whispered at her shocked and confused expression.

The sedative only took moments to knock her out. But just a few mumbled thoughts filtered through to me before she drifted off.

I can't let them die.

Give myself to Victor.

Anger welled up in me as I realized she'd been planning to sacrifice herself to keep everyone safe. Any guilt I felt about what I was about to do next evaporated.

I couldn't think of what would have happened if Gary hadn't told me that Scarlett had overheard my conversation with Blake. For her own good I was going to keep her safe, and I'd do whatever I had to.

I picked her up gently and carried her downstairs into the basement of the house where cells were located. I'd gotten Jake to get one ready for her.

I didn't know how I was going to face her once she woke up. She was going to be hurt and angry. I had no idea if it was something she would ever be able to forgive me for.

Inside the cell, I laid her on the bed gently. I pressed a gentle kiss to her forehead, and let my eyes drift over her for a few moments before I turned and left the cell. I locked it behind me and left the room.

Outside in the hallway, I leaned against the wall next to the closed door and slid down the wall. I waited anxiously for her to wake up. I'd already set in motion my plans to protect her. I couldn't do this to her without coming up with a plan to keep her safe.

Finally, a few hours later I heard her gasp as I was pacing the hallway. She was awake and it was time to face her. The anger that I felt at the knowledge she had decided to give herself to Victor still simmered under the surface as I opened the door and stepped into the room.

She looked so fragile that I wanted to open the door and go to her, but I stopped myself.

"Take it easy, the effects will take a few minutes to wear off," I warned her when I saw her struggle to sit up.

Slowly I watched her piece what happened together and her eyes shot to mine. The hurt in her eyes nearly undid me. What had she expected me to do? Open the door and shove her in Victor's direction?

"I don't understand..." she began to say as she walked slowly to face me through the bars. She reached out to hold one of the bars.

"Don't touch the bars," I warned her. She stopped her hand just in time.

"What's going on?" she asked.

"The bars are covered in wolfsbane," I revealed. She clearly had no idea what that was.

"It'll burn your skin if you touch it," I told her. "It's a security precaution we take to keep werewolves from escaping."

"I don't understand," she whispered again. She looked at me like I'd just kicked a puppy.

"After you came downstairs last night I knew there was

something up, I just had no idea what. I went to talk to Jake and Gary came to me. He told me that you'd overheard what Blake and I had been talking about. I had this dreaded feeling that you were going to do something stupid."

I waited for her to say something but she remained silent. I watched as anger ignited in her eyes. She was pissed.

"I began to understand why you were acting so strangely. I decided it was in your best interest to keep you confined so you wouldn't try and do something stupid. I knew you wouldn't be able to sit back and do nothing."

I paused for a moment as I tried to control my anger.

"It was only after I injected you with a sedative and I heard your jumbled thoughts did I realize how far you were prepared to go," I said, and my voice broke on the last word.

She kept silent.

"Do you have any idea what he might do to you?" I yelled at her when I finally snapped. "Do you have any idea what that would have done to me...your brother...or Gary?

It would have broken me. Did she not understand that?

CHAPTER TWENTY-SIX

CADE

She looked sad for a moment and then her emotions disappeared from her face.

"And you really thought that I'd just stand back and do nothing while you gave yourself over to a fucking lunatic!" I shouted.

The fear of losing her scared me more than anything and I couldn't believe how close I'd come to that.

"I would have started a war to get you back," I stated to her. I was still so angry. I ran a hand through my hair as I dropped my eyes from her face and fixed them on the floor. It hurt to look at her.

"How long was it going to take for you to tell me that you'd figured out that Victor was behind the rogue attacks?" she asked, her anger becoming more visible.

"It was only when Kyle told you about your parents and Victor that things started to make more sense. Jake confirmed it last night. A couple of the rogues were in our territory and Jake tracked them to the border of Victor's territory. He saw them talking to some of the pack members from Victor's pack. It explains how he was able to get the rogues to work together. He is an alpha," I said as I shoved my hands into the pockets of my jeans.

"So when were you going to tell me?" she asked. We both knew I had no intention of telling her anything.

"You weren't going to tell me, were you?" she asked as she put her hands on her hips.

"I didn't want to worry you," I replied. It was weak, but it was the truth.

"How could you keep that from me? I had a right to know," she shouted, finally losing her temper. Her eyes glinted with anger.

"And when you found out? What did you decide to do?" I responded as my anger flared again.

"Do you really expect me to stand back and do nothing while the people I love get slaughtered trying to protect me?" she said as she struggled to contain her rage. "I heard what you and Blake said. You'd be going into a fight that you would lose."

My gaze lifted to hers.

"You didn't even give me a chance to come up with a solution," I replied, hurt. "Instead you decided you were going to go and hand yourself over to a monster."

She had no idea what I was capable of when it came to keeping her safe. I would do anything.

"You can't keep me locked up," she argued.

My gaze held hers.

"Yes, I can," I stated. I could keep her locked up for as long as I needed to and there was nothing she could do about it.

"I'll hate you for it," she warned. I knew she wasn't going to be happy about what I'd done but her words still cut through me.

"If hating me is the only way to keep you alive, I can live with it," I lied. "You can't hate me if you're dead."

I didn't know how I'd be able to cope with her hatred for me. But the most important thing was to keep her alive, even if it made her hate me.

She reached for the bar and she screamed in pain. I tensed as I watched my mate in pain. Everything in me screamed for me to go to her but I fought against it. I couldn't show how much her pain affected me or she could potentially use it as a bargaining tool.

"I'll send Curtis to check on you," I said tightly as I fought against my basic urge to protect her.

"You told me you love me," she said in a hurt tone that tore at my heart.

"I'm doing this because I love you."

She might not like it, but it was the truth. I gave her one more look before I forced myself to turn and leave.

Once I stepped outside the room, I leaned defeated against the wall. Doing this to her was tearing me apart but for her own safety I had to keep strong. I reached for my phone and dialed Curtis.

"I need you in the basement," I ordered him before I cut the call.

He didn't keep me waiting for long. I sent him in to look at Scarlett's hand.

It was easier to keep away from her than face the hard reality that she hated me.

Besides, I had plans to make. Blake and I had joined our packs. It was agreed that it would only be a temporary arrangement until Victor was taken care of. I had the larger pack so it was decided I would remain as the alpha and Blake would take the beta role.

The rest of the pack had to be shuffled slightly to accommodate the new roles.

I'd also arranged for a couple of guys to watch over Scarlett's house until everything died down.

Jake appeared in the study.

"She is still refusing to eat."

I needed to do something. I had hoped I'd be able to talk her into eating but I knew it would be a long shot.

She was lying on the bed staring at the ceiling when I entered.

"You have to eat," I told her, but she ignored me.

I had to do something. I couldn't let her try and starve herself to prove a point. It couldn't be an empty threat; I had to be prepared to follow through with it.

"If you refuse to eat I'll have to get Curtis to sedate you and put you on a drip," I warned, hoping that would be enough to get her to eat something.

Silence hung in the air between us.

"You have till tomorrow morning, otherwise you leave me with no choice."

I left, hoping that my threat would work. The thought of getting Curtis to sedate her and put her on a drip against her will made my heart hurt.

A little later Gary came to me and offered to try and talk some sense into her. I hoped that he would be able to but I wasn't surprised when he walked out of the room shaking his head.

"She won't listen."

That night I tried to get some sleep, but I was restless without Scarlett. I spent some time in my study and then I found myself standing outside the door to her cell. I missed her and I wanted to touch her. But I had to hold firm.

A little later that morning I got her a plate of food, hoping she would finally give in and eat something. She was sitting in the bed leaning against the wall when I walked in.

"Here is your breakfast," I said.

She remained silent.

"Scar."

It was only one word but with that one word I pleaded with her to eat. I didn't want to be the bad guy, but if she forced me, I would be.

"I'm giving you an hour. If you haven't eaten anything I will follow through on my threat," I said, giving her a final warning.

I expected her to ignore me but when she got off the bed and walked over to the bars I was surprised.

"Let me out," she instructed in a firm tone.

"No," I replied.

Then to my horror she reached for the bar covered in wolfsbane.

"Don't," I commanded but there was nothing I could do but watch as she wrapped her hand around the bar. She held on even though I could see the pain evident on her face.

It was like someone was ripping my heart out of my chest.

"Let go!" I yelled. As painful as it was, she didn't—she was determined to make me let her out and she'd use whatever she could to weaken my resolve.

"Stop it!" I yelled more urgently as my eyes fixed on her hand, which was still holding onto the bar tightly as her face filled with pain and determination.

Finally, to my relief, she let go and dropped to the floor, holding her injured hand to her chest.

"Let me out," she requested, still in pain.

She'd injured herself to make me let her out. I was prepared to do anything to keep her safe and she was prepared to do anything to get out.

I had no choice. She'd forced my hand.

Anger at her actions made me throw the plate against the wall in frustration. I watched it shatter as I fought to control the anger boiling inside of me.

I looked at her one last time before I walked out.

I called Curtis as I stalked to my study. I told him to sedate Scarlett and put her on a drip. I tried to keep busy strategizing with Blake in my study when I heard Jake call out to me through the mind-link.

We're under attack!

SCARLETT

For the first time since Cade had drugged me I tried to call to him through the mind-link.

Cade.

I got no response. Was he so angry with me that he was ignoring me?

I heard movement by the door of the cell and held my breath as I waited to see who it was. The lock turned and the door opened.

My jaw dropped open in surprise as Keri walked in. There was no sign of the outgoing and friendly girl that I'd taken an instant liking to. And in her place was a stranger void of any emotion.

"Keri?" I questioned my friend, not quite believing my eyes.

She didn't answer or acknowledge me as she turned back to the open door—and in walked an older guy. That feeling of power hit me; I'd only ever sensed that around Cade, Blake and Kyle. The guy was an alpha as well.

He was tall and well-built with brown hair streaked with some gray at the roots that was cut neatly short. He was dressed in a dark formal suit. His dark brown eyes swept over me triumphantly like he'd won and I was his prize. Fear began to seep into me. His smile was chilling and cruel.

He stepped forward.

"You are as beautiful as your mother," he said as he stepped forward to touch my cheek. I jerked my face away from him.

Horror filled me when I finally realized who he was.

Victor.

He was the man that had murdered my parents. Hurt, anger and an array of various emotions began to build up inside of me.

The last thing I remembered was Curtis injecting me. It didn't add up. Curtis was human. Why would he be working for Victor? Victor watched me with a satisfied smile.

"Have you figured out how I got you?" he asked, looking mildly entertained.

My eyes flickered to Keri, who was still watching me with stone-like features. She was Keri, but she was different. There was something different about her. Then it hit me.

I smelled her scent. Keri was a werewolf. How was it possible? I'd been around her for weeks and I'd never smelled a scent on her. In a school full of werewolves, no one had known that she was a werewolf.

Victor's smile deepened as he watched me for a reaction.

"Wolfsbane is a very handy herb," he drawled. "It doesn't just burn our skin and make an effective way of keeping us confined. In small doses, administered to a werewolf, it suppresses some of the werewolf traits."

"Isn't that right, darling?" he said to Keri. Darling? Was Keri his partner or something? He was old enough to be her father but some people liked that. I watched as she looked to Victor. For the first time, I saw a flicker of emotion briefly pass over her face. I recognized fear and nervousness.

"Yes, Father."

What?!

Keri was Victor's daughter? I looked incredulously from him to her. Keri's features were void of any emotion and Victor smiled at my obvious surprise. Her father was the man who had murdered my parents in cold blood. My initial shock and surprise was slowly replaced by the anger and hatred for who he was and what he'd taken from me.

"Curtis?" I asked.

"Yes, Curtis. He is a werewolf from my pack."

Victor had given them wolfsbane to suppress enough of their werewolf features, so that none of the other werewolves would pick up on them.

"Why?" So many questions were running through my mind.

"I like to keep tabs on the packs that surround mine; it just makes sense to keep an extra eye on them. You must have heard the saying, 'keep your friends close and your enemies closer'."

He'd planted them as spies to keep an eye on Cade and Blake, and their packs.

"You planted the spies before I moved here," I realized out loud.

"Yes. Finding you was an added bonus," he said as he cocked his head to the side. He studied me for a moment like I was something precious to him, which made my stomach turn.

"When my daughter reported back that a new werewolf had moved into town I was very curious about you," he began to explain. "She took a couple of photos of you and when I saw them I knew who you were straight away. There was no mistaking those features."

He took a step closer and caressed my cheek with his knuckles. My skin crawled at his touch.

"I had no idea how your parents managed to hide your existence from me. But that is irrelevant. I have you now, and that is all that matters."

This guy was off his rocker. 'Fucking lunatic' was an apt nickname for him.

"Don't think for a minute that if you'd done things differently this wouldn't have been the ultimate outcome," he assured me with a smugness I wanted to wipe off his face. "From the time I found out about you, this was inevitable."

I felt a sinking feeling in my stomach.

"How did you get me away from Cade?" I asked the burning question. I hadn't been able to figure that out. I was never going to be okay. In my mind there were only two ways this was going to play out and neither was going to be good for me, but I needed to know that Cade was safe.

He studied me for a moment and touched my mating scar on my neck.

"Cade had no idea that when he requested Curtis to sedate you that he was making it easier for me to get you. We created a distraction and Curtis managed to sneak you out without anyone noticing. They had bigger problems to concentrate on than the fact that you're missing."

"What do you mean?" I asked as a sense of foreboding settled over me.

"I have decided that it is time to expand my territory. I'll get rid of the smaller packs and any werewolves that don't get killed in the process will be integrated into my pack by force."

Oh. My. God.

I put my hand over my mouth as I realized that the reason why he hadn't answered was because our pack was under attack. Panic began to build up in me. What if it was worse?

What if he'd been injured? Or worse? No, that wasn't something I could contemplate. He had to be okay. There was no other option.

I closed my eyes and tried to reach Cade again through the mind-link.

Cade! Please answer me. But I got no response.

I opened my eyes and Victor laughed at me.

"There is no point trying to mind-link with your mate. I've dosed you with the wolfsbane, so you aren't able to communicate with him."

Victor studied me for a moment. My eyes flickered to Keri for a moment but she was indifferent to me, her gaze fixed on her monster of a father.

"From this moment on you belong to me," he told me. "And I will never let you go."

He could hold my physical body by force but he couldn't hold my heart: that already belonged to Cade.

"I belong to Cade," I stated, holding his unwavering gaze. "And nothing you ever do will change that."

His eyes fastened on me, and before I could react his hand connected with my cheek. The force was so hard that I felt my teeth shake. I flew back from the force of the hit and my hand went to my stinging cheek.

Through the pain, I glared at him.

"If I have to I will beat it out of you," he warned me. "You don't know what I'm capable of, so don't test me."

I knew exactly what he was capable of. I fisted my hands to try and keep control of my temper because I knew I was about to lose it. My mind began racing through the options I still had. I was contemplating shifting into my wolf form and trying to attack Victor before he could shift and fight me back.

"Don't even think about it," he warned. The change happened so suddenly that I was convinced he had a split personality.

"The dose of wolfsbane also stops you from shifting into

your wolf form."

My situation was getting worse and I was running out of options. I had to do something.

My gaze did a sweep of the immediate area around me as Victor turned to say something to Keri, but there was nothing within reach that I could use as a weapon.

"We need to move her," he informed Keri and she nodded.

CHAPTER
TWENTY-SEVEN

SCARLETT

"You stay here," he instructed Keri. "I will be back soon."

He turned to give me one last appreciative gaze, which made my stomach sink with foreboding. I knew what he was going to do to me the minute he got me alone and I couldn't help the shiver of fear up my spine at the thought.

The door closed and Keri turned to face me.

"Why did you have to come back?" she asked me angrily as she glared at me like I was the one at fault. "If you hadn't come back things would still be okay. But now everything is going to change and who knows who will still be standing when it ends."

I was stunned by her words. I stood up and faced her.

"How is this my fault?" I asked, shocked at her words.

"If you'd never come back, he wouldn't be starting a war with the surrounding packs... it's because of you this is happening. He knows Cade will fight for you, so he attacked first. But this isn't just about attacking your pack, he will wipe out the other packs to make sure there is no support for Cade and in the process he will take them over," she revealed angrily. "People are going to die."

"Their deaths won't be on my conscience, they will be on yours for doing nothing to stop your crazy father."

A few moments of strained silence settled between us. She flickered a quick nervous look at the door.

"I have no choice," she whispered and then she pressed her lips together.

"Help me get out and we can stop it," I tried to reason with her but she was shaking her head at me.

"I can't go against him," she said in a determined voice. The glimpse of the girl that had been my friend disappeared into the cold heartless bitch in front of me. I tried to take another angle as I began to run out of time.

"What about Blake?" I asked. I had no idea if her feelings for him were real.

Her features remained stone-like.

"He will die along with the rest of them," she stated calmly.

She was going to do nothing to help me while her father slaughtered innocents.

Any connection I'd ever formed with her vanished in that moment and I viewed her as the enemy. She'd never been my friend and if she was willing to do nothing while her father carried out his war, then as far as I was concerned she was on the wrong side.

For a split second her eyes glazed over and I knew she was concentrating on the mind-link and not on me. It was now or never.

I couldn't shift to my wolf form because of the wolfsbane but I had to try something. Whatever I was going to do I had to do before Keri had a chance to fight back.

I launched forward and punched her in the face. Her

head hit the wall and she dropped to the floor, holding her nose.

I rushed to her, needing to incapacitate her before she could call for help. I put my arms around her neck and squeezed her air supply off. She struggled against me but I held on.

She clutched desperately at my arms, leaving scratches as she fought to breathe. Just as she stopped struggling and her body went limp I released my hold on her.

My heart began to speed up with adrenaline and fear.

I stood up but faltered—Victor filled the only exit out of the room. He watched me calmly as he stepped into the cell and glanced at his daughter, who lay on the floor.

"That wasn't very nice," he said, like he was scolding a child. I took another step back. He had me cornered and I had no options.

"If you'd killed her I would have been angry," he told me as he stepped closer. His hand slipped into the inside of the jacket of his suit and he pulled out a syringe filled with some liquid.

I knew it didn't matter what that liquid was, but I couldn't let him inject it into me.

"It would have annoyed me if I would have had to replace her," he said calmly as he stepped closer.

He was a monster; any doubt that I might have had evaporated. He didn't care about Keri. She was just another soldier in his army. I felt a moment's sympathy for the girl lying unconscious on the floor. I couldn't imagine what it would have been like being raised by someone as evil as Victor.

"I'm going to inject you with wolfsbane and then I'm going to take you away until I've taken over the additional territories," he told me. "Cade will be dead and you will belong only to me."

My heart squeezed at his words. I didn't want to live if I had to do it without Cade. It wasn't something I could comprehend. He had to stay alive and he had to be safe.

I was out of time and I was out of options but there was no way I was going to let Victor take me without a fight. Without another thought I lurched forward, taking him by surprise. I grabbed the syringe from his hand and slammed it into his knee and pushed the liquid into his body.

He grabbed both my arms and threw me down onto the floor like I was a rag doll. I landed with a thud and rolled onto my back, struggling to catch my breath.

He shook his head at me slowly as he pulled the syringe from his leg without flinching and dropped it to the floor.

"You really shouldn't have done that." He said it so coolly that it scared me.

"It's a good thing I don't need to shift into my wolf form to teach you a lesson," he told me in a deadly calm tone as he walked to me and picked me up by my arms.

Even though he couldn't shift, he was still strong enough to tear me apart limb by limb and there was little I could do to defend myself.

Fuck!

But even in a situation where the odds were stacked against me, I wasn't going to lie down and take it. I was going to fight with every last breath I had.

His fist connected with my mid-section and I stumbled backward. The next hit to my face, which connected with the back of his hand, sent me stumbling backward, making me lose my footing and I fell. I landed on the floor, winding me of the breath in my lungs. My back ached from the hard landing and I rolled onto my chest to try and get to my feet before he landed another blow.

I didn't see his foot until it connected with my stomach and I screamed as pain exploded in my abdomen. I rolled onto my back, clutching the damaged tissue.

"I will break you and then I will build you up again. You will do as I say or you will face the consequences," he said as he picked me up again and set me down on unsteady feet. There was no doubt in my mind that consequences meant death.

"Fuck you," I spat at him. His eyes darkened with anger.

His fist hit my stomach and I bent over gasping, my arms across my abdomen. As I lifted my determined gaze to his, he backhanded me and I landed on the floor.

I tasted blood in my mouth as I groaned in pain. None of my training had prepared me for the absolute ruthlessness of this monster.

My eyes landed on the still form of Keri. Had he broken her to build her back up like he was trying to do to me? Realizing how evil Victor was I couldn't help feel a little sympathy for Keri even though she'd betrayed us.

"Have you had enough?" he taunted as he took pride in surveying my injuries.

Somehow, I rolled onto my hands and knees and I pulled myself up again.

"You should have stayed down," he said with a sigh as he stepped forward.

My stomach hurt so bad I couldn't stand up straight and my face throbbed with pain but I wasn't going to give him the satisfaction of staying down.

I thought about Cade and how much I loved him. I prayed that he and the rest of my loved ones were safe.

I was no match for Victor but I couldn't bow my head to him to save my life. I couldn't let him take me because I would never survive. I made the decision there and then to go out fighting.

"Was that the best you could do?" I taunted at him.

I hoped that it would be over soon. His eyes darkened as

he took a menacing step closer.

"No...I can do much better than that," he promised with a cruel smile as his hands tightened into fists.

The sound of a groan stopped him and he turned to look at Keri as she started to come around.

"Get up," he instructed a dazed Keri but he didn't offer to help her up.

She blinked a couple of times before she sat up. She was still a little wobbly as she stood up with her hand against the wall for support. I tried not to feel guilty at what I'd done to her. I had to remember that despite my feelings of sympathy she was the enemy.

Her father gave her a disappointed look before he turned to fix his gaze on me.

"There is no escaping. This is your destiny," he ranted on. I wiped the blood that dripped from my nose. My face hurt and I tasted my own blood on my tender lips.

This guy wasn't playing with a full deck of cards. At that moment another guy entered the cell. He was built like Hank, big and bulky. His gaze didn't waver as his eyes passed over me briefly before he looked to Victor.

He seemed unperturbed by the scene in front of him.

"The helicopter is ready," he informed his boss.

A helicopter!

I began to panic. I couldn't let them get me into a helicopter. Who knew where they would take me.

"Get everything we need together and start loading the helicopter," he told the guy. The guy turned and left to do what he'd been ordered.

"Help him," Victor instructed Keri in a stern voice. She bowed her head slightly.

"Yes, Father," she replied obediently. Her eyes flickered to mine briefly just as she turned to leave.

I was alone with Victor. I tried not to show the fear that

I felt when his eyes met mine. My face and stomach throbbed. I took a tentative step back as he approached me. I felt like a wild animal he was trying to corner to capture.

"Have you finished fighting me?" he asked mildly as he surveyed my beaten form.

"I'd rather die than go with you," I spat at him.

He cocked his head to the side and studied me for a moment.

"There are worse things than death," he replied in a deadly tone and I felt fear begin to build up further inside of me.

What is worse than death?

"I can show you a new level of pain that will make you beg for death," he revealed with a glint his eye. I had no doubt that he would enjoy every moment of it.

I was on my own, there was no one coming to help me. Everyone would be too busy fighting for survival. It wasn't in me to just keep my mouth shut and do as I was told, so there was no way I was going to go quietly.

I believed Victor when he told me he could keep me in so much pain I'd beg for death. My only option was to force his hand by making him angry. If I made him lose his temper maybe he'd kill me quickly.

I didn't like to believe I was giving up. I looked at it more like I was going out fighting a battle I couldn't win.

"I won't go with you," I told him with all the determination I could muster. More blood dripped down my face and I wiped it away with the back of my hand.

"I can make you," he told me calmly. "Besides, I've got grand plans for you."

He is crazy.

"The first time I saw your mother I knew I had to have her. There was no alternative. It didn't matter that she was already mated to your father," he explained. I felt pain in my heart at the thought of what he'd put my parents through.

I didn't have to imagine how that felt because he was going to do it to me. He was going to take me by force irrespective of the fact that that I was already mated to Cade, the one destiny had chosen for me.

"You will take the place that I wanted your mother in. You will become my mate and you will bear my children," he informed me. I nearly threw up at the thought of what he was saying.

"I have a mate," I replied defiantly. I felt proud of the man fate had chosen to be my mate, Cade. I couldn't imagine being mated to this crazy nut.

"He won't survive the attack. For all you know he could be dead right now," he replied with a cruel smile. His voice was level but I could see his jaw clench slightly. He was calm on the surface but anger simmered beneath.

Was it enough anger to make him lose control and end it quickly for me? I thought about Cade and my heart squeezed at the thought of never seeing him again. All I could do was hope he was safe.

"And I'll fight you every step of the way," I assured him as I fisted my hands and took a fighting stance.

"I warned you," he said in a resigned tone.

His first swing I managed duck away from but the second connected with my stomach. I felt my feet lift off the floor with the force of the blow and I landed on my back with a thud, knocking the breath from me.

I groaned as I tried to roll onto my stomach to get back up.

"I can make this go on forever," he said as he stepped closer. I believed him and that's why I was going to push him to end my life. My body could only take so much before it gave in. Even now the pain in my stomach was excruciating and my face throbbed with pain.

For a moment I closed my eyes and thought about my parents. He'd taken their lives and he was going to take mine. If nothing else, I would find peace with them.

I leaned against the wall for support as I lifted myself to stand.

"You're just like your mother," he murmured as he watched me. "Defiant until the end."

Pride swelled up inside, knowing that my mom had fought against him just like I was. She hadn't just given up.

"Even your father fought hard to save your mother's life," he continued. From the time they'd been murdered, I'd always wondered which one had died first.

"Your mom died first and I made your father watch," he said with pride and I felt my heart break.

"He begged me to take his life instead," he sneered at me. I swallowed hard and tried to ignore the sting of tears at the thought that my dad had done everything he could and it still hadn't been enough. He'd been forced to watch my mother die.

That was horrific.

My temper snapped as he smiled at my reaction. Hank always said that with speed I'd be able to fight. Although I was injured I managed to take him by surprise. I got a hit to his face but it was like hitting a brick. He retaliated by grabbing me by the arms and throwing me against the wall. I felt the impact on my body and I screamed in pain. I landed with a thud on the floor.

"That wasn't very nice either," he said to me as he wiped the blood from his mouth. Even in my haze of pain I smiled at the fact that I'd made him bleed.

Lying on the floor unable to get up, I rolled onto my stomach. It hurt to breathe. I wiped more blood from my face as I groaned in pain. It felt like I'd been hit by a truck. I wanted to stay where I was because everything hurt, but giving up wasn't an option.

I looked up. I noticed the empty syringe on the floor and then it struck me.

Bloodied and in pain I could barely get onto my hands and knees to try and stand up. But in that moment I knew I had another option.

It was an option that could save me.

CHAPTER TWENTY-EIGHT

SCARLETT

I closed my eyes briefly for a moment. Nothing happened.

Fuck!

Pain exploded in my side as Victor kicked me. The force of it flipped me onto my back and I screamed out in pain as I clutched my stomach. I couldn't take much more. I had to do something now.

"I will break you," he assured me arrogantly as he stood over me. Through my haze of pain I watched as a cruel smile spread across his face. He was enjoying this.

I had to try again before it was too late. My body had already taken a serious beating and I didn't know if I had enough strength to do what I had to. Even in the pain I was in, I got to my knees and I lifted myself onto my shaky legs.

"No you won't, asshole," I spat back and his eyes darkened in anger as he reacted to my provocation. His smile disappeared from his face as his eyes narrowed at me.

In the instant he stepped forward to hit me again, I closed my eyes and this time something happened.

I shifted into my wolf form. The change was excruciating with the added injuries but I remained on all fours. Victor stopped, taken slightly aback at the sudden change. Anger turned to surprise on his face.

I saw the moment the realization hit him that he wasn't in control of the situation anymore. The balance had tipped in my favor. Through my wolf eyes I glared at him as I growled a warning.

He took a step back. I watched as he tried to shift into his wolf form but the wolfsbane I'd injected into his leg earlier prevented him. Fear crept into his features as I took a step closer and growled again.

That injection had been meant for me; the wolfsbane had been wearing off. Without that dose, the existing wolfsbane in my system was negligible and I was able to shift into my wolf form.

His eyes flickered to the door, the only escape out of the room, but before he could try and run I jumped in front of the open door. I could smell his fear in the air as I stepped forward slowly cornering him like he'd done to me only moments before.

The injuries from the beatings were forgotten as adrenaline began to pump through my veins. Victory was within my grasp. My wolf senses fixed on the target in front of me.

"You don't have the stomach to kill someone," he taunted me with a confidence that he clearly didn't feel. The perspiration beginning to form on his forehead and the nervous flicker of his eyes were telltale signs that he didn't believe it and that he was afraid.

I'd never killed anyone before but he was different. He wasn't some innocent person whose death would bring me lifelong guilt. He was the ruthless murderer of my parents. His death would be the justified revenge for what he'd done to my parents and to countless other people.

Payback is a bitch.

I let my eyes take in the sight of the monster one last time before I lunged forward and attacked him. He raised his arms to ward off the attack but in wolf form I was stronger. I knocked him to the ground. Desperately he tried to stand up again but I jumped against him and he landed on his back with a thud as he hit the floor again.

His arm stretched out and his fingers closed around the empty syringe. I wanted to laugh out loud. What damage did he think that would do against me?

I allowed him to stand up. He was shaken and he held the syringe tightly in his right hand. If he thought for a moment that a syringe was going to stop me, he was crazier than I thought. But on the other hand I was glad he wasn't giving up so easily. I wanted an excuse to tear him limb from limb and he was giving me one.

He smiled as he filled the syringe with air. What was he planning?

I growled just before I leaped at him again. I knocked him down to the floor again and I stood beside him, growling.

It was then I noticed the syringe was missing from his hand. I'd probably made him drop it when I'd attacked him.

He groaned as he lay on the floor. He'd shown me no sympathy when our roles had been reversed so I wasn't going to show him any now.

I could make it quick but after hearing what he'd done to my parents I wasn't going to kill him quickly; instead, I was going to make him suffer. I growled and I bit down on his arm. He screamed and tried to pull away but my teeth hooked into his flesh and I refused to let go. His blood seeped into my mouth as I bit down harder.

The wolf inside of me took over, and I began to rip into him. Piece by piece he screamed and begged but I wasn't going to stop until I couldn't hear his heart beating anymore. The only outcome for him was death. There was no way I was going to allow him to leave this cell alive. My actions became more frenzied as I bit him over and over again.

Finally, bloodied and barely hanging on, he lay unmoving on the cold floor as I stood beside him. His blood dripped from my mouth and covered most of my fur. His body was full of bite marks and a pool of blood was beginning to form around his body. His eyes met mine one last time.

It was time.

I didn't hesitate for a second. I wrapped my powerful jaws around his neck and bit down, allowing my teeth to sink into his flesh. He didn't make a sound as I tore at his throat with my razor-sharp teeth.

I stepped back. His eyes were open but unseeing. He was dead.

My nightmare was finally over.

The adrenaline wore off and exhaustion made me collapse on the floor. I shifted back and the pain that I'd been able to block out rushed back and I gasped.

Pain in my shoulder made me look to see the syringe embedded into my skin. The syringe was empty. I realized he'd injected me with air.

I had no idea what that meant. I winced as I pulled the syringe out and threw it on the floor beside Victor's dead body.

Time was running out and I had to get out of there before anyone from Victor's pack came looking for him.

With strength that I didn't know I had, I got onto my hands and feet and I stood up. For a moment I swayed but then the dizziness passed. Every part of my body hurt and I wanted to get away quickly but the severity of my injuries stopped me.

I shuffled out of the cell and into a hallway. I tried to be as quiet as possible as I moved down the hall. At a set of stairs, I peered upward, but there was no one. Slowly I climbed the stairs, step by step. Blood mingled with sweat dripped off my face, and I wiped it with my hand.

The top of the stairs opened up into some sort of room that looked like it was used for storage. I moved through the room past the boxes that filled its entire length. I turned the handle of the door and opened it cautiously.

I'd managed to kill Victor, but if Keri or another member of his pack discovered me now I would be as good as dead.

The door led outside. The sun was shining and I squinted to be able to see. I was near a forest. I let my eyes scan the grassy area but I had no idea where I was. There were no other buildings.

I'd at least expected to hear a helicopter but there was silence.

Suddenly I dropped to my knees and swayed. I couldn't go on anymore.

Scar!

For a moment I thought I was imagining things and then I heard it again.

Scar!

I felt the sting of tears as I scanned the area and then I spotted him. His wolf form was magnificent and I felt a tear slide down when it sank in that he was safe. He ran to me as fast as he could.

I felt a pain in my heart and I gasped at my chest. My body crumpled to the ground.

And then there was nothing, and my pain was gone.

CADE

We're under attack!

As soon as the thought hit my mind I went into alpha mode. My main concern was to keep my pack and Scar safe.

I heard Blake issue commands to some of the werewolves that had remained on his property. He wanted every werewolf that wasn't ordered to look after the females and children to get to us as soon as they could.

I began to issue orders to Jake through the mind-link as Blake and I rushed out of the study.

Get the off-duty fighters together. I'm on my way.

The on-duty fighters would be fighting the attacking wolves already here. Hopefully, they hadn't breached the gate yet.

Once outside the house, we both shifted.

The gate at the bottom by the compound was untouched but I could hear the snarls and growls of wolves fighting just outside. My fighters were struggling to hold off the incoming attack.

I knew that it was Victor's pack attacking us before the scent of the invading werewolves hit me.

I was out of options. Even with the additional fighters from Blake's pack we didn't have anywhere near enough fighters to defend ourselves.

At the closed gate, I turned to face my fighters.

I was taken aback to see nearly all the females from my pack in human form surrounding the fighters, who had all shifted into wolf form.

We want to fight, requested one of the females via the mind-link.

I didn't want them to but I didn't know if I had a choice.

If the fighters couldn't keep the attacking pack out of the compound they would slaughter or enslave them. With the additional numbers of females that could fight we might have a chance to survive the attack.

I looked to Blake.

We have no choice, he thought.

For a moment I thought about Scarlett and her constant fighting with me to allow females to fight alongside their male counterparts. It was finally about to happen and she wouldn't see it.

She was safe in the cell being sedated so that Curtis could put her on a drip. Through my actions I'd left her unable to protect herself but I couldn't think about that now.

I turned back to face my pack.

Only females that can shift will be allowed to fight: if you want to fight, shift into your wolf form, I instructed through the mind-link.

I watched as the females from my pack began to shift. I was astounded at how many shifted into their wolf forms. Only a handful of females remained.

You protect the children, I instructed to them. Someone needed to stay behind to keep the kids safe.

Take the children to the bunker.

It was built into the main house. I looked to one of the females that was to remain with the children. Her name was Sue.

Tell Curtis to move Scarlett into the bunker and take Gary with you.

I had to do everything I could to keep her safe. If she were in the bunker with the kids it would give her added protection, although nothing would keep her safe if we didn't win this fight.

We can't hold them off much longer, Jake informed me desperately through the mind-link.

Open the gates, I instructed to a couple of fighters. Adrenaline began to pump through my veins as I watched the big iron gates swing open.

My fighters were outnumbered but they were doing their best to keep the attacking pack at bay. They'd formed two lines of fighters that surrounded the gates, and as the wolves attacked they fought them off, keeping them from breaking the line of defense.

I looked back quickly to the members of my pack.

Attack! I commanded.

I turned to start running toward the middle of my line of fighters. They allowed us to pass as I led the rest of my pack against the vicious aggressor pack. The gates closed behind us, giving the weaker members of our pack added protection.

In that moment, I gave in to the animal inside of me. When the first wolf attacked me I ripped into its throat and it was dead before it hit the floor. One by one I tore into the attacking wolves with no mercy.

Blake was taking out as many as I was. His jaw locked around a wolf and he tore its throat out. The wolf slumped to the floor. But as hard as we were fighting I feared it wouldn't be enough.

Scarlett is missing.

The thought came to me through the mind-link from Sue, the female I'd instructed to tell Curtis to move Scarlett into the bunker.

I hesitated for a moment. A wolf I hadn't seen coming because of the distraction leaped into the air and was about to take me down.

Blake shot in front of me, taking a hold of the wolf by its throat. He threw it down on the ground. It whimpered but it never got back up.

Where is Curtis? I asked Sue, feeling a franticness I'd never felt take over me. I wanted to rush back to the house and look for her but I couldn't leave my pack.

I can't find him, she answered worriedly.

Every possible scenario flitted through my mind but nothing I came up with made sense. Why would Curtis and Scarlett be missing? Had he moved her somewhere else?

At that same moment, I don't know if it was fate or just pure luck but I smelled the scent of another pack. I looked up to see Kyle and his pack surround Victor's pack from the opposite side. Relief and fear flooded through me at the same time.

I need to go and find Scar, I said to Blake.

Go! he replied as he growled at a werewolf about to attack him.

I didn't waste another moment, and I ran back into the compound. It was only when I reached the main house did I shift back into human form.

It had to be a mistake. She had to be somewhere. True to Sue's words, though, the cell that had held Scarlett was empty.

Fuck!

My heart was beating so fast I could hear it pounding in my ears. I was living one of my worst fears. The only option that seemed to make sense was that Curtis had betrayed me and taken Scarlett. He was human; so I had no idea why or where he would take her.

It made no sense.

An overriding fear that I'd left her vulnerable to being taken clutched at my heart.

Cade! Blake shouted to me through the mind-link. *One of the guys I had watching Keri just reported back.*

I had no idea that he'd had someone watching her.

They saw her get into a car, and the driver of the car was Curtis.

Why would Keri be getting into a car with Curtis? If

Curtis was with her did that mean Scarlett was with them?

I'll go check it out. Who is watching them? I asked so that I would know who to mind-link with.

Gabe.

Gabe was a member of Blake's pack that had joined with mine.

Where are you? I asked Gabe through the mind-link. Gabe gave me the address but told me that they were on the move.

It looks like they are on their way into Victor's territory, he told me.

Victor! I knew he had to be behind this.

I mind-linked to a couple of my pack's fighters to order them back to the compound. I had no idea what was going on but there was no way I was going in without some sort of backup.

If I fucked up, Scarlett could die.

Minutes later we all got into a couple of cars and raced out of the property. I drove the car as fast as I could. Time was of the essence and I couldn't waste even one moment.

They have just entered Victor's territory, Gabe told me, and gave me directions to the area.

It took me thirty minutes before our cars pulled up alongside Gabe's and we all got out.

Curtis and Keri are werewolves, Gabe informed me as I came to a standstill beside him. The statement threw me. I had no idea. How had they been able to cover that up?

They belong to Victor's pack, he told me.

From where we stood I spotted them loading some stuff into a helicopter. It was time to take action. We shifted into our wolf forms and then we crept up and surrounded them before they could run. They were outnumbered and they knew it.

I shifted as my fighters, who were now in human form as

well, held Keri and Curtis in front of me. They looked at me defiantly.

"Where is she?" I spat at Curtis but he refused to talk. It was hard to think that I'd trusted him. The betrayal I felt—I pushed it down. I couldn't let that cloud my mind.

I was about to make him talk with the persuasion of my fists when I got a faint whiff of a scent.

It was Scarlett. I could smell her.

I shifted so that I would be able to smell her scent better and I followed it through the field. It got stronger.

Scar! I called out to her. Then I spotted a building and, at the open door on her knees, was Scarlett. Relief filled me at the sight of her. She was alive.

Scar! I called out to her again as I ran as fast as I could to her. Two of my fighters followed behind me.

I watched with horror as she clutched her heart and gasped in pain. She crumpled to the floor like a broken doll.

I shifted the moment I reached her. I reached for her and lay her gently on her back. I scanned her face frantically trying to figure out what had happened.

The bruises and blood made my heart crack. She'd been beaten badly.

"Scarlett, talk to me," I said, desperation creeping into my voice. I had no idea what was wrong.

Then I heard her heart stop beating.

CHAPTER
TWENTY-NINE

SCARLETT

I gasped and filled my lungs with air. My chest hurt as the numbness in my body gave way to pain. I groaned. My throat was sore and it hurt to swallow.

"Scar," I heard someone whisper. Disorientated, I tried to figure out who the source of the voice was. My eyelids felt so heavy and I struggled to open them.

"Come on, Scar, open your eyes," the voice pleaded in a whisper. The voice was so close.

The sun blinded me for a moment as I opened one eye. Then I saw a face appear above me.

Cade. His eyes were filled with concern and I swear I saw moisture by his eyes. I wanted to reach out and brush it away but it hurt when I tried to lift my arms.

Everything rushed back in that moment: Curtis kidnapping and taking me to Victor, discovering Keri was a werewolf and Victor's daughter. One after another I relived them as they flitted through my mind.

I clutched at my chest when I remembered the pain and then the nothingness. I felt my heart pounding in my ears at the fear of what had happened.

Cade leaned closer.

"It's okay, Scar, I've got you," he soothed.

"Cade..." I said in a hoarse voice.

"You're okay," he assured me as he pressed a kiss to my forehead.

I remembered the syringe and Victor injecting me with air just before I killed him.

"What...happened?" I managed to ask.

Cade brushed my hair from my face gently.

"You died...your heart stopped beating...I panicked so I did the only thing I could think of, I started CPR," he explained. "Just when I didn't think you were going to pull through I heard a faint pulse. Somehow you came back."

Then I realized what the moisture by his eyes was. They were tears, tears he'd cried because he thought he'd lost me. I lifted a finger and brushed the tear from his face.

"We need to go," said one of the members of our pack.

I remembered Victor telling me about attacking our pack. I reached out and clutched Cade's shirt.

"The pack?" I gasped, feeling panicked.

"Everything is okay. The fight is over and we won," he told me with relief.

"We'll talk about everything later," he said. "We are still in enemy territory and we need to get out of here before someone sees us."

I wasn't sure what happened or who took over from Victor now that he was dead.

"I killed Victor," I whispered.

"You killed Victor?" Cade repeated in disbelief.

"He is in the basement of the building," I told him. His eyes pierced mine and for a moment an array of emotions passed through them. First fear, then anger and finally pride shone in his eyes.

"Go and get the body," he instructed one of the guys.

He looked back down to me, and his eyes softened.

"Let's get you home," he said. One of the guys stepped forward to pick me up but Cade shook his head.

"I've got her," he said and he lifted me as gently as he could into his arms. I bit on my lip to keep myself from crying out in pain when the small action jarred my aching body.

I clutched at his shirt and buried my face against his chest, savoring the smell of him. I felt safe. After going through everything that I had, I was finally safe.

I was light and effortless to carry for his arms. When we reached some cars I saw Keri and Curtis being put into the back of one of the vehicles. At that moment my eyes connected with Keri's. Her face was void of any emotion. I wanted to be angry with her and I wanted to hate her, but I couldn't.

If I'd grown up with a father like Victor I would have turned out the same. What I felt for her was sympathy. Victor had been a very cold and cruel man and to have been brought up with that must have been a never-ending nightmare.

Someone opened up the back door to the other car and Cade got in the back seat with me. I curled up against him and he put a protective arm around me. The car ride back was long but Cade held me the entire time, soothing me with words.

By the time I saw the familiar surroundings of his house I was in a lot of pain, but I felt relieved. Cade helped me out of the back seat, and then I was standing with his arm around me, supporting me, when Blake came rushing out the door.

"I'm so glad to see you," he said, sounding relieved as his eyes fixed on me.

"And I'm glad to see you," I replied, giving him a weak smile.

A sound from behind us pulled Blake's attention away.

The other car had parked behind ours and the fighters held Keri and Curtis.

My heart hurt a little when Blake's eyes narrowed and fixed on Keri. He smelled her werewolf scent. I didn't know if he'd been told before now about what or who she was.

His features changed from happiness and relief to betrayal and anger. He knew that she was a werewolf and must have guessed that she belonged to Victor's pack. Soon he would find out that she hadn't just betrayed him, but that she was also the daughter of their biggest enemy.

There were a few moments of strained silence.

"Lift your shirt," Blake ordered her softly, like no one else standing around them existed. For a moment I was confused at his request; then I realized what he wanted to see.

Was it possible? Not once had it ever crossed my mind that they might be mates.

Her gaze fell to the floor as her fingers reached for the hem of her shirt and she lifted the material slowly.

My eyes flickered to Blake, who had an unreadable expression on his face, but I saw his jaw tighten. The calmness on the outside hid the turbulent emotions in him.

My gaze went back to Keri.

Her birthmark was a half-moon-shaped birthmark. Blake's pack had been the silver moon pack. My eyes flickered from the birthmark to Blake's face.

He stared at the birthmark like someone had sucker-punched him, and then raised his eyes to hers. Keri's eyes remained on his as she anticipated his reaction.

He never said another word. Instead he gave her a look of disgust and revulsion before he turned and walked away. I looked back to see a tear slide down Keri's face.

There were no words to describe the scene I'd just witnessed. I couldn't help but feel sorry for both of them.

I looked to Cade and his eyes were fixed on the retreating back of his best friend. Cade swung his angry gaze to the fighters that held the prisoners.

"Take them to the cells," he commanded. The fighters steered the prisoners into the house and they disappeared inside.

This whole situation was so complicated and I didn't know if they would be able to work through it. I couldn't imagine what they were going through. I was glad that Cade and I didn't have the obstacles that they did.

"Scarlett," I heard someone say and I turned to see Kyle rush forward. Gary stood behind him, looking anxious.

"Easy there, she's injured." Cade put his hand out when Kyle tried to pull me into a hug.

"Sorry, it's just...I'm...so glad to see you," he said as he ran a hand through his hair.

"Let's get her upstairs," Gary said like a concerned parent as he stepped forward and touched my hand.

"I'm okay, just a little sore," I said as Cade lifted me gently back into his arms.

Gary and Kyle followed Cade as he carried me into the house all the way up to our bedroom. At the doorway, they both stood as Cade laid me down on the bed.

"I'll be back later to check on you," Kyle assured me with a smile before they both left.

Cade closed the door and turned to face me.

Jake. You're in charge for the moment. Blake is busy and I'm taking care of Scarlett, he told him through the mind-link.

No problem, Jake replied.

"I want to shower," I said as I tried to get up. He rushed over and helped me to my feet.

"You should be resting," he insisted but I glared at him.

"I'm smelly and dirty," I grumped. "I'll feel better once I've had a shower."

He let out a sigh as his arm slipped around my waist.

"Let's go," he said as he helped me into the bathroom.

We stripped off our clothes and he got into the shower with me. I leaned my head against the wall as he gently soaped me down and then rinsed me off. My chest still hurt and my stomach still ached.

Outside the shower he dried me off with a towel. I couldn't help but gasp when I saw my face in the mirror. I looked awful.

"It will look better tomorrow," Cade soothed as he stood behind me.

He helped me into one of his shirts before he carried me back to the bed.

Someone from the medical center came to look me over. They'd wanted me to go stay in the medical center for the night under observation but I'd refused. Cade told them he would watch over me. I was told to rest and they gave me some painkillers.

Once they left, Cade got into the bed with me. I was starving so he brought me some food which I ate quickly.

"So what happened?" I asked as I put the empty plate on the bedside table. My eyelids felt so heavy. My mind wanted answers but my body wanted to sleep.

"Sleep, Scar," he instructed gently as I shifted to lay my head on his chest. "We can talk tomorrow."

The pills helped ease the pain and I drifted to sleep.

When I woke up I was lying on my stomach. Cade was awake and lying next to me, watching me.

"Hi," he whispered and he pressed a kiss to my forehead. For a moment I smiled and then all the memories of the previous day came back to me.

I rolled onto my back and groaned. I wasn't in as much

pain as yesterday, but it would be a few days before I healed totally. I wondered what my face looked like today.

"How are you feeling?" Cade asked with concern.

"I'm still in a little pain but I'm sure I'll be better by tomorrow," I assured him as I sat up and leaned against the headboard.

Cade slipped out of the bed and walked into the bathroom. I wasn't sure what he was doing until he came back with a glass of water. He handed the glass to me and picked up the tablets the nurse had told me to take. He dropped two into my hand.

I swallowed the tablets and handed the glass of water back to him.

"So tell me what happened with Victor," Cade said as he sat down on the bed beside me.

"That guy was crazy," I began. I decided not to go into the details of what he had in store for me. Talking about it would only upset Cade.

"He told me how he got me out of the house without anyone noticing. The last thing I remembered was Curtis sedating me, and the next thing I remember is waking up in a cell being held by Victor. He told me he was launching an attack on the pack and I was so worried. I remembered you said that you wouldn't be able to fight off an attack by him."

"It could have been so much worse but the girls insisted they wanted to fight, and then your brother arrived with his pack," he revealed.

"I told you girls could fight," I gloated with a smile. He smiled and shook his head.

"Fine. You were right."

"Say that again?" I teased. He playfully glared back at me.

After a few moments, our playful mood turned serious.

"I'm sorry," he whispered as he reached over and caressed

my cheek.

"Why are you sorry?" I asked as I studied his features.

"I was supposed to be there to protect you and I failed," he stated. His voice was filled with regret.

"Victor was determined to get me and he would have done anything to do it. Besides, you had no idea Curtis was working for him," I said, trying to ease the guilt he felt. "We were both wrong but I can't say I was happy when you locked me in the cell."

I remembered how angry I'd been. I didn't have that anger anymore. Maybe it was because, despite everything, things had worked out.

"Will slapping me make you feel better?" he asked in a serious tone. I contemplated it for a moment.

"I can't say that hadn't crossed my mind more than a few times while I was in the cell," I admitted. "But I'm over it."

I shrugged and he smiled at me.

"That's the problem. We're both so stubborn and so intent on protecting each other that we end up doing stupid things," I said.

"I know I could have done things differently but I was scared," he explained as he ran an agitated hand through his hair. "When I found out you had overheard us I knew you were going to do something drastic and I couldn't let you do that."

There were several moments of silence.

"The thought of something happening to you…it's like trying to breathe without air," he said, trying to put into words how much I meant to him.

"I get it. I feel the same way about you. But what you did to me was horrible. Don't ever do that to me again," I warned him. "We are probably going to face other problems and we need to learn to deal with them together."

"You're right. We need to learn to work things out

together," he echoed.

"Did Victor tell you how Keri and Curtis managed to hide the fact they were werewolves?" he asked.

"He'd been injecting them with wolfsbane," I answered. "It suppressed their werewolf traits. It was how I defeated Victor."

His eyes darkened with anger and he remained silent. I reached for his hand and took it into mine.

"He meant to inject me with the wolfsbane to keep me from mind-linking or being able to shift. But I managed to get the syringe and I injected him with it. He wasn't able to shift but I was. He was able to get the empty syringe and he filled it with air. Then, just before I killed him, he injected it into me."

I gave him the shortened version. He didn't need to know all the painful details.

"That explains why you collapsed. It had something to do with the air in your bloodstream," Cade said.

I was so thankful it hadn't killed me.

"How did you find me?" I asked, still confused as to how he knew where I was.

"I discovered you were missing," he explained. He reached for both my hands and held them in his. "It had to have been Curtis but I wasn't sure why. Luckily Blake had someone watching Keri. He was worried about her and when he found out from the guy watching Keri that she and Curtis had gotten into a car together, I knew you had to be with them."

It was still hard to believe that Curtis had been working for Victor.

"The guy tailed them onto Victor's territory and he also discovered they were both werewolves. He told me where they were and I got some guys and got there as soon as I could."

He paused for a moment.

"When I saw you, you crumpled to the ground. I was scared."

It was still hard to believe I'd come that close to dying.

"I think the fact that you are a werewolf, and heal quicker than a human, is the only reason you survived," he finished. He squeezed my hands.

"What is going to happen to Keri?" I asked as I bit my lip. He'd brought Victor's body back for a reason. And despite the fact that Keri had betrayed us, I didn't want something bad to happen to her.

"She is now the alpha female of Victor's pack and hurting her will start another war. Besides, whether I like it or not, she is Blake's mate," he said as he rubbed his temple.

We'd overcome so much but I was so glad that we weren't in their shoes.

"Why did you bring Victor's body back with us?" I asked. There was no way I ever wanted to see that man again even if it was in a body bag.

"We need to prove that he is dead so that Keri can take over," he replied.

"Why do I have the feeling that we are only safe for the moment?" I said.

"There is no guarantee that the change of leadership from Victor to Keri isn't going to have some effect on the surrounding territories."

I gave him a questioning look.

"Victor was a brutal sadist but at least we all knew where we stood with him. Keri will take over his leadership but the problem is no one knows what type of leader she will be. Treaties will have to be renegotiated."

It was werewolf politics.

He leaned forward and touched his lips to mine. All thoughts of what we were talking about vanished. As he pulled back, I held his face and kissed him harder. I took control and I pushed my tongue into his mouth and caressed his tongue. I needed more.

He groaned against my lips.

"You need to rest," he said as he tried to pull away but I wasn't having that. I snaked my arms around his neck and pulled him closer.

"I need you," I told him as I pressed my lips against his.

He was still for a moment and then his arms wrapped around me and he held me firmly against him. He was careful not to hug me too tight.

"For you, anything."

My heart swelled at his words.

"I love you," I said.

"I love you too," he said as his eyes took in my face.

CHAPTER THIRTY

SCARLETT

The next couple of days after killing Victor, Cade was very overprotective; it was almost suffocating. The only reason I didn't put a stop to it was because I knew nearly losing me had scared him and constantly being around me fussing was helping him work through it.

After two days of being confined to my bed, I'd had enough. I was going stir-crazy lying in bed watching mindless TV. I was getting out of bed when Cade walked into the room and he frowned at me. He held a tray of food.

"Where do you think you're going?" he demanded as he walked to me and set the tray down on the bedside table.

"I'm not spending another day in bed," I told him. He was about to open his mouth and argue but the glare I sent in his direction made him stop and shut his mouth.

Almost all of my bruises were gone and physically I was feeling okay. And after two days, I was bored stiff. I needed to get out, get some fresh air.

I was dying to be able to shift into my wolf form and run in the forest.

"I'm fine," I stated with my usual determination, and Cade knew there was no fighting me on it.

"At least have some breakfast first," he told me. I raised an eyebrow but he held my gaze.

We were both so headstrong, and when we clashed it could be explosive.

"Okay," I relented, getting back into the bed.

He set the tray on my lap and I surveyed the food. I had just eaten a spoonful of cereal when someone knocked on the door.

I looked up to see Gary, and I smiled.

"I thought I'd just stop by to see how you're doing," he said, walking into the room.

"I'm fine, in fact I will be out and about today," I told him and I saw him shoot a look to Cade who just shrugged.

"Okay. If you get a chance, come and pop into the gym. I want to show you the setup," he said, looking so excited about his new role in the pack.

After the fight with Victor's pack, all the women had insisted that they wanted to be allowed to fight, so changes had been put into place. Women didn't just train to protect themselves; they also trained to fight with their male counterparts as equals.

With the increase in fighters, Hank had been overwhelmed and Gary had offered to step in to help. Obviously he couldn't physically fight against a werewolf, but he helped with the strength-building exercises using the gym equipment while Hank concentrated on the fighting of werewolf against werewolf.

It gave him a sense of purpose that had eluded him from the time he'd found out about the supernatural creatures.

"I will," I promised him. He bent down and gave me a

quick kiss on the cheek before he left.

I looked to Cade with a satisfied smile and he rolled his eyes at me.

"You don't get to say it anymore," he told me and shook his head. My smile widened playfully.

"I don't have to say it anymore," I shot back, and he glared at me.

I was right, I said to him through the mind-link. He never said anything about not mind-linking it. He rolled his eyes at me. I never tired of reminding him and he hated it.

"Come on, eat so you can go and see the setup," he said, trying to get me to concentrate on eating my cereal instead of gloating.

The only reason I dropped it was because I really wanted to see the females in the pack fighting alongside the male werewolves. From the time I'd found out I was a werewolf, I'd been fighting Cade to allow females to fight and he'd fought me on it.

Now that I'd won, I wanted to see it with my own eyes.

I finished my cereal quickly and while Cade took the tray back to the kitchen, I got dressed.

Just as I got to the bottom of the steps, Cade walked up to me.

"Are you sure you're okay to be out of bed?" he asked, his eyes scanning my features for any tiredness.

"I'm fine," I assured him.

He reached for my hand and we walked side by side out of the house.

The flurry of activity in the gym when I entered made me smile excitedly. Females were training alongside the men and I saw a girl put a guy flat on his back on the sparring mat. I'd never felt so proud before.

For a while I just stood there, taking it all in.

I couldn't wait to start training again but I knew it would

be a couple more days before Cade would let me. I didn't need his permission. Having someone in your life meant considering their feelings in every decision you made. It was taking some getting used to but I was getting there.

After a visit to the gym, I stood in front of the gates of the compound that led into the forest. I could feel the need to shift and run wild.

"You ready?" Cade asked beside me as he told the guards to open the gates.

"Yes," I breathed as I closed my eyes and shifted into my wolf form. This time it didn't hurt when my body changed.

I looked beside me to see Cade had shifted and was standing beside me.

Still so beautiful, he said to me through the mind-link.

My heart smiled at his words. I never tired of hearing him say that to me.

I'd only shifted a few times but I felt more comfortable in my werewolf form than my human form.

I looked back to the forest and shot off. The feel of the ground beneath my paws felt wonderful as my powerful legs pushed me forward to a speed that made the forest blur beside me.

The smell and the sounds made me feel peaceful inside as I bounded through the forest with Cade following closely behind me.

After a little while of whizzing through the forest, I began to feel tired so I stopped, feeling my lungs burn from the exertion.

Are you okay? Cade asked, sounding concerned as he came to stand beside me. He nudged me with his wet snout and I looked at him.

I'm great. I was trying to catch my breath but I felt wonderful.

For a few minutes we stood side by side, taking in the

serenity and the calmness around us.

It was in that peaceful moment with just the two of us that I realized how lucky we were to get through everything we had, unscathed.

I turned to look at Cade and I managed to study him for a moment or two before he turned to catch my gaze.

I love you.

He nudged me gently. *I love you too. So damn much.*

My heart melted at his words. For a few minutes we stood, still feeling each other's emotions.

Time to go back, Cade said through the mind-link. As much as I didn't want to admit it, he was right.

I hadn't been out for a while, and I didn't want to tire myself out.

The run back to the pack was quick and as we ran into the compound the gates swung closed.

I shifted back into human form just as Cade did. The more I shifted, the easier it seemed to happen. It was almost like creating a habit that could be done without concentrating on the thought too much.

While we walked back to the house, I asked about Blake.

"Have you heard any more from Blake?" I asked. Was it too soon to hope that he and Keri had managed to put the betrayal and lies behind them?

"Yeah," Cade answered. "He is trying to put what happened behind them and move on."

Keri and Blake had been the most important thing on my mind, but unfortunately I couldn't fix them. I would try to help them but they would need to work through their problems together.

Despite everything Keri had done, I didn't believe for one moment that she was evil like her father. Blake would just need a little time to see it for himself.

She was the one destiny had chosen for him and there

would be no second chances. If he couldn't get it to work with her he would spend the rest of his life mateless.

I walked up to Cade and hugged him. The touch of his skin against mine made me feel calm and complete. I didn't know what I would do without him. Cade pressed a kiss to my forehead.

"Come on," he said, releasing me and taking my hand in his. "I have a surprise for you."

My curiosity was piqued as he led me back into the house and into the formal lounge.

My eyes were on the stranger watching me from the fireplace.

There was no doubt. I knew who he was and I swallowed hard as I took a step closer to him. I hadn't been expecting to see him.

He stood, stunned, looking at me like he was looking at a portal to the past. He looked like an older version of my father, with dark hair flecked with gray.

"You look just like your mom," he said hoarsely, and I smiled at him. I liked that I looked like her, it was like a part of her still lived on in me. But my similarity to my mom wasn't just skin deep. I'd fought bravely against Victor like she had, but I'd survived; she hadn't.

He stepped closer as his eyes caressed my face. I couldn't believe how similar he looked to my father. He took another step closer and hugged me. It was hard to keep my emotions in check as I hugged him back.

"I'm so glad you've come home," he whispered as he hugged me tighter.

He was right. I was home. It was more than just a town on a map. It was the people who surrounded me that made it my home and I knew I belonged here.

I smiled and hugged him as I thought of how much I'd gained in such a short span of time.

I'd gained family.

I pulled away gently and turned to face Cade, who was standing beside me with an encouraging smile. I'd gained the love that would carry me through to forever.

He held his hand out to me and I put my hand in his. Just being with him was enough to make me feel that my life was complete.

We would never be one of those quiet, getting-along type of couples. We fought and we were both strong and stubborn. We would disagree and we would have to find a way to sort it out but I had no doubt I would enjoy every minute of it.

Cade and I visited with my family for a while. I asked Uncle Nate so many questions about my mom and dad. I was too young to remember a lot about them so I was transfixed as he relayed childhood memories of my father getting up to mischief and getting into trouble.

"The day he found out your mom was his mate, he was so happy," Uncle Nate said with a faraway look in his eyes. It was like he was looking back at the memory.

I wished that for a moment I could see back in time at that memory with him.

The way he spoke of my parents and the way he relayed the past, it felt like I was getting to know my parents better.

I hung onto every word, hoping to savor the feeling of getting to know my parents better through the memories of them. I wanted to remember my parents not by the way that they had died, but by the way that they had lived.

When I closed my eyes I didn't want the image of my parents to be of them lying dead. I wanted to remember them by the way they'd looked at each other with the type of love that I only now understood. The way that I looked at Cade.

I lost track of time as we all sat in the formal lounge listening to Nate talk about my parents.

He relayed one story after the other, never tiring of

telling me everything he could remember. I think he also enjoyed taking a walk down memory lane.

Gary joined us. I could tell by his expression that Uncle Nate's resemblance to my father was uncanny.

Cade introduced them and they shook hands. Gary sat down beside me as Nate started to tell us about the day my mom found out she was pregnant.

"She was so happy and excited," Uncle Nate said with a look of sadness.

It was late. I yawned and Cade looked at me.

"You're tired," he stated as he stood up and extended a hand to me. I allowed him to pull me to my feet.

"You can visit more tomorrow," he told me. I nodded in agreement. The truth was I was exhausted and in need of rest. There were so many times that I'd fought him constantly over everything but now there were times when I was okay with him bossing me around. But only sometimes.

I said good night and hugged everyone. Cade led me upstairs to our room.

In the bathroom, Cade helped me strip my clothes off and we got into the shower. He kissed me under the running water and I wrapped my hands around his neck and pulled him closer.

The intense flutter of excitement went into overdrive when his tongue swept against my lips and opened them, allowing him access. Our tongues tangled and I groaned.

I pulled him closer, needing more.

"I want you," he whispered.

"Then take me," I told him as I pressed my lips firmly against him.

In the shower, under the steady stream of water, he loved every inch of me, and I'd never felt so cherished before.

Breathless afterward, he soaped me down and rinsed me off. He switched off the water and got out of the shower to dry me off with towel.

I loved those moments when he took care of me.

Tired and satisfied, he tucked me into my side of the double bed. He got in the other side and I laid my head on his chest as he wrapped an arm around me. He switched off the lights and for a few moments in the darkness, I just enjoyed the happiness I felt.

"Thank you for my surprise," I said.

"You're welcome," he said as he squeezed me closer.

"It's still hard to believe how much my life has changed," I murmured, thinking about when I'd first moved here.

Never in a million years when I first set eyes on Cade did I ever imagine that he would turn out to be the best thing that had ever happened to me.

"I know," he said.

There were more changes to come. We'd decided to keep my house and use it as another location for the pack. Plans were already in place to start building a similar setup to the compound on my property.

My stuff would be moved to Cade's house, although he now referred to it as 'our house', which made me feel all warm and fuzzy inside.

"I love you," I whispered, needing him to know how much he meant to me.

"I love you too," he said, pressing a soft kiss against my temple. I loved it when he did that, it made me feel adored.

I'd been so against the idea of having a mate. I'd thought that it was taking away my right to choose my own partner for life but fate and destiny had matched me perfectly with Cade.

"What are you thinking about?" he asked.

"How lucky you are to have me," I teased.

He laughed and I lifted my head to look at him, still grinning. Even though it was dark, the light from the moonlight illuminated his features.

I reached out and touched his face, loving the way the connection between the two of us made me feel.

His laughter faded.

"Are you sure you wouldn't be happier with someone more easygoing?" I asked. I knew sometimes I could be hard to handle.

"No. That would be boring. I know every moment with you is going to be unforgettable."

Feeling overwhelmed by his words, I kissed him.

I'd learned in my short life that happiness wasn't guaranteed.

I'd defeated Victor but that didn't mean we wouldn't face other problems in the future. We were werewolves and our way of life was dangerous, but I knew I could face anything with Cade by my side.

I trailed my fingers down his cheek and touched his lips with my finger.

It was hard to believe that I'd fought this so hard in the beginning. I had believed that you couldn't be with someone without losing your independence and some of who you were.

But I'd learned that I was wrong: I could still be the same person with my independence left intact. If someone truly loved you, they loved you just the way you were.

And this was true love.

About the Author

Regan discovered the joy of writing at the tender age of twelve. Her first two novels were teen fiction romance. She then got sidetracked into the world of computer programming and travelled extensively visiting twenty-seven countries.

A few years ago after her son's birth she stayed home and took another trip into the world of writing. After writing nine stories on Wattpad, winning an award and becoming a featured writer the next step was to publish her stories.

Born in South Africa she now lives in London with her two children and husband, who is currently doing his masters.

If she isn't writing her next novel you will find her reading soppy romance novel, shopping like an adrenaline junkie or watching too much television.

Connect with Regan Ure at www.reganure.com

Printed in Great Britain
by Amazon